Roberts Bartholow

The treatment of diseases by the hypodermatic method

A manual of hypodermic medication

Roberts Bartholow

The treatment of diseases by the hypodermatic method
A manual of hypodermic medication

ISBN/EAN: 9783742828743

Manufactured in Europe, USA, Canada, Australia, Japa

Cover: Foto ©Andreas Hilbeck / pixelio.de

Manufactured and distributed by brebook publishing software
(www.brebook.com)

Roberts Bartholow

The treatment of diseases by the hypodermatic method

A MANUAL OF HYPODERMATIC MEDICATION.

THE

TREATMENT OF DISEASES

BY THE

HYPODERMATIC METHOD.

BY

ROBERTS BARTHOLOW, M.A., M.D., LL.D.,

Professor of Materia Medica and General Therapeutics in the Jefferson Medical
College of Philadelphia; Fellow of the College of Physicians of Phila-
delphia; Member of the American Philosophical Society; Honorary
Member of the Medical and Chirurgical Faculty of Maryland,
of the New York and Ohio State Medical Societies;
Cartwright Lecturer for the year 1880, etc., etc.

FOURTH EDITION, REVISED AND ENLARGED.

PHILADELPHIA:

J. B. LIPPINCOTT & CO.

LONDON: 16 SOUTHAMPTON STREET, STRAND.

1882.

TO

COL. JOHN M. CUYLER,

SURGEON U. S. ARMY,

I DEDICATE THIS EDITION OF MY MANUAL,

IN GRATEFUL REMEMBRANCE OF PERSONAL KINDNESS,

AND TO

TESTIFY MY ADMIRATION OF HIS MORAL AND

INTELLECTUAL GIFTS,

HIS FIDELITY TO PRINCIPLE,

AND

HIS GREAT PROFESSIONAL AND ADMINISTRATIVE

CAPACITY AS A MEDICAL OFFICER

OF THE ARMY.

JE pense même, à raison de ces circonstances, que l'absorption sous-cutanée, qui n'a été employée jusqu'ici sur l'homme que par exception, devra devenir méthode générale pour l'administration de tous les médicaments énergiques, et à l'état de pureté.

BERNARD.

WHO that has suffered from a painful local affection can think of the alleviation of his sufferings which follows from the subcutaneous injections of an anodyne without gratitude?

SIR W. JENNER.

DIE neueste Zeit, mehr und mehr einer nicht skeptischen aber rationell critischen Auffassung in therapeutischen Dingen zuneigend, hat diesen gewaltigen Apparat pharmaceutischer und dynamischer Mittel grossentheils über Bord geworfen, und beschränkt sich auf wenige, aber in eminenter Weise bewährte, locale Methoden. Dieser glückliche Uemschwung knüpft sich zum Theil an die Einführung der *hypodermatischen Injectionen*, welche die symptomatische Behandlung der Neuralgien ausserordentlich vereinfacht und vervollkommnet, die meisten älteren Verfahren ersetzt und überflüssig gemacht haben.

EULENBERG.

PREFACE

TO THE FOURTH EDITION.

THE rapid progress made in therapeutical science renders necessary frequent revision of any work devoted to its exposition. This is especially true of hypodermatic therapeutics, which deals with the active principles,—the newest products of chemical research, which may be made available for this method of administration. Hence, since the publication of the third edition of this manual, so much has been contributed to this subject, that many changes, and considerable addition of new material, has been found necessary. I have rewritten much of the work, and have added new matter to the extent of one hundred and fourteen pages of text. As heretofore, I have incorporated those new contributions to therapeutics which seem so well grounded as to be permanent additions to knowledge.

In the substitution of the term *hypodermatic* for the familiar word *hypodermic*, my action may or may not be generally approved, but the change is urgently demanded in the interests of a correct nomenclature. To make the attempt at substitution successful it will be necessary to have the co-operation of medical authors. The unanimity of scholars in regard to the incorrectness of *hypodermic* is surely sufficient justification for combined effort.

When referring to the subject of "iridium points" for needles, I did not know the precise origin of the application of this remarkable metal for this purpose. I have learned since the printing of that part of the work that we owe this important improvement to Dr. William Judkins, of Cincinnati.

R. B.

1500 WALNUT STREET,
PHILADELPHIA, PA.

PREFACE

TO THE THIRD EDITION.

SEVERAL years having elapsed since the publication of
the second edition of this manual, important alterations
have been rendered necessary by the advance in knowledge. But few changes seem desirable in the first part,
devoted to "History, Technology, and General Therapeutics," but many changes and numerous additions have
been made in the second part, or "Special Therapeutics."
Chapters have been added on the following topics: The
Morphia Habit and its Treatment, Duboisia, Pilocarpine,
Chloroform, Chloral Hydrate, Apomorphia, Aquapuncture;
and all of the other chapters have had important additions made to them, and some of them have been entirely
rewritten. The size of the volume has been considerably
increased, and its usefulness enhanced, it is believed, by
these alterations and additions.

As this is now the only work on the subject in the English language before the profession, and as this embodies the
results of the most recent investigations, the author ventures
to express the belief that it must continue to be useful to
those for whom it was originally intended. The exhaustion
of two editions and the demand for a third indicate that

7

the manual supplies an existing want. The author has, therefore, felt encouraged to increase the size and enlarge the scope of the manual, so as to make it still more worthy of the approval of the medical profession.

The hypodermatic method has been greatly extended in range since it was first employed for the relief of pain. The applications of various agents by this mode to the treatment of different morbid states are even more important than the use of anodynes, and it is probable, as other active principles are discovered, the method will receive still greater extension. As, however, no good can exist in this world without a corresponding evil, the usefulness of the subcutaneous medication is embarrassed by a most serious abuse in the employment of the hypodermatic syringe for the purpose of narcotic stimulation. It is no exaggeration to say that this abuse is becoming a gigantic evil, to the extent and dangers of which the medical profession should be fully alive. The author has set forth this subject, as amply as the limits of such a manual will permit, in a chapter on the morphia habit, and he begs now to add another warning in regard to the danger of the lengthened use of morphia subcutaneously; for no matter how much the original prescription may have been justified in the condition of the patient, and how conscientious the physician in his efforts to prevent abuse, if the habit be formed, the mental and moral degradation which ensues will always be referred to as the blunder or the crime of Dr. So-and-so.

R. B.

1509 WALNUT STREET,
   PHILADELPHIA.

PREFACE

TO THE SECOND EDITION.

THIS edition is not a mere reprint of the first. Numerous and important additions have been made in various parts of the work. I have sought to incorporate every real improvement in hypodermatic medication which has been announced since the appearance of the first edition. Much has been proposed that does not appear to me to be of permanent value, and hence I have omitted it, in conformity with my original design of keeping on the strictly practical side of my subject. Whilst I have omitted much that seemed wanting in the essential quality of utility, I have not felt at liberty to reject from consideration any remedy a knowledge of whose uses might aid the physician in an emergency.

Now that the first enthusiasm which attended the introduction of this method has died away, we are in a position to estimate accurately its true merits. It is gratifying to me to observe that the judgments pronounced in the first edition, in regard to the various agents employed in this way, have been confirmed by a larger personal experience and by the general voice of the medical profession. The hypodermatic method is, certainly, a very important addition to our resources, and no physician can be considered as doing justice to his *clientèle* who does not give them the advantage, in suitable· cases, of its great curative value.

In conclusion, I have to express my obligations to the reviewers for their very favorable notices of the first edition, and to the medical profession for the estimate which they have placed on my labors.

R. B.

27 WEST 8TH STREET,
CINCINNATI.

PREFACE

TO THE FIRST EDITION.

As a teacher of Therapeutics, and as a practitioner, it has frequently been brought to my notice that the information existing in our language on the subject of hypodermatic medication is exceedingly meagre. I have been urged by students and practitioners to prepare a convenient manual, to embody in small compass what is really known of value on this subject. This little work is the result.

Those who do me the honor to read my book will find that I have drawn largely upon my personal experience in the use of the hypodermatic method. This fact, together with the necessity I was under not to enlarge my work beyond the boundaries of a " manual," will, I trust, excuse the apparent dogmatism of my statements. As, however, the experience and observation of one individual, how great soever may have been his opportunities, must necessarily, in so extensive and important a subject, be incomplete, I have not neglected the contributions of English, French, and German physicians to this department of practical medicine.

I am indebted to the present resident physicians of the Good Samaritan Hospital for important aid. Drs. De

Courcey and Rutter, with a scientific zeal which does them honor, submitted themselves to experiments in order to elucidate some important points in the physiological action of morphia and atropia. Dr. Galbraith made and recorded the observations.

Dr. J. S. Unzicker, of this city, a very capable physician and pharmaceutist, has placed me under obligations for numerous careful experiments, to determine what agent, if any, is best suited to prevent change in solutions prepared for hypodermatic use.

R. B.

CINCINNATI, OHIO.

TABLE OF CONTENTS.

13

THE TREATMENT OF DISEASES

BY THE

HYPODERMATIC, OR SUBCUTANEOUS, METHOD.

HISTORY OF SUBCUTANEOUS MEDICATION.

WITH the opening of the present century began attempts to utilize the skin as a medium for the introduction of medicaments into the blood. Chrestien, of Montpellier, who is also celebrated for his researches on the medicinal value of the salts of gold, published in 1804 a treatise on the iatraleptic method. This work was translated into German by Bischoff the following year. Various papers of minor importance appeared in French and German literature during the first quarter of the century. Lembert, in 1828, and Richter, in 1835, discussed, in more or less elaborate essays, the endermic method, and Madden, of Edinburgh, in 1838, published an experimental inquiry into the physics of cutaneous absorption. It is in a high degree probable that Madden's research had its inspiration in the recent developments in regard to the curative effects obtained by the inoculation and implantation of medicines. About 1836, Lafargue had published the results accomplished by his method; that is, the insertion of morphia into the skin along the trajectory of the nerve affected with neuralgia. Lafargue invented a needle-trocar, with which he could effectively deposit morphia in the form of a paste in the skin. Ascribing the curative results of this practice to the pustules that formed at the site of the inoculations, he studied with care their development and structure. Although it was early discovered that the .benefit derived from the inoculation of morphia was in no way related to the pustules produced, the good results of the method were most conspicuous, and attracted wide-spread attention at that time. Valleix, Cazenave, Malgaigne, Hayem, and others in France, Langenbeck, Bertrand, and Von Bruns in Germany, Rynd in Dublin, and Drs. Washington and Taylor in New York, repeated the practice of Lafargue, in some instances modifying the method. These observers, and probably the most of· those who practised the inoculations, were not concerned, as was the originator of the method, as to the mode of development and the special forms assumed by the pustules, but referred the curative effect to the action of morphia on the sensory nerves of the part. It is not surprising, then, that modifications in the mechanical details were soon introduced. In 1839, Drs.

Taylor and Washington, of New York, on becoming acquainted with Lafargue's method and the important curative effects obtained from the inoculations, also inserted morphia along the course of the affected nerve in cases of neuralgia. Instead of inserting morphia in paste by the inoculation plan, they injected a solution of morphia beneath the skin with an Anel's syringe, an opening having been made previously for this purpose. Anel's syringe, the real progenitor of the modern hypodermatic instrument, is a small syringe having an elongated tapering nozzle, fine enough for entrance into the lachrymal duct. To convert this into an instrument for subcutaneous injection it is only necessary to put a cutting point on the small extremity of the canula.

About the same time, and no doubt influenced by Lafargue's successful practice, Dr. Rolland, as Dr. Wilson * informs us, "cured a case of neuralgia by inserting $\frac{1}{16}$ grain of morphia in four punctures over the deltoid." It was also, there is reason to believe, the publication of Lafargue's results which induced Mr. Rynd, of Dublin, to set about the invention of a complicated instrument for introducing under the skin a solution of morphia by its own gravity. Besides the inoculation method, the endermic use of morphia began to be discussed and to be much employed about the twentieth year of the present century.

---

* St. George's Hospital Reports, vol. iv. p. 19 (Foot-note).

Brown-Séquard has always advocated the endermic method, which he holds is in some respects
superior to the subdermic. Sieveking * has found
the endermic plan work well in cases of persistent
neuralgia, and this experience extends back beyond the period when was brought forward the
hypodermatic method, with which he compares
the endermic. There was, therefore, an abundant
experience in the local use of morphia just before
the introduction of the hypodermatic method. It
was not, however, until the experiments of Dr.
Alexander Wood, of Edinburgh, were published,
that the method of subcutaneous insertion of
morphia began to be properly appreciated.
Doubtless also in imitation of Lafargue, Wood
began in 1843 the use of a crude syringe (similar
to the Anel), with which he injected a solution
of morphia through an opening previously made
in the skin. In 1855, or twelve years after the
first attempts to execute his conception, Wood
published† an account of his method. It is certain, however, that the physicians of Edinburgh
had become familiar with subcutaneous medication by personal communication with Dr. Wood
before any account of it had appeared in the
journals of the day. During this time Mr. Rynd,
of. Dublin, was carrying on his investigations,
and he affirms that "the subcutaneous injection

---

* The Lancet, 1861, vol. i. : "Clinical Remarks on Neuralgia."

† The Edinburgh Medical and Surgical Journal, 1855.

of medicinal substances to combat neuralgia was first used by myself in Meath Hospital in 1844."

It is obvious that the practice as thus far developed had for its chief, if not only, object, to obtain the local effects of morphia. Even so late as 1861, Dr. Sieveking was concerned chiefly about the local action in the endermic and subdermic application of morphia. We find that Dr. Wood began with the same notion, for he strongly insisted on the importance of injecting the medicament into spots painful on pressure. "The local effect depends," he says, " much upon the affinity between the particular medicine administered and the tissue to which it is applied." Not, like Lafargue, seeing a relation between the forms of pustules and the curative action on the nerves affected, but an " affinity" between the morphia and the morbid state of the nerves, Wood attributed the cures effected by the new method to the local action. He did not fail to observe, as, indeed, he graphically described, the systemic or general effects which so speedily follow the subcutaneous injection of morphia.

The question of priority of discovery has been warmly disputed. As is usual when great improvements are made in the arts and the sciences, the way to discovery is prepared by the work of many investigators. The inventor finally coordinates the results of his predecessors, and adds the experiment or the needed acquisition which completes the discovery. Wood estab-

lished his right to be regarded as the discoverer
of the hypodermatic method, by using the syringe
for injecting a solution of morphia, and by the
publication of his experiments and their results.
Mr. Rynd, who claims to have been the first to
employ the new method, must be ranked with
those who were working in the same direction,—
like Drs. Taylor and Washington of this country,—but who failed to make public their improvements or discoveries in time to substantiate
a claim to priority. Dr. Sieveking asserts that
" Dr. Kurzak, of Vienna, was the first, he believes, to employ the subcutaneous or hypodermic
method, which was then largely used by Dr.
Wood, of Edinburgh." * There is no reference
to the authority for this statement, hence we are
compelled to resort to contemporaneous German
works for evidence. The treatise of Prof. Dr.
Eulenberg,† the most thorough and elaborate
which has thus far been published on this subject,
and which is peculiarly rich in its bibliographical
lists, contains no reference to Dr. Kurzak's claims
to priority, or to any work done by him on this
subject. Dr. Eulenberg also in a more recent
publication‡ on the same topic, Dr. Erlenmeyer,§

---

* The Lancet, 1861, vol. i. p. 105. *Supra.*

† Die hypodermatischen Injectionen der Arzneimittel, etc.
Berlin, 1867, p. 10.

‡ Percutane, intracutane, und subcutane Arzneiapplication,
Allgemeine Therapie, i. 328.

§ Die subcutanen Injectionen der Arzneimittel, p. 1.

and Dr. Lorent* are equally unmindful of Kurzak's claim to be recognized as the discoverer of hypodermatic medication.

How far, if at all, the progress of physiological research influenced the endermic and subdermic application of remedies cannot now be stated with precision; nevertheless there are some important facts which have a distinct relation to the subject under consideration. The first research into the action of a medicament made by the physiological method was conducted by Magendie, about 1819, upon the *upas* and *nux vomica,* and on *strychnia.* In the course of this research Magendie first demonstrated that poisons acted by absorption into the blood. To ascertain the general effects of the remedy being examined, he introduced some of it *under the skin of the thigh,* and then observed the actions as they occurred. This experiment was performed in 1819.† In the course of this research, also, he tested the rate of absorption from different parts, including the veins. Subsequently, Bernard, pursuing his investigations into the action of curara, and also in his studies of the poisons, introduced the medicament, the subject of experiment, under the skin.‡ It was, therefore, perfectly well known

---

* Die hypoderm. Inject. nach clinischen Erfahrungen. Leipzig, 1865, p. 1.

† Ann. de Chim. et de Physiol., vol. xvi., 1819.

‡ Leçons sur les Effets des Substances toxiques et médicamenteuses. Paris, 1857, p. 272.

to physiologists that medicines introduced under the skin were rapidly absorbed, producing their characteristic effects, at the time when Lafargue was studying the forms of pustules caused by the endermic application of morphia, and Mr. Rynd, of Dublin, was inventing an instrument for the more efficient introduction of morphia into the skin.

It is the more surprising that the progenitors of the hypodermatic method should have referred the curative action of morphia to the local impression, since they observed that it produced the most decided systemic effect. Although Wood directed that " the instrument is not to be put into the place where the patient complains of pain, but into the spot where you find you can awaken pain on pressure," he accurately describes the rapidity and extent of the narcotic impression. The injunction to insert morphia into the spot painful on pressure had its origin in the practice of Valleix, who, in his work on neuralgia, then in the first flush of its popularity, had recommended the method of Lafargue. That Wood fully appreciated the extent of the systemic effect of morphia when administered hypodermatically is evident in the following passage :

" It is truly astonishing how rapidly it affects the system. If you throw in a large quantity of morphia, you will see the eyes immediately injected and the patient narcotized, and in a few minutes afterwards you will see him in a profound sleep."

Making such observations, it is impossible that he should be unaware of the effect of the remedy thus administered on the centres of conscious impressions; but he yet attributed the curative effect in neuralgia to the local action.

It was reserved for Mr. Charles Hunter to demonstrate the important fact that the application of the injection to the painful points, as contended for by Wood, was really unnecessary, and that equally good effects followed the introduction of the injection into a distant part. Mr. Hunter's first paper appeared in 1859, and was entitled " Experiments relative to the Hypodermic Treatment of Disease." These experiments, made on animals, demonstrated that hypodermatic injections " acted by absorption; that they acted quicker than by the endermic method, or than stomachic doses; that they acted more effectually; and that a small injected dose was equivalent to a much larger one by the stomach." Mr. Hunter was permitted to use the method of Wood on two patients afflicted with neuralgia, in care of Dr. Pittman in St. George's Hospital. As " both had abscess in the neuralgic site, from the continuance of the localization," the point of introduction of the injection was varied, and it was found,—" first, that in neuralgia equal benefit followed distant injection of the cellular tissue as followed the injection of the neuralgic site;

secondly, that localization was not necessary to benefit a given part; and, thirdly, that for certain reasons it was better not to localize,—the chief being: 1, the infliction of unnecessary pain; 2, the almost certain risk of irritating, thickening, or inducing matter in the part from repetition; and, 3, it became evident that a large class of neuralgia would be excluded from this treatment if it was necessary to inject the neuralgic site."

Great praise must be awarded Mr. Hunter for his success in demonstrating these important conclusions, and for popularizing his method. His industry in collecting facts and presenting them to the profession was indefatigable. His views were perseveringly advanced, with an intelligent appreciation of the nature and importance of his facts. He read papers before societies; he published articles in the "Medical Mirror," "Lancet," "Medical Times and Gazette," and "British and Foreign Medico-Chirurgical Review;" he issued a pamphlet* containing all of his previous papers and some additional facts, and he enlisted, by personal effort, many of the physicians and surgeons of London in a trial of the new therapeutical expedient.

It was thus, chiefly through the efforts of Mr. Hunter, that the method of Wood, previously

---

* On the Speedy Relief of Pain and other Nervous Affections by means of the Hypodermic Method. Churchill, London, 1865.

confined to Edinburgh and to Dublin, became naturalized in England. Mr. Hunter's papers in the " Medical Times and Gazette" attracted the attention of Courty, of Montpellier, and Béhier, of Paris, who popularized the new method in France. It was soon after tried and reported upon favorably by Scanzoni, of Wurtzburg; Oppolzer, of Vienna; Graefe, of Berlin, and numerous other eminent authorities on the Continent. In 1865 a small treatise, by Dr. Lorent, of Bremen, appeared at Leipsic. A monograph, by Dr. Erlenmeyer, passed to the third edition in 1866. In 1867 the second edition of the elaborate work of Dr. Albert Eulenberg was published in Berlin. Dr. Eulenberg gives a list of two hundred and twenty articles and essays in various languages, but chiefly in German, which appeared on this subject from 1855 to the date of publication of the second edition of his work. From these facts may be seen the extraordinary extension which has been given to this method of treatment on the Continent.

The method of Wood, as illustrated by Hunter, met with a more favorable reception on the Continent than in the country of its origin. According to Dr. Anstie,* "it is still very much unappreciated" in England. It is true that the principal English physicians and surgeons think highly of the method, and now employ it largely,

---

* The Practitioner, July, 1868.

but, as Dr. Anstie informs us, there are "practitioners who will not admit that there *can* be any particular advantage in it which the old way of giving medicines does not offer."

The hypodermatic method, soon after its publication by Wood, was introduced into the United States.   Dr. Fordyce Barker, of New York, whilst in Edinburgh in 1856, was presented by Prof. Simpson with a hypodermatic syringe. Soon after his return home, in May, 1856, he used this instrument, and was, consequently, the first in this country to practise the method of Wood. Prof. Barker's syringe was the model from which Tiemann's instruments were made.   In August, 1857, the late Prof. George T. Elliot published some observations on the hypodermatic method. It thus appears that the new mode of using medicines was known and employed in New York when Dr. Ruppaner's articles appeared in 1860 in the "Boston Medical and Surgical Journal," the first on this subject published in this country.

Not only was the hypodermatic method as taught by Wood early naturalized in the United States, but, as we have already shown, it was practised in New York before Wood made public his discovery, or before the earliest date assigned by Mr. Rynd, of Dublin, for his use in this way of remedial agents.   Dr. Isaac E. Taylor, in a communication to the "New York Medical Gazette,"*

---

* April 23, 1870.

shows that Dr. Washington and he used practically the same method in the New York City Dispensary so long ago as 1839. The idea was suggested to them by the results of Lafargue's method of inoculation. Instead, however, of inserting the solid medicament by means of a grooved needle, as was Lafargue's practice, these gentlemen punctured the skin with a lancet, and by means of an Anel's syringe threw a solution of the medicine under the skin. This mode of operating was the same practically as that suggested and used by Wood in 1855.

When the first edition of this work was published (1869), I was not aware of the above facts in regard to the introduction of the hypodermatic method in this country. It affords me sincere pleasure to attribute to my own countrymen the credit to which they are justly entitled.

Definition.—Mr. Hunter, in 1859, proposed the word *hypodermic* as the name for the new method, in imitation of terms already in use, as *epidermic*, etc. The word hypodermic is compounded of two Greek words, ὕπο, *under*, and δερμα, *the skin*. This word is condemned by all scholars, who are unanimous that the term should be—in accordance with the rules of construction—hypodermatic. That eminent philologist and Oriental scholar, Mr. Fitzedward Hall, D.C.L., assures me that under no circumstances is hypodermic allowable. It is, however, so firmly established, and in such universal use, that the substitution of the more correct term can be accomplished only by combined effort. In former editions of this work I have followed almost universal custom in using *hypodermic*, but in the present edition, and in the fourth edition of my " Practical Treatise on Materia Medica and Therapeutics," I have departed from custom to do my part towards the introduction of the more correct phrase, *hypodermatic*. The word *subcutaneous* expresses the same idea, and is in all respects appropriate.

By this method the medicament is introduced beneath the skin, usually into the subcutaneous

30

areolar tissue, but also into the muscles. Further, the instrument may be employed to inject medicines into the serous cavities, into the veins, into the parenchyma of organs, and into the tissues of morbid growths. Although these topics are in some respects foreign to subcutaneous medication, it is my purpose to include them in the present edition, since the same process is followed practically in all cases when the hypodermatic syringe is the instrument employed. The method consists in—

1. A suitable solution of the medicament;

2. An instrument for injecting the solution beneath the skin, into the subcutaneous areolar tissue, or into the tissues of muscles, organs, or new formations.

THE SOLUTION.—A medicine employed for hypodermatic use should be capable of perfect solution in the vehicle, which is usually distilled water. Particles of medicine undissolved are not only not in a condition to be readily absorbed, but also act as irritants to the tissue, producing inflammation and abscess.

The solution should be free from dirt or foreign matter of any description, and should be neutral, or, at least, without decided acid or alkaline property. Any substance which will coagulate the blood, or produce violent irritation, is unfit for hypodermatic use.

A solution, even of a neutral substance, should not be too concentrated. Pure distilled water is entirely harmless, and the quantity of fluid injected is, within certain limits, a matter of indifference, provided suitable care be used in selecting the site and in injecting. Concentrated solutions, *cæteris paribus*, are more apt to produce local irritation than dilute solutions. Moreover, if the solution of a powerful alkaloid be very concentrated, a drop too much injected may produce dangerous symptoms. In ordinary syringes, a few drops remain at the bottom of the cylinder and in the needle; hence it is difficult, in using a very concentrated solution, to inject the precise amount desired, or, indeed, to approximate to it very closely.

Solutions may be *extemporaneous* or *permanent.* For reasons to be detailed presently, extemporaneous solutions are generally to be preferred. The agent to be injected should be dissolved, at the moment when required, in clean water. Distilled water is not essential, is not even better than ordinary river-, spring-, or well-water free from visible impurities. Distilled water quickly becomes cloudy on exposure to air, because of the growth in it of a minute but visible vegetable organism. I find, after ample experience, that river-water that does not contain recognizable impurities is perfectly suitable for the solution of alkaloids and other agents used subcutaneously. If distilled water be employed for making the solution, it should be freshly distilled.

For the purpose of preparing extemporaneous solutions, powders of a given weight are made in advance. It is, unfortunately, quite impracticable to properly subdivide and make into powders those alkaloids that are given in hundredths of a grain. Morphia, morphia and atropia, pilocarpine, apomorphia, and some others may be put up in powders for solution as required, but the same arrangement is not practicable for many other remedies. Gelatine tablets, containing a definite measure of the medicament incorporated with gelatine when fluid, have been in use for several years, especially in England. The gelatine disks or tablets are slow to dissolve, and the absorption of the gelatine is imperfect, so that local irritation is apt to result from them.

The most important improvement lately made in this respect is the "hypodermic tablets" prepared by Messrs. Wyeth, of Philadelphia, at the suggestion of Dr. S. Augustus Wilson, of the same city. They are compressed pellets, containing definite measures of the agents usually employed mixed with sulphate of soda. The compression is effected by a machine, and the tablet, when complete, is a circular disk, about one-fifth of an inch in diameter and a line in thickness. The quantity of sulphate of soda in each tablet is one-fourth of a grain, which is intended to furnish a proper basis and to aid in the solution of the alkaloid. All agents now employed hypodermatically are put up in this form and furnished to " the trade" in quantity. When it is proposed to use a tablet subcutaneously, it is dissolved in sufficient water, preferably in warm water, and is then drawn up into the syringe in the usual way. Tablets that have become old dissolve slowly, and careful and patient trituration is necessary to effect perfect solution.

Permanent solutions are prepared from formulæ and kept on hand for use as required. The most carefully prepared solution rapidly deteriorates by keeping. In a few days a faint cloud appears, and soon after the solution becomes turbid. The cloudiness and turbidity of an alkaloid solution, made with pure distilled water and free from visible impurities, are due to the development of a minute organism,—*the penicilium.* This plant grows partly at the expense of the alkaloid, and hence whilst the solution increases in turbidity it declines in power. Filtration removes the visible impurities, but a solution which has once been turbid is ever afterwards unfit for subcutaneous injection. A solution long kept, although it may not be turbid, or if turbid has been filtered, will, when injected, often cause an indurated and painful swelling, which remains for months, and is slowly absorbed or suppurates. In some cases a cyst forms at the site of such an injection, slowly enlarges, and when finally emptied is found to contain gelatinous, purulent matter, with a small slough of connective tissue.

If permanent solutions are to be used, it is

extremely desirable to prepare them with menstrua that will not undergo change, or to make such additions to ordinary solutions as will prevent the growth of the penicilium. The distilled waters of cherry-laurel and of eucalyptus have been used successfully, and solutions made with them do not exhibit any change for several weeks at least. They are not irritating, and do not affect the system in the quantity required for subcutaneous administration. The imitation cherry-laurel and eucalyptus waters, prepared by triturating the oil of bitter almonds, and eucalyptol, with magnesia and water, are far inferior for this purpose to the waters made by distillation; nevertheless, in the absence of the genuine, the artificial water may be used for a short period.

The addition of certain antiseptics to the aqueous solution of alkaloids is an efficient method of preventing change. Two to four minims of carbolic acid to the ounce of solution of morphia will act efficiently for several weeks in preventing the growth of penicilium. A minim of carbolic acid to the drachm of solution is not enough to act injuriously, and will continue an antiseptic action for several months. This agent increases a very little the pain and smarting which attend the injection at the first moment, but then a state of lessened sensibility follows. Two to four grains of salicylic acid to the ounce of solution will also prove effective in preventing change, but it increases the irritation

—the smarting — which attends the injection. Resorcin may be substituted for salicylic acid, as it is almost free from irritating qualities and is equally as effective as an antiseptic. Boracic and benzoic acids, like carbolic acid, have the power to stop the growth of the penicilium, but are more irritant than the latter and than resorcin. The mineral acids are effective both to prevent change and to increase the solubility of many of the alkaloids, but they are much too irritating to be employed for the preparation of solutions for subcutaneous injection. Indeed, the acids are responsible for most of the abscesses, the slough-ing, and the tetanus which have followed the in-jection of medicaments. My conclusion is that it is far better to make extemporaneous solutions than to rely on any formula, how well adapted soever it may appear to be to the purpose in view.

THE SYRINGE.—The instrument used by Wood in his first experiments was a Fergusson's syringe, intended for the injection of liquor ferri chloridi into nævi. This instrument, like the Anel's and the Pravaz syringe (French), required a pre-liminary opening to be made in the skin, through which the canula could be passed. Mr. Hunter made a most necessary and important improve-ment when he had a cutting point put on the canula for transfixing the skin.* The details of

---

* On the Speedy Relief of Pain and other Nervous Affec-tions, etc. Pamphlet. London, 1865.

the manufacture have been further elaborated, and now very perfect instruments can be obtained. The material of which the barrel is constructed is glass, hard rubber, celluloid, Ger-

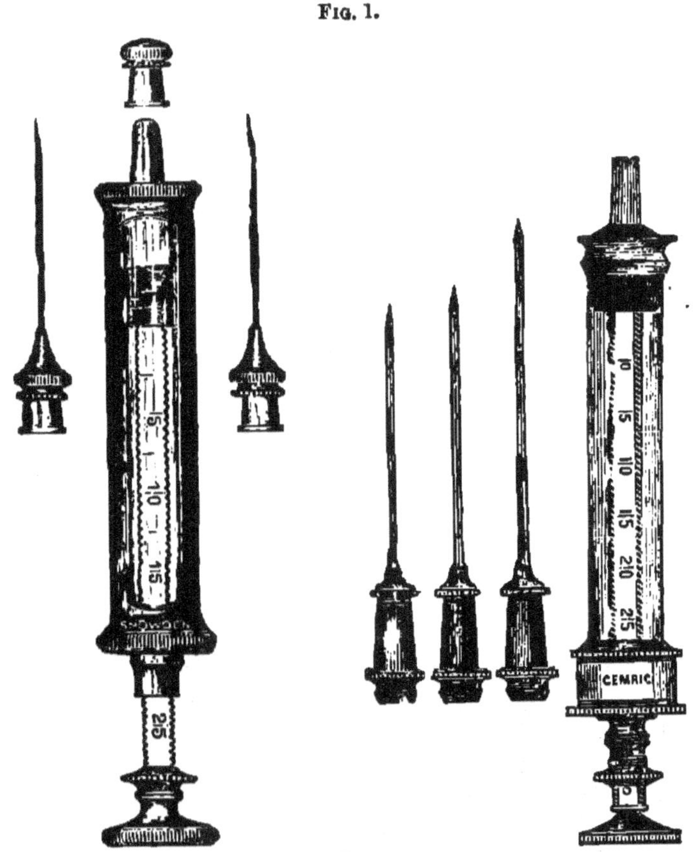

Glass Syringes.

man silver, pure silver, or gold.   Glass is fragile, and the bore of glass tubing is so unequal that it is difficult to obtain a piece uniform in calibre throughout.   The fragility is corrected by enclosing the tube in metal, leaving a slit through which

the contents can be inspected and the graduation
read.   In the original glass syringes, and in the
inferior ones now made, the mountings of the
cylinder are fastened on by sealing-wax or other
cement, and hence loosen easily, and leak, or
give way altogether.   The new material known
as " celluloid" is well adapted to the making of
cylinders.   As it is moulded in a soft state, perfect uniformity in the calibre can be secured, and
as it can be made transparent, the contents are
visible.   Although possessed of a transparency
almost equal to glass, it is not fragile, and will
not break by falling on a tiled or stone floor.   On
the other hand, it is soluble in chloroform, and
when the syringes made of it require repairs
they can be made only at the shops of the celluloid company.   Hard rubber is a suitable material for syringes, but they are usually made very
poorly.   An exception to this statement is the
syringe of Leiter, of Vienna, made so that the
parts fit accurately without screws, and hence
very readily cleaned and very durable.   Of course
the contents of a hard rubber syringe are not
visible, but the graduation of the piston may be
accurate.

Silver, according to my experience, is the best
material for making hypodermatic syringes.   It
is practically indestructible, and is not acted on
by any fluid introduced into the tissues.   The
barrel can be constructed with a uniform bore,
and an accurately-fitting piston assured.   The

objection to it is that its contents are invisible; but the piston-rod can be graduated with the utmost nicety. German silver may be substi-

Fig. 2.   Fig. 3.

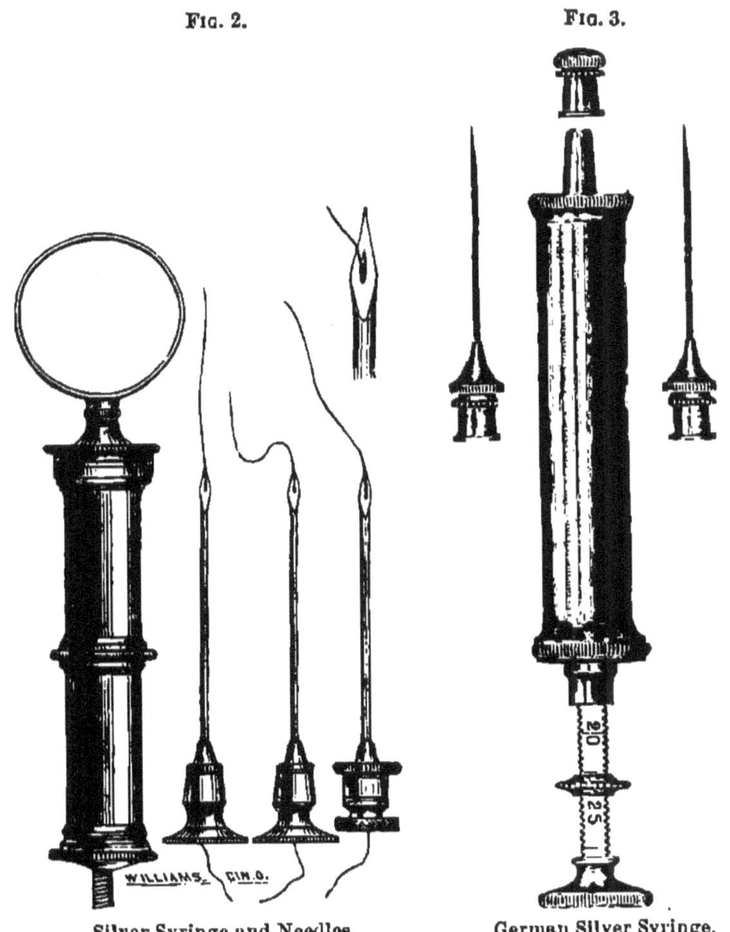

Silver Syringe and Needles.   German Silver Syringe.

tuted for pure silver, as no solutions are injected that would corrode this material. Gold has also been utilized for the construction of syringes. They are beautiful in appearance, durable and satisfactory in usage, but they are expensive, entirely out of proportion to their utility.

The needle is a very important part of the instrument. The needles furnished with most instruments are too large, and have an abrupt shoulder at the cutting extremity, which makes

Fig. 4.

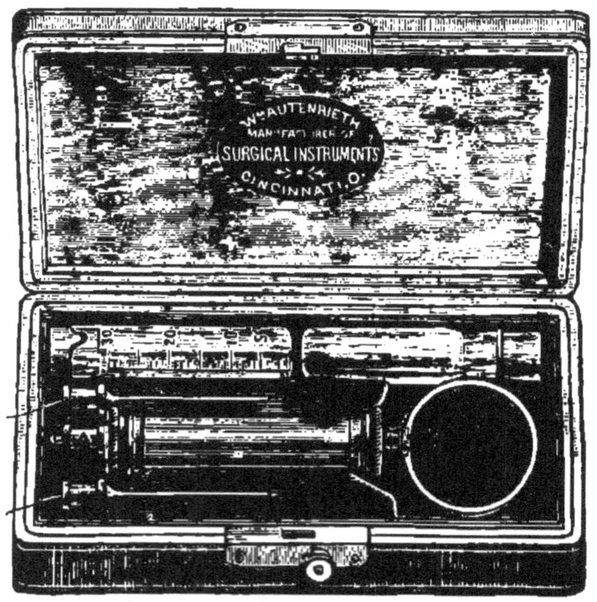

The Author's Silver Syringe, with Gold Needles, Iridium Pointed, as made by Wm. Autenreith, Cincinnati, Ohio.

the perforation of the skin difficult. The needle should be as small as possible, and the cutting part should have a lancet-shape, but without the groove or depression which some makers put in. The best needle is made of gold, with a hardened or an iridium point, as now made by Mr. Autenreith, of Cincinnati. Steel is the usual material, but it is more apt to cause after-troubles, such as nodules, abscesses, etc., because it undergoes oxidation, especially when put away damp. The needle should have a wire passed through it when not in use, for the double purpose of excluding any solid particles and preventing the closure of the calibre. Every instrument should be provided with several "rimmers,"—long, tapering, and

Fig. 5.

Rimmers.

very fine steel rods used by watchmakers,—which are very useful for cleaning out obstructed needles. As in the intervals of the use of syringes the piston dries and will not work properly, the barrel should be closed by a cap, which is put on or screwed on when the needle is removed. A few drops of water may be drawn in, and then the cap adjusted. In this way the piston is kept moist and in working order as effectively as if it were in frequent use. Dr. Whittaker, of Cincinnati, first proposed to use them. Weiss, of London, has invented a new piston, which promises to be very useful. It is made of hard rubber, thin enough to be flexible and adapt itself to the barrel of the syringe, so that no leather packing is required. The superiority of this piston in neatness, cleanliness, and effectiveness is obvious.

4

Undoubtedly the utmost circumspection is necessary in the use of the needles,—for diseased blood, or specific virus, may be transmitted from one person to another. Besides the cleanliness enjoined, the practitioner must see to it that needles used in infected persons must not be again employed in those free from infection.

Box containing Syringe, Needles, and Hypodermic Tablets, proposed by Dr. J. W. White, and made by Gemrig.

There are several methods by which the hypodermatic syringe may be charged with the required dose of the solution. The fluid may be drawn up into the barrel by aspiration, or the cap of the barrel may be unscrewed, the piston removed, and the solution poured into the barrel. The former is more convenient. If air enter when the fluid is being drawn up, it may be readily expelled by inverting the barrel and moving up the piston until a drop of the fluid presents itself at the orifice of the needle. In using a glass instrument which is graduated, more of the solution should be drawn into the barrel than it is contemplated to administer, and, fixing the eye upon those divisions of the scale representing the amount to be injected, the piston is made to traverse slowly the proper space. In filling my silver instrument I pursue the following method: I pour into a minim-glass the proper quantity of the solution. The needle being screwed into its place, I insert the point into the solution and draw the whole amount into the barrel of the syringe by slowly elevating the piston, inclining to one side the minim-glass, in order to take up the last drop. If air have entered, I invert the syringe and push up the piston slowly until it is all expelled. An allowance of one minim should be made for loss when more than ten minims are used.

Mode of Injecting.—Take up between the thumb and forefinger of the left hand a loose fold of skin in some convenient situation. Push in the needle with a quick and decided motion, at a right angle to the direction of the fold. The resistance ceasing, it will be known that the needle has perforated the skin, and the point of the needle may also now be freely moved about in the subcutaneous areolar tissue. It is better to pass the needle for an inch or more under the skin, to have sufficient space for the fluid. The injection must be made slowly, drop by drop, so that the fluid may diffuse itself without rupturing any small vessels or the fibres of the connective tissue. When all has been injected, withdraw the needle slowly, pressing at the same time upon the puncture to prevent escape of the fluid. A few minutes' pressure will suffice to retain the fluid, and to arrest the little bleeding which sometimes takes place. A bit of isinglass plaster may also be applied to the puncture, but this is generally unnecessary. By some persons the fluid is always injected into a muscle; and this is the method of using strychnia in paralysis, but it is not frequently adopted for other agents employed hypodermatically. To inject into a muscle, for example the brachialis anticus, make it tense by flexing the forearm, and then by a quick motion thrust the needle directly into the muscle. It is claimed for this method that it is less painful and less liable to be followed by abscess than by the injection under the skin, but it is obviously improper if any considerable amount of fluid is to be injected.

In practising the hypodermatic injection, it is important to avoid puncturing a vein. Serious depression of the powers of life, fainting, and sudden and profound narcotism have been produced by injecting a solution of morphia directly into a vein. Fatal collapse might be induced by injecting air into a large vein along with the solution.

Bony prominences should also be avoided, for in these situations the skin is not sufficiently loose to permit the ready entrance of the fluid, and inflammation and abscess will follow a too forcible injection.

The puncture should not be made, as a rule, into inflamed parts. I have known a bad phlegmon produced by injection into the tissues of an inflamed wrist.

It is not necessary to follow the original method of Wood, and inject into those points in which pain can be awakened by pressure. Some exceptions to this rule undoubtedly exist, as will hereafter be shown, but they are not numerous. The arm, the outer face of the thighs, the calves, the abdomen, and the back are suitable places for the injection. The arm, about the insertion of the deltoid, is generally selected. Eulenberg makes the assertion that the effect is slower when the injection is made in the back than in any other situation.* I have not been able to observe any difference in the rapidity of effect as influenced by the site of the puncture. If, as sometimes happens, the patient prefer injection into the painful part, it will be well to yield to his prejudices, provided no contra-indication exist thereto.

If the patient be timid and intolerant of pain, the sensibility of the skin may be lowered by

---

* Die hypodermatische Injection, etc., op. cit., p. 62.

ether or rhigolene spray. A piece of cotton cloth moistened with chloroform and held on the skin a few minutes is nearly as effective as the douche, and much more convenient. Sometimes redness and swelling take place at the site of the injection. This is best relieved by a cold wet compress.

REMEDIES ADMINISTERED BY THE HYPODERMATIC METHOD.

Source.	Preparation for Subcutaneous Use.
Opium.	Morphia and its salts. Codeia and its salts. Narceine. Apomorphia.
Belladonna.	Atropia and its salts. Homotropine.
Duboisia.	Duboisine and its salts.
Hyoscyamus.	Hyoscyamia and its salts.
Alcohol.	Whiskey, Brandy. Diluted Alcohol.
Chloral.	Chloral Hydrate.
Chloroform.	Chloroform.
Ether.	Ether.
Nux Vomica.	Strychnia and its salts.
Ergot.	Aqueous Extract (Ergotin). Sclerotinic Acid. Ergotinine. Fluid Extract.
Ustilago Maidis.	Fluid Extract.
Digitalis.	Digitaline and its salts. Tincture of Digitalis.
Conium.	Conia and its salts. Conia and Morphia.
Tabacum.	Nicotine and its salts.
Aconite.	Aconitia and its salts. Napelline.
Physostigma.	Extract. Eserine and its salts.

CURARA.	{ Curara. Curarine.
HYDROCYANIC ACID.	Hydrocyanic Acid.
COLCHICUM.	Colchicia and its salts.
PILOCARPUS.	Pilocarpine and its salts.
MUSCARIA.	Muscarine and its salts.
CAFFEA.	Caffcine and its salts.
CINCHONA.	Quinia and its salts.
CARBOLIC ACID.	Carbolic Acid.
RESORCIN.	Resorcin.
ARSENIC.	Liquor Potassii Arsenitis.
MERCURY.	{ Corrosive Chloride of Mercury. Peptonate of Mercury.
SILVER.	Nitrate of Silver.
IODINE.	{ Lugol's Solution. Tincture of Iodine.
IRON.	{ Ferrum Dialysatum. Liquor Ferri Sulphatis.
WATER.	Aquapuncture.
PEPSIN.	Glycerite of Pepsin.
AMMONIA.	Aqua Ammoniæ.
SALINES.	{ Salts of Sodium and Potassium.

LOCAL AND SYSTEMIC EFFECTS OF SUBCUTANEOUS INJECTIONS.

All agents injected under the skin, even water, produce some irritation at the point of puncture. Smarting, burning, followed by redness, and a more or less extensive swelling or wheal, are the usual phenomena. Very acute pain is caused when a nerve is punctured. When a few drops only are injected, there may be some trivial redness to indicate the point where the needle entered, and no after-swelling or irritation. The resulting wheal, when considerable fluid is injected, resembles the swelling of urticaria or of erythema nodosum. An indurated nodule may form, to suppurate slowly, and discharge after some weeks or even months. In such a case more or less sloughing usually occurs, including the areolar tissue and a portion of the skin, a depressed cicatrix resulting. Sometimes a frank abscess, sometimes an induration, and, rarely, a cyst are produced by the injection. There can be no doubt that, if the proper precautions are taken, and the tissues of the individual injected are sound, no induration or inflammation will result from the injections. If the rules already laid down for the preparation of solutions are not complied with; if the syringe or needle is dirty or rusty; if injury is done by rough handling; or if the patient is in a cachectic state, the local accidents above described may happen. Inflammation has resulted from partial puncture of the skin and forcing in the fluid violently. In some of the reported cases, all accessible parts of the body have been covered with cicatrices, partly-healed sores and ulcers, and recent abscesses. Making due allowance for the sensational spirit in which these cases have been narrated, there are still facts enough to show conclusively that through carelessness in the preparation of solutions, in the treatment of the syringe and needles, and in the method of injecting, inflammation and abscesses will result. The puncture of a vein may cause some loss of blood, or the formation of a purpuric spot, and the fluid may be thrown directly into the blood, or be drawn into the vein through the opening made by the needle. In the former case there will be an almost instantaneous action of the medicine; in the latter, slower yet rather quick and powerful effects. These will be described when the remedy concerned is under discussion. In a few instances, the injury of nerves at the site of former punctures has induced tetanus, but the nervous system was prepared by the disease for which the injections were originally used, or by the cachexia induced by the chronic morphinism.

The systemic effects produced by the hypodermatic injection of remedies must now be compared with the stomachal administration. A remedy entering the blood through the stomach is affected in its physiological and therapeutical action by the condition of that organ. Disease— for example, gastric catarrh—may hinder if not entirely prevent diffusion through the mucous membrane. The rate and extent of absorption are influenced by the presence of other ingesta, by the state of repletion of the veins, and by the condition of the liver. The digestive fluid undoubtedly exerts a chemical action on many remedial agents, forming combinations sometimes more, sometimes less powerful. Again, as the state of the nerves has an important influence on absorption, it is obvious that those remedies which depress the activity of nerves must constantly lessen by repetition the power of the stomach to convey them into the circulation. On the other hand, when a medicine suitable for the purpose is thrown under the skin, its physiological and therapeutical effects are produced in the fullest degree and in the most characteristic form. It follows that the therapeutical properties of a drug must differ not only in degree, but also in kind, according as it enters the blood through the stomach or by the subcutaneous areolar tissue. Experience and observation abundantly demonstrate the truth of this statement. The subcutaneous use of certain drugs has developed very valuable therapeutical properties, which the stomachal administration had not even suggested. Bernard * affirms that this mode of administering remedies, which has hitherto been the exception, must become the general method for the use of active principles. The advantages of this method over other methods, considered from the point of view of practical therapeutics, are manifold.

The effect is produced more speedily, and the whole effect of the quantity introduced.

The results are more permanent and curative.

Gastric disturbance rarely occurs, and irritation of the stomach is avoided.

The administration may be made to persons unwilling or unable to swallow.

It follows, then, that remedies suitable for this purpose may be used hypodermatically, to produce—

1st. All of the physiological and therapeutical effects which can be accomplished by them when given by the stomach; and,

2d. The physiological and therapeutical effects peculiar to this method.

The hypodermatic method may be employed for—

1st. A local action only.

2d. The general or systemic effects.

---

* Archives Générales, 1864.

LOCAL EFFECTS.

To cure nævi, aneurisms, varicose veins, etc., by coagulating the blood (liq. ferri subsulphatis; liq. ferri perchloridi, etc.).

To destroy morbid growths, goitre; or irritant injections into substance of tumors (tinct. iodinii iod. ; acetic acid in cancer, etc.).

REMOTE OR SYSTEMIC EFFECTS.

As a cerebral sedative..........
- In Insomnia.
- Melancholia.
- Mania.
- Puerperal mania.
- Delirium tremens, etc.

As a moderator of reflex action.............................
- In Epilepsy.
- Chorea.
- Eclampsia.
- Hysteria.
- Tetanus.
- Hydrophobia, etc.

As a motor excitant............
- In Paralysis, etc.

As an anodyne...................
- In the various forms of Neuralgia, etc.

In affections of thoracic viscera...............................
- Spasmodic cough.
- Whooping-cough.
- Asthma.
- Angina pectoris.
- Bronchitis.
- Pleuritis.
- Pericarditis, etc.

In affections of digestive system...............................
- Dyspepsia.
- Vomiting of pregnancy.
- Sea-sickness.
- Cholera morbus.
- Colic.
- Intussusception.
- Enteritis.
- Peritonitis.
- Hepatic colic.
- Scirrhus, etc.

<table>
<tr><td rowspan="7">In affections of the genito-urinary apparatus............</td><td>Dysmenorrhœa.</td></tr>
<tr><td>Uterine colic.</td></tr>
<tr><td>Nephritic colic.</td></tr>
<tr><td>Spasmodic stricture.</td></tr>
<tr><td>Spasm of sphincter vesicæ.</td></tr>
<tr><td>Spermatorrhœa.</td></tr>
<tr><td>Chordee, etc.</td></tr>
<tr><td>In fevers........................</td><td>Periodical fevers, etc.</td></tr>
<tr><td rowspan="2">In blood diseases.................</td><td>Rheumatism.</td></tr>
<tr><td>Syphilis, etc.</td></tr>
<tr><td rowspan="4">As an antidote....................</td><td>Opium.</td></tr>
<tr><td>Belladonna.</td></tr>
<tr><td>Strychnia.</td></tr>
<tr><td>Physostigma, etc.</td></tr>
</table>

THE ALKALOIDS OF OPIUM.

MORPHIA AND ITS SALTS.

History.—Morphia was the first remedy used subcutaneously. After the inoculation experiments of Lafargue, first published about 1836, Dr. Alexander Wood, of Edinburgh, began in 1844 to insert a solution of morphia under the skin. Although this is the origin of the subcutaneous method as now practised, it is perfectly demonstrable that Magendie, in the course of his physiological experiments, was in the habit of inserting poisons under the skin, to procure their characteristic effects, long before the earliest date assigned for the origin of the hypodermatic method.

The Preparation.—A solution, a "hypodermic tablet," or a powder of given weight may be used. There is no general agreement as to the salt of morphia which is best; but as the sulphate is most soluble, and, when neutral, not more irritating than any other salt, it should be preferred. The muriate is much used in Germany, and Eulenberg's formula is as follows:

> ℞ Morphiæ muriatis, gr. iv ;
> Acidi muriatici, gtt. iv ;
> Aquæ destil., ʒi. M.

In this formula the acid serves to increase the solubility of the morphia and to prevent the development and growth of the *penicilium*. It has already been set forth that acid solutions are highly irritating, and have produced much mischief by exciting a local inflammation, followed by suppuration and sloughing. The committee appointed by the Medico-Chirurgical Society to examine the subject of subcutaneous medication reported in favor of a solution made with acetate of morphia, dissolved by the aid of sufficient acetic acid and afterwards carefully neutralized with liquor potassa. The committee wisely remark: "In using drugs which require an acid to render them soluble in water, it was found that very acid solutions are apt to irritate, and the solutions were, therefore, carefully neutralized. Very alkaline solutions should be avoided for the same reason." * Dr. Anstie, in his much-quoted paper on " the Hypodermic Injection of Remedies," says that " morphia should be used in the form of acetate, dissolved with a minimum of acetic acid in hot distilled water, five

---

* The Medico-Chirurgical Transactions, vol. 1 p. 565.

grains to the drachm."* Dr. Lawson recommends a solution of the muriate, in the proportion of ten grains to two drachms, so that six minims contain a half-grain of morphia.† "This solution," says Dr. Lawson, "is always solid at ordinary winter temperature and generally so in summer, and it must be heated before each injection." A more recent English writer, Dr. Wilson, after making an elaborate review of the subject, concludes "that the solvent for morphia should be distilled water without any admixture of acid."‡ This expression of Dr. Wilson now represents the common sentiment of practical physicians, and the use of acid as a means of increasing the solubility of morphia or of preventing change in the solution has been abandoned. Much difference of opinion yet obtains as to the degree of concentration of the solution. The formulæ above given, so concentrated as to require heat to effect a solution, are not to be commended. The precipitation which takes place on cooling, and the danger of giving an overdose, are insuperable objections. The physicians replying to Dr. Kane's queries § have, with few exceptions, resorted to rather dilute solutions, sometimes after unfortunate experiences with more concentrated. My personal observation is in

---

* The Practitioner, July, 1868.

† On Sciatica, Lumbago, etc., p. 93.

‡ St. George's Hospital Reports, vol. iv., 1869.

§ The Hypodermic Injection of Morphia, New York, 1880.

favor of a rather dilute solution. The acetate and muriate of morphia, advised by some authors and practical physicians, are really less desirable, as they are less soluble than the sulphate. On the whole, we cannot improve on the formula of Magendie, and this, which I have recommended in former editions of this manual, continues to maintain the first place in my judgment:

R Morphiæ sulphatis, gr. xvi ;
Aquæ, ℥i.   M.
Sig.—Fifteen minims contain one-half a grain.

The advantages of this formula are the complete solubility and sufficient concentration for the fullest effect of the morphia.

As in all solutions of morphia, and indeed of the alkaloids in general, a change takes place too subtile for recognition by our present means of investigation, by reason of which solutions of some days' duration become unfit for use, the addition of an antiseptic is necessary when the preparation is intended to be kept. Besides this change of unknown character, the penicilium develops in solutions of alkaloids at the expense of the principal, not only weakening the strength, but also rendering the solution highly irritating. From two to four minims of carbolic acid may be added to the above formula, or for simple water may be substituted cherry-laurel or eucalyptus water, as has been elsewhere suggested.

For reasons explained when solutions in general were under discussion, it is preferable to have at hand the materials for extemporaneous solutions. A "hypodermic tablet" or a morphia powder of the required strength is conveniently carried, and as regards liability to accident, is much superior to any permanent solution. Since I have adopted the method of extemporaneous solutions I have not had occur the hard nodules and the points of suppuration and sloughing, which were not infrequent when permanent solutions were employed. A number of those responding to the inquiries of Dr. Kane * report a like experience, — that the abscesses formerly quite common when a permanent solution was used ceased to be produced when the solution was made at the time of injecting.

THE DOSE.—The dose of morphia for hypodermatic use varies from $\frac{1}{12}$ to $\frac{1}{2}$ of a grain. *In commencing, it should not exceed one-third of that ordinarily administered internally.* It is prudent in all cases to test the physiological capabilities of the patient by a small dose before resorting to the maximum amount. Patients vary in their susceptibility. Women are, as a rule, more easily affected than men. One-twelfth of a grain is a sufficient dose for many of the conditions requiring an injection. Persons habituated to the use of the drug, or those suffering pain, will bear a

---

* Supra, p. 47.

larger quantity. The maximum doses may be administered with safety if combined with atropia (see *post*). As Brown-Séquard has indicated, large doses of morphia, when combined with atropia, exert a more decided curative effect in obstinate neuralgias. It may be necessary in such cases to give $\frac{1}{2}$, or even 1 grain of morphia, with $\frac{1}{48}$ of a grain of atropia.

In order to maintain a constant physiological effect, but slight increase of the dose is necessary. This is one of the greatest advantages of the hypodermatic method, especially in cases requiring the protracted use of morphia.

Hypodermatic injections of morphia are rarely advisable in the case of children, yet as their utility is unquestionable in certain convulsive disorders of early life, it may be necessary to employ them. From $\frac{1}{60}$ to $\frac{1}{20}$ of a grain, according to age, may be regarded as a safe quantity, but the administration of so powerful a remedy should not be undertaken without careful consideration of the dangers involved.

So many accidents have happened from the incautious or improper use of morphia hypodermatically that I must repeat the injunction to proceed cautiously. Before deciding on the dose, ascertain if the malady requiring it be one in which a special susceptibility to the action of morphia exists. Is it a case of tumor or abscess of the brain? of chronic alcoholismus? of idiosyncrasy in respect to the cerebral effects? of weak heart? of obstructive pulmonary lesions? of deficient excretion? etc. If any of these conditions be present, the dose must be small. On the other hand, if the habit of opium-taking have been formed, if there be excessive pain, or if the case be one of uræmic convulsions, the dose may be large.

PHYSIOLOGICAL ACTIONS.—The effects of morphia injected beneath the skin are *local* and *systemic*. At the moment the injection is practised, pain is produced by the penetration of the skin, and a sensation of smarting and burning follows as the fluid diffuses through the subcutaneous tissue. · The latter sensation is the greater the larger the amount of fluid, the more concentrated the solution, and the more irritating the salt of morphia used. Under the usual circumstances it is not severe or persistent. Besides a little redness at the site of injection and some tenderness, no other local symptom appears when a few drops are inserted, and these results cease in a few hours. When, however, ten minims or more are administered, considerable swelling is produced, a large wheal forms, and the part is tender for several hours. Repeated injection at one point will produce much irritation, tenderness, and even inflammation. The accidents resulting at the point of injection under some circumstances will be described hereafter.

The effect of morphia on the tactile and pain sense of the part into which it has been injected

has been much disputed. In coming to a conclusion the various results which may be produced by the injection must have due consideration. Frequent injections or a single irritant
injection may induce such a local congestion as to
exalt the functional irritability of the peripheral
nerves, when, of course, the tactile and pain sense
will be exalted. An unirritating morphia injection lessens the tactile and pain sense for some
distance about the point of insertion, as has been
affirmed by Eulenberg,* Chouppe,† and others.
On the other hand, when local irritation and congestion have resulted, the opposite condition obtains, as has been stated by De Renzi,‡ Mitchell,
Morehouse and Keen,§ and others. In this way
may be explained the contradictory observations
made on this important point. Further support to the view of the local action of morphia is
given by the effects which follow the application
of a solution to a nerve-trunk, for when a nerve
is so treated its power to transmit impressions is
lessened.

The local effects of morphia are quite subordi-
nate to the systemic. The rate of diffusion of
morphia is very nearly the same for the connective tissue of any region. Any differences that
may exist are due to the number of vessels in

---

* Die hypoder. Injectionen, etc., *supra.*
† British Med. Journal, April 10, 1875. (Abstract.)
‡ New York Med. Journal, vol. xviii. p. 214. (Abstract.)
§ The Amer. Jour. of the Med. Sciences, July, 1865.

the part and to an accidental intra-venous injection. As the round of the circulation is made
within a minute, the effects become manifest
within that time, into what part soever the solution may be thrown. When, unhappily, the
solution enters a vein, the effect is not instantaneous, although very prompt. Under ordinary
circumstances, within a minute after the injection is practised, the cerebral effects, which vary
with the dose, the idiosyncrasies of the individual, and usage, are experienced. A feeling of
giddiness, faintness, depression, and nausea, accompanied by pallor of the face and contracting
pupils, is the effect experienced at the first onset
of the morphia impression by those not habituated to it. A deadly faintness, anxiety and
alarm, extreme pallor, cold surface, and weak
circulation are not infrequently produced in susceptible subjects on being injected for the first
time by even so small a dose as the twelfth of a
grain. Usually the preliminary depression and
pallor are succeeded by a flushed face, a feeling
of heat and fulness of the head, increased action
of the heart, tingling and redness of the extremities, and a general sense of discomfort. Very
often some pain is felt in the abdomen, due to
the movements of gas, and loud borborygmi
occur. The mouth grows dry and pasty; the
taste loses its acuteness, and the mastication
and swallowing of food become awkward and
difficult. The pupil contracts, and vision is

rather hazy. The sense of hearing is obscured somewhat by the *tinnitus*. A minute dose will not impair the equilibrium, although more or less dizziness occur, but a full dose will render walking uncertain, even prevent the necessary co-ordination of the muscles. There will be present, indeed, the usual symptoms and appearance of intoxication. Various odd sensations are experienced. One has an overpowering sense of muscular fatigue; another has a feeling of weight on the nape of the neck and the shoulders; a third has a splitting headache, with resounding *tinnitus* and incessant and severe vertigo; a fourth feels a sudden glow, then a sinking at the epigastrium, sudden nausea and vomiting occur, after which he is languid, exhausted, but has a sense of comfort; and a fifth is merely depressed and gloomy. There are but few who experience the traditional exhilarating effects, in which the mind is filled with delightful visions and the body is pervaded with an exquisite sense of well-being. By him to whom there are denied the higher joys of morphia intoxication, a grateful sense of freedom from all bodily discomforts, and the added feeling of delightful existence quite independent of surrounding circumstances, seem to be experienced. It is in this sense of all-pervading present comfort that the fascination of opium apparently consists, rather than in active exhilaration of the mind. When to the sufferer not only relief but a pleasing existence is given, when from the weary fatigue is made to vanish and work becomes a pleasurable exertion, and when for the disappointments and troubles of life a peaceful calm and content are substituted, it is not surprising that those in whom these transformations have been wrought should ardently desire their continuance.

The first stimulating effect of morphia on the cerebrum is of very variable duration. In some persons a condition of somnolence follows in a few minutes, and then more or less profound sleep persists for many hours. The sleep is often accompanied by vivid—usually horrifying—dreams; there is much talking and agitation, and in some persons a somnambulistic state is induced. Other subjects, again, fall into a deep sleep, with snoring, even stertorous, respiration. A large proportion of those taking morphia have but snatches of light sleep, with long intervals of wakefulness, and many are kept wide awake in a very active mental state, but experience a profound sense of comfort and peace. Those made actively wakeful usually are very drowsy and sleep heavily after the immediate effects of the morphia have declined. When the action has begun, the circulation, respiration, and temperature are characteristically affected.

Mr. Hunter * first pointed out the effect of morphia administered subcutaneously on the pulse

---

* On the Speedy Relief of Pain, etc., p. 33.

and respiration. "In mania," he says, "I have reduced the pulse from 120 to 80 in four minutes," and he also observed "the diminished rate of respiration." I have been most fortunate in securing the co-operation of some *internes* of the Good Samaritan Hospital, who submitted themselves to experiment in preparation for the graphical representation of the results of the morphia action.

In the accompanying diagram are represented the effects on the pulse, respiration, and temperature of Dr. Rutter, who had received, whilst in a perfectly normal state, one-fourth of a grain of morphia subcutaneously. In the febrile condition of the system the temperature-curve would not contain the elevation which marks the above tracing, but a depression corresponding to those of the respiration and pulse. A considerable rise in the blood-pressure also is produced. A sphygmographic tracing may or may not have scientific value. So much depends on the adjustment of the instrument, on the amount of spring-pressure, and on the nervousness of the patient, that perfectly accurate sphygmograms are somewhat difficult to accomplish. Those subjoined were obtained from Dr. Drake before and after the administration of one-fourth grain of morphia hypodermatically. The first or normal tracing was taken with a spring-pressure of 200 grammes, the sphygmograph being fitted with the modifications of Dr. Burdon-Sanderson, which permit a

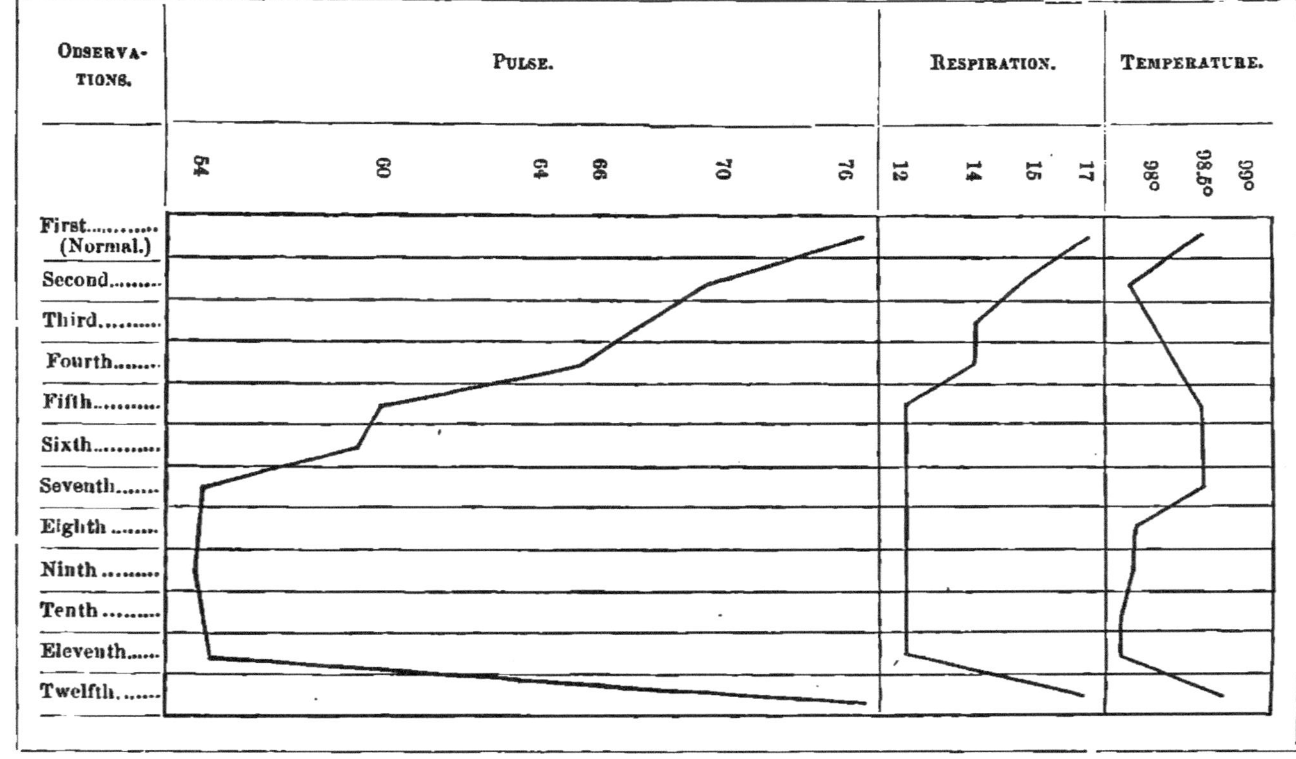
OBSERVATIONS.
PULSE.
RESPIRATION.
TEMPERATURE.
54
60
64
66
70
76
12
14
15
17
98°
98.5°
99°
First (Normal.)
Second
Third
Fourth
Fifth
Sixth
Seventh
Eighth
Ninth
Tenth
Eleventh
Twelfth

more accurate adjustment of the spring than is possible in Marey's instrument.

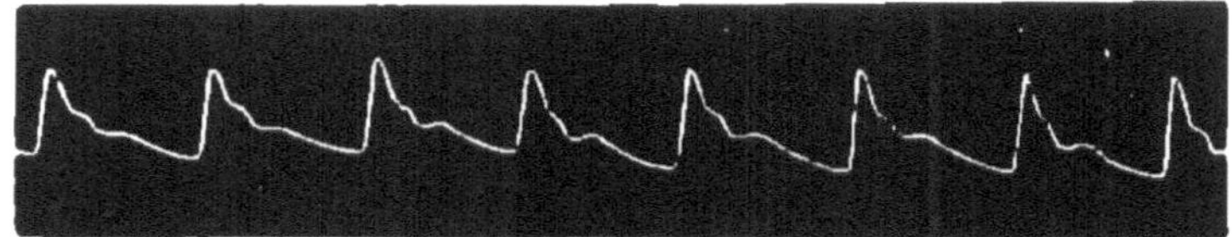

Tracing of normal pulse.—Spring-pressure of 200 grammes.

Soon after taking the normal tracing, the medicament was given and the apparatus remained *in situ.* When the usual effects were produced at their maximum, the second tracing was taken at the same spring-pressure. There being no

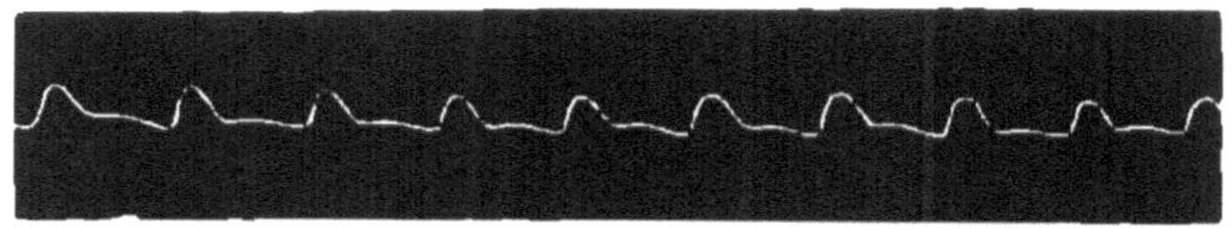

Tracing of pulse after the subcutaneous injection of morphia.—Spring-pressure, 200 grammes.

change in the conditions of the experiment, except the administration of morphia, the result must represent the true effects of this agent. The second tracing, as compared with the first, exhibits the following deviations from the normal :

The altitude of the wave is less, the ascent more oblique, the summit more rounded, and the dicrotic rebound less distinct,—peculiarities indicating a considerable rise in the tension of the arterial system.

Ophthalmoscopic examination of the fundus

oculi made when the effects of morphia are at
their maximum, discloses an increased vascularity
of the retina and a somewhat cloudy or blurred
state of the papilla. The drum membrane also
exhibits a more considerable injection than is
normal. The increased tension of the vascular
system begins to decline soon after it attains
the maximum; the pulse then becomes quicker
but softer, and secretions previously suspended
flow freely. Itching of the nose is very usual,
and some subjects experience a general itching
of the surface during the whole period of the
action. Moisture appears on the skin about the
time the pulse relaxes, and considerable sweating persists up to the end of the ·morphia influence. The tongue moistens as the skin perspires,
and doubtless, also, the gastro-intestinal mucous
membrane then resumes secretion and excretion.
Probably, also, during the period of its maximum action, morphia suspends or enfeebles the
activity of the pancreas and liver. Digestion is
stopped for a time if a full dose of morphia be
given after a meal, and, as a rule, constipation
results; but this is by no means invariable, for
in some instances the bowels continue to act
regularly, and occasionally constipation has been
removed by morphia injections. The diminished
excretion of bile is shown by the yellowness of
the conjunctiva, the muddy tint of the skin,
and the lighter color of the fæces. The urine
also has a higher tint than normal, due to the

presence of bile-pigment and to the greater density. The rather scanty urine is referable to two factors,—to the diminished functional activity of the kidneys, and to the increased diaphoresis.

With the decline in the morphia narcosis, some patients experience headache, confusion of mind, anorexia, and nausea; but these results are not so constant as after the internal use of this agent. If the injection be administered at night, the nausea and vomiting are experienced on rising in the morning. Perfect quiet, a cup of hot coffee taken before rising, an ice-bag to the cervical spine, and a full dose of bromide of potassium, may be administered for the relief of these symptoms when they are severe.

The extent and persistence of the foregoing physiological effects will depend upon the quantity of morphia injected. Very large doses excite not only immediate disturbance in the functions of the brain, but secondary disturbances in the process of elimination of the narcotic from the blood. The occurrence of these unpleasant and depressing effects of the morphia narcosis is an additional reason for cautious tentative experiments in any case in which the physiological tolerance of this agent is unknown.

Phenomena somewhat different in character, as well as in degree, from those which I have described under this head, follow the subcutaneous injection of large doses. The following symptoms were observed by me after the injection of one grain of sulphate of morphia:

In ten minutes the patient had fallen asleep so soundly, sitting upright in bed, that he could not be aroused. At the end of an hour I found him in a state of profound narcotism, his pulse 50 and feeble; respiration 10 and labored, with stertor; skin cold and sweating; face pale and ghastly. The conjunctivæ were deeply injected; pupils minutely contracted, and insensible to the strongest gas-light. No reflex movements could be excited by touching the eyes, or by irritation of the fauces. These formidable symptoms were relieved by the subcutaneous use of atropia, the physiological antagonist of morphia.

ACCIDENTS.—Although morphia, when rightly administered subcutaneously, may be freely used, accidents do occur, and a clear conception of their causes and character becomes necessary. These accidents may be local or systemic: local, due to the site, manner of injecting, and condition of the subject; systemic, the impression of the remedy on the cerebral, respiratory, and circulatory organs.

The local irritation produced by subcutaneous injections has been briefly referred to in connection with the solutions. Improperly prepared solutions of morphia, long-kept solutions, a rusty and dirty needle, the forcible introduction of a large quantity of fluid, are fruitful causes of local inflammation and induration or abscess. Repeated injection at the same site sets up a hyperplasia of the subcutaneous connective tissue, resulting in the formation of indurations, which may slowly suppurate, or induce such a highly vascular state of the parts that finally injections here become very dangerous.

When a vein in the skin is perforated by the needle, a very sudden and powerful impression is produced, if, as usually happens, the morphia solution be sucked into the vessel. If the needle enter a vein and the solution be thrown directly into the blood-current, the effect produced is still more sudden and powerful. The interval between the act of injecting and the effect of the morphia is greater in the former case; in the latter, the effect may seem to be instantaneous, almost. The difference being quantitative rather than qualitative, there need be no separate consideration of the effects resulting from the two modes of the accident. There are three kinds of results: slow and feeble action of the heart, contraction of the arterioles, and therefore anæmia of the brain, causing syncope; the same conditions, associated with weakened contractile power of the cardiac muscle, resulting in failure of the heart; and profound narcotism, terminating in paralysis of the respiratory centre.

When the injection is making, the vein perforated, no difference in the operation is observed, except the escape of blood; when the injection is delivered into a vein, the fluid passes in with an unusual readiness. Dizziness, oppression of breathing, singing in the ears, a fearful apprehension, intense throbbing in the head, dimness of vision, are immediately experienced; the face becomes deadly pale, the eyesight dim, the pupils contract, the pulse is small and slow, the respiration shallow and sighing, and thus, on the instant, the patient falls unconscious in a syncopal state. After a time consciousness is slowly regained, vomiting occurs, intense headache and vertigo are felt, and on every attempt to sit up the faintness comes on again. There are great differences in the duration of these symptoms, according to individual peculiarities; they may continue from an hour or two to twelve hours or longer, and, after the subsidence of the effects directly due to the morphia, more or less indigestion, constipation, hebetude of mind, and stupor persist for several days.

If the heart muscle have undergone the changes produced by myocarditis, fatty degeneration, or fatty infiltration, or the right heart be dilated and weak in consequence of obstructive pulmonary lesions or other causes, the syncopal state induced by the injection of morphia may speedily result in death. In such cases, immediately on receiving the injection, the patient turns pale, reels, falls into unconsciousness, and, with a deep sigh, expires. Such a sudden termination is, however, not common. More frequently the fatal result is due to excessive action of the remedy,—to coma and suspension of the functions of the respiratory centre. Such cases pursue the course of opium narcosis. The patient after receiving the injection passes into a condition of stupor, presently becomes profoundly insensible, the reflexes are abolished, the pupil minutely contracted, the respirations slow and shallow, the face pale, and the skin relaxed and cold. The rapidity of the effect depends on the amount administered, the point of insertion, and the susceptibility of the individual receiving the injection.

Idiosyncrasy is an important factor in determining ill results. There are persons, women especially, so susceptible to the action of opium and its alkaloids, that the minutest quantity will produce unpleasant effects. In such subjects a small medicinal dose will cause faintness, extreme vertigo, nausea, and profound depression of the vital powers, lasting from a few hours to several days. In such cases, even on the following day, great depression, faintness, and nausea occur on attempting to assume the upright position, and a dazed, confused, and " groggy" condition of the head continues for some days longer. In the subjects of this peculiar susceptibility, a full medicinal dose may cause a fatal result by syncope.

Chronic alcoholism develops a state in which ordinary medicinal doses may cause a dangerous narcotism or sudden failure of the heart. The structural changes which occur in the brain, especially in the medulla oblongata, in the walls of the heart, and in the kidneys, explain the nature of these results.

Habit diminishes the danger of accidents. When, in the case of a morphia-taker, a strong solution is sucked or thrown directly into a vein, the following effects are observed: an intense tingling occurs over the body generally, but especially over the extremities; often extensive wheals appear; the skin is swollen and deeply red; the action of the heart becomes rapid and tumultuous, and all the arteries of the body beat vehemently; an intense headache, with strong throbbing, occasions extreme distress, and is increased by every movement. Such symptoms will persist for a half-hour or longer, and not infrequently are followed by nausea. Notwithstanding enormous doses may be taken with impunity, they may be dangerous when, after a period of reduced quantity, considerably larger doses are suddenly administered. Several deaths have been caused in this way. Hence those reducing their daily allowance must be warned of the danger incurred by taking a dose considerably larger, although within the limits of former indulgence.

The treatment of the various accidents caused by the subcutaneous injection of morphia includes prophylactic as well as therapeutical expedients. No physician should administer a morphia injection without first assuring himself of the quantity. Deaths have been caused by the administration of approximate quantities. The rules with regard to dose, already given, should be carefully adhered to. The condition of the patient, idiosyncrasies, and existing diseases should be ascertained. Morphia should always be given with atropia, unless some contra-indication of the latter exist. It has been proposed to put a ligature about the limb, in readiness to be tightened should it be found that a vessel has been entered. It need hardly be observed that such preparations are too suggestive to be made with nervous subjects, and are rather unbecoming. As the symptoms occur only when the remedy reaches the brain, a ligature may fail to be useful. The person injected should lie recumbent, and if faintness comes on, the head should be lowered below the body. The measures of chief importance for the cases of syncope are inhalation of ammonia (cautiously), artificial respiration, and stimulation of the chest muscles by the faradic current, enemata of turpentine or alcohol, the intravenous injection of ammonia, and inhalations of amyl nitrite or its subcutaneous injection. The condition of narcosis requires the subcutaneous use of atropia to counteract the respiratory and cardiac depression, faradization of the chest muscles, the subcutaneous use also of caffein, stimulant enemata, etc.

THERAPY.—The subcutaneous injection of morphia may be used to relieve pain, to relax spasm, to subdue inflammation, to cure specific diseases, and to antagonize toxic agents. An anatomical arrangement seems best adapted to embrace all of the therapeutical facts under these several heads. Accordingly, I shall consider the uses of morphia in—

Diseases of the brain and nervous system, of the respiratory and circulatory system, of the digestive apparatus, of the genito-urinary organs, and of constitutional or specific origin; in certain surgical diseases and operations, and as a physiological antidote.

Diseases of the Brain and Nervous System.

Psychical Disorders.—Mr. Hunter was the first to indicate the utility of, and to employ, the hypodermatic injection of morphia in the treatment of *psychical disorders.* He enunciated an important truth in the following observations: "For derangements of the cerebral nervous system we have in the hypodermic method a means of treatment far superseding in its immediate efficacy any other mode of medication." In another place he further remarks, " In this class of cases [mania] a single dose, administered beneath the skin, will at once break the neck of the disease. It will often at once stop the delirium, correct the mental aberration, and remove the exhaustion." * Notwithstanding the striking advantages thus shown to result from the hypodermatic treatment of mania, some years elapsed before it came to be employed. Indeed, so late as May, 1869, we find a distinguished asylum superintendent † repeating the expression of Dr. Anstie, "that despite the satisfactory working of the hypodermic method, and the greatly increased power of handling remedies which it gives us, it is still very much unappreciated." Dr. Robertson believes that "this remark applies to the employment of the hypodermic injection of morphia in the treatment of mental disease." According to the same authority, Dr. Mackintosh published a paper in 1861 on "The Subcutaneous Injection of Morphia in Insanity," and the reports of the Somerset Asylum contain allusions to the advantages of this method. Lorent,‡ Erlenmeyer,§ and Eulenberg‖ support the observations of Hunter by their individual experiences. Maudsley,¶ who places opium at the head of all the remedies employed in the treatment of insanity, considers the subcutaneous injection of morphia "a valuable expedient." Reissner,**

---

* On the Speedy Relief of Pain, etc., pp. 18, 19.

† C. Lockhart Robertson, in Practitioner, May, 1869, p. 272.

‡ Die hypodermatischen Injectionen, etc., op. cit., p. 16.

§ Die subcutanen Injectionen, etc., op. cit., p. 28.

‖ Die hypodermatische Injection, etc., op. cit., p. 154.

¶ Reynolds's System of Medicine, vol. ii. p. 60.

** Bulletin Général de Thérapeutique, Jan. 30, 1870, p. 89.

who has experimented largely with the hypodermatic method in the various forms of mania,
comes to conclusions less favorable than those
above expressed. In acute mania he had no
permanent good results. Dr. Vix has, however, adduced a remarkable case in which a
single injection of morphia cured a recent case
of acute mania. In melancholia, Reissner's results were not more favorable than in acute
mania. In chronic mania the effects were
variable: some patients were calmed for weeks
and months; in others large doses were without
benefit. Reissner considers general paralysis
unsuited for the action of morphia, and that it
is contra-indicated in cases of mental disorder
complicated with heart or stomach disease,
rigidity of the arteries, tuberculosis, and in
certain epileptics.

More recently, Dr. O. J. B. Wolff has attempted a more accurate determination of the
indications for the use of morphia subcutaneously in mental diseases. The state of the arterial tension is Wolff's guide to the use of morphia. If the sphygmograph shows a low state of
the arterial tension with a slow pulse, small doses
are indicated. On the other hand, as large doses
of morphia, by over-excitation, cause paresis of
the sympathetic, these are indicated when the
pulse is quick and tension high. He advises
caution in the use of large doses in the obese
and the aged. He thinks the subcutaneous in-

jection of morphia very useful in both curable and incurable cases.*

Krafft-Ebing reports excellent results from the use of morphia subcutaneously in cases of lypemania, especially when there exist at the same time neuralgic troubles. He has been equally fortunate by this method in the treatment of " moral hypochondriasis complicated with hyperæsthesia of the spinal cord," and " in forms of mental alienation determined sympathetically in the predisposed by neuralgias and neuropathies." The existence of a neuralgic element constitutes an indication for the use of morphia subcutaneously in simple mania and in hysterical mania. Krafft-Ebing considers the same mode of treatment the most efficacious for the relief of the insomnia so common in the insane.† My own experience, which has been limited, however, is very favorable to the subcutaneous injection of morphia. In a case of acute melancholia, characterized by insomnia and intense restlessness, I found this method of treatment exceedingly useful. A grain of morphia reduced the pulse from 140 to 96, quieted the agitation, and procured sound and refreshing sleep.

Robertson in the paper referred to gives three typical cases of different forms of insanity—recent mania, chronic mania, and melancholia—in

---

* Archiv für Psychiatrie und Nervenkrankheiten, Band ii.
† Bulletin Général de Thérapeutique, Jun. 30, 1870, p. 474.

which the hypodermatic injection was successful. The indications for the employment of this method are the following:

Prolonged wakefulness.

Maniacal excitement.

Obstinate and persistent refusal of food, or drink, or medicine.

Destructive and suicidal tendencies.

Mandsley adds a caution here, which I transcribe for the benefit of my readers: "It will be well to have in mind that neither opium by the mouth, nor morphia hypodermically injected, will always quench the fury of acute mania, and that successive injections of morphia, followed by brief snatches of fitful sleep, have been followed, also, by fatal collapse."

The evidences of the beneficial effect of the injection are the following:

Prolonged and healthy sleep.

Less excitement on awakening.

Illusions or delusions less strong.

Willingness to take food.

Absence of any tendency to collapse, although pulse, temperature, and respiration are reduced.

To produce the best results, larger doses than those I have indicated as proper in general are necessary in the treatment of mania. Hunter administered $\frac{1}{2}$ and 1 grain; Robertson speaks of $\frac{1}{2}$ grain of the acetate of morphia injected every four hours, and in one case of 1 grain injected night and morning. In cases which have occurred under my observation, extraordinary tolerance of the morphia was exhibited; and in that case to which I have made special reference, 1 grain was found necessary to procure sufficiently prolonged sleep.

It is in the beginning of mania that the hypodermatic injection of morphia is most conspicuous for good. The timely use of the syringe may avert this disorder in that critical period when the occurrence of unusual excitability and sleeplessness indicates that an outbreak is imminent. This observation is especially true of puerperal mania. The introduction of chloral hydrate has modified somewhat the treatment of maniacal affections by the subcutaneous use of morphia; but, as Wolff has shown, each has its own sphere of applications.

Delirium Tremens.—We owe to Mr. Hunter the first suggestion of the hypodermatic treatment of *delirium tremens.* It was afterwards employed by Ogle, Semeleder, Lorent,* Eulenberg,† Ruppaner,‡ and others. Dr. Anstie, in an able paper on " Alcoholism,"§ thus formulates his views as to the utility of this method:

" Opium should never be administered by the stomach, but always in the form of morphia

---

* Op. cit.
† Op. cit.
‡ Hypodermic Injections, 2d ed., p. 132.
§ Reynolds's System of Medicine, vol. ii. p. 90.

hypodermically injected, in the dose of $\frac{1}{10}$ to $\frac{1}{4}$ or $\frac{1}{2}$ grain."

The treatment of delirium tremens has undergone a radical change within the past few years. This is well expressed in the following observations by Dr. Anstie:

"In former times—indeed, a very few years since—the notion universally prevailed that the delirious symptoms were owing to the exhaustion which was chiefly kept up by want of sleep; and, consequently, that the production of continuous sleep for several hours was the sole and all-important means of cure. It was therefore the custom to ply the patients with larger and larger successive doses of opium, with the view of drowning the delirium in narcotic stupor. Great mischief arose from this wide-spread belief and practice. In the first place, it has often happened that the patient, without ever sleeping at all, has passed first into a condition of coma-vigil, next of stertorous breathing, and at last sunk, fairly poisoned with opium."*

I have quoted these strong but just expressions to warn my readers against the abuse of the hypodermatic injection of morphia in the treatment of delirium tremens.

The following are the indications for the use of this method in this disease:

---

* Reynolds's System of Medicine, vol. ii. pp. 88, 89.

The condition of "horrors," or wakefulness, preceding delirium.

Excessive and uncontrollable vomiting of food, drink, and medicine.

Mild cases, in which there is little tendency to depression of the vital forces, in which the assimilation of food proceeds satisfactorily.

It is contra-indicated in severe and protracted cases, with great depression of the vital forces and non-assimilation of food;

In cases in which serious organic lesions of liver or kidneys have occurred;

In cases in which the delirium tremens is consecutive to traumatic or other serious lesion of brain.

In **cerebro-spinal meningitis** opium is the best remedy, especially in the onset of that disorder, and according to Radcliffe* the hypodermatic injection of morphia is the best method of administration.   Erlenmeyer,† who appears not to have had any personal experience with the hypodermatic use of morphia in this disease, refers to the experience of Bois.   According to Eulenberg,‡ Niemeyer used this method as a palliative in an epidemic at Rastadt and Carlsruhe.   It relieved the pain and cramps, and quieted the extreme restlessness (*gross Unruhe*), which are marked

---

* Reynolds's System of Medicine, vol. ii. p. 702.

† Die subcutanen Injectionen, op. cit., p. 31.

‡ Die hypodermatische Injection, op. cit., p. 156.

phenomena in these cases. Dr. B. Arnold, of
Donzdorf, reports favorably of its use in these
cases.* According to Stillé,† the opium treatment was very serviceable in the disease as he
observed it in Philadelphia. The author's experience is fully confirmatory of the published observations. He has witnessed remarkable cures
effected by the timely, and even heroic, use of
morphia subcutaneously. It is especially serviceable in the early stage—stage of irritation—
and ceases to be useful when depression of function—paresis—occurs.

In the psychical disorders *insomnia* is a prominent symptom, for the relief of which the morphia injection is especially indicated. When insomnia is the substantive disorder, a combination
of morphia and atropia is better than morphia
alone,—a fact which I shall develop in a future
chapter.

In the treatment of **coup-de-soleil, sunstroke,**
very unexpected and gratifying results have been
obtained by Dr. Hutchinson at the Pennsylvania
Hospital.‡ He injected one-fourth of a grain of
the sulphate of morphia, which produced almost
instant relief, and was followed by rapid recovery.

Hysteria.—In England Hunter,§ in Germany

---

* Schmidt's Jahrbücher, vol. cxxvii. s. 163.
† Epidemic Meningitis. Philadelphia, 1868.
‡ Pennsylvania Hospital Reports, vol. ii. p. 291.
§ On the Speedy Relief of Pain, etc., l. c.

Lander and Fronmüller,* were the first to employ the hypodermatic method with morphia in the treatment of hysterical convulsions. Lorent † recommends it in *hysterical melancholy.* In my own experience, no remedy has acted so promptly and satisfactorily in terminating a hysterical paroxysm as this. One-twelfth to one-eighth of a grain of sulphate of morphia is sufficient for this purpose; but in this disease, owing to the craving for narcotic stimulation, it is not proper to administer a remedy efficacious indeed, but so apt to induce appetite for its repetition.

Epilepsy.—Brown-Séquard was the first to indicate the utility of hypodermatic injections of morphia in epilepsy. He combined with it atropia. Results as important as they were unexpected have followed this method. It has been found that not only are the paroxysms in violent cases quickly relieved, but permanent benefit also has been obtained by diminishing the number, frequency, and severity of succeeding attacks. This remedy disputes with bromide of potassium the first place in the amelioration and cure of epilepsy. One may succeed when the other fails; both, of course, fail frequently. It is important, then, to have clear notions as to the kind of cases in which one or the other should be preferred.

As has been pointed out by S. W. Duckworth

---

* Eulenberg, l. c.   † Op. cit., p. 17.

Williams,* Russell Reynolds,† and myself,‡ bromide of potassium is more effective in cases of *grand mal* in which the paroxysms occur frequently, with great violence, and during the daytime, and less effective in those which occur chiefly at night. The bromide is more effective in epileptoid convulsions symptomatic of " coarse organic lesion of the brain." It is less effective in the *petit mal* and in convulsive *tic*.

The hypodermatic injection of morphia is preferable in epilepsy the paroxysms of which occur at night, in the *petit mal,* and in convulsive *tic*. It is not proper, as a general rule, in cases of epileptoid character dependent upon cerebral lesion.

When the paroxysms succeed one another rapidly, and are violent, the injection may be made during an attack, and without loss of time. Ordinarily two or three times a week will suffice, and, whenever practicable, the onset of an expected attack should be anticipated. A very marked amelioration in obstinate cases may be thus induced. With the decline in number and violence of the seizures there will be witnessed under this treatment most gratifying improvement in the mental condition. For the treatment of epilepsy, seven or eight minims of my solu-

---

* On the Bromide of Potassium in Epilepsy and Certain Psychical Affections. Pamphlet.

† The Practitioner, vol. i. p. 5.

‡ Fiske Fund Prize Essay, 1871, p. 38.

tion, or one-fourth of a grain, will be a sufficient quantity for each injection. Notwithstanding the good effects of this practice, the certainty of inducing a morphia habit by frequent repetition of the narcotic impression is a serious objection to the method, and it is, consequently, rarely employed at the present time.

Scanzoni was the first to use the hypodermatic injection of morphia in *eclampsia*. This practice was followed by Lander, Hermann, and Lehmann, with good results.* The injection is much safer than the inhalation of chloroform, almost as prompt in its effects, and quite as efficient in suspending the morbid reflex excitability. In the convulsions of infancy, whether dependent upon reflex irritation of teething, worms, indigestible food, etc., the hypodermatic injection of a small quantity (one-thirtieth to one-sixteenth of a grain) of sulphate of morphia will promptly terminate the paroxysms. This treatment must be conducted with caution in very young subjects. It will be prudent in any case to attempt relief by the ordinary measures, especially by the removal of the cause of irritation, before resorting to so powerful an agent. The dose for this purpose should not exceed one-sixteenth of a grain, and may be sufficiently powerful in one-half this quantity (one-thirty-second of a grain).

* Erlenmeyer, op. cit., p. 35.

One of the most important recent contributions to our therapeutical resources is the demonstration, made by Prof. Loomis, of New York, of the remarkable curative power possessed by the hypodermatic injection of morphia in the *convulsions of albuminuria.* Heretofore the presence of albumen in the urine has been held to contra-indicate the use of the preparations of opium; but the observations of Loomis have established the fact of an antagonism between the action of morphia on the one hand and of that condition of the intra-cranial circulation which occurs in albuminuria on the other. In albuminuria the arterial tension is low, the perivascular lymph-spaces are distended with serum, and the brain-substance is anæmic. In this state of things Traube found a sufficient explanation of the convulsions which by others were supposed to be caused by uræmia.

In the treatment of uræmic convulsions, considerable doses of morphia are not only well borne, but are demanded by the conditions present. For an adult half a grain may be administered at once, and this must be repeated promptly if the convulsions continue, or if they recur after having ceased for a time. As much as two grains may be injected within a few hours in severe cases. The author must, however, repeat the caution that such heroic medication must not be undertaken without due consideration and an accurate diagnosis.

Chorea.—Hunter[*] and Levick,[†] of Philadelphia, employed the hypodermatic injection of morphia in this disease with success. When the jactitations are incessant and violent, preventing sleep and causing injury to the soft parts, the patient wearing out at length, the use of morphia subcutaneously has undoubted value. It is useful in those cases in which Trousseau[‡] was in the habit of prescribing enormous doses of morphia internally. But over ordinary cases of chorea, as Dr. Bristowe[§] has shown, "specific forms of treatment have little or no real influence," and suitable hygienic means will as certainly conduct the case to a favorable termination. Nevertheless, in the very violent cases to which I have referred there is no means of treatment equal to the hypodermatic injection of morphia. Generally speaking, such cases require the maximum doses, as Trousseau's use of ten, twelve, and even fourteen grains of morphia daily with success sufficiently indicates. Commence with one-fourth of a grain, and increase according to the effect produced: it will rarely be necessary to exceed one grain at a single injection.

Tetanus and Hydrophobia.—Hunter used the hypodermatic method in cases of traumatic teta-

---

[*] Loc. cit., p. 27.   [†] American Journal of Med. Sciences.
[‡] Clinique Médicale de l'Hôtel-Dieu, tome ii. pp. 195, 196.
[§] The Practitioner, No. X., April, 1869, p. 195.

nus, "giving sleep and diminishing the spasms," but without permanent relief, death ensuing in each. Ruppaner* injected two cases with the liq. opii comp., which very much assuaged the sufferings of the patients, but did not retard the fatal termination. He urgently recommends further trials with this agent. More favorable results were obtained by others. Thus, Eulenberg† used it with success in a case of traumatic tetanus. In idiopathic tetanus, and in trismus neonatorum, more favorable results have been obtained, but these forms of trismus are much more amenable to treatment than the traumatic. Demarquay‡ obtained good results in the treatment of cases of tetanus during the second siege of Paris, by a new mode of using subcutaneous injections. He carried the needle deeply into the contracted muscles, and, if possible, to the point of entrance of the nerves. He thus injected the masseters, the muscles of the neck, the sterno-cleido-mastoid, the sacro-lumbar muscles, etc. He used in this way one to two grains of the muriate of morphia daily, with the effect to relax the spasms and permit the nourishment of the patient. Of three cases treated in this way, two recovered and one died; but the fatal result in this case was due not to the tetanus, which was relieved by the injections, but to pyæmia. The subcu-

---

* Hypodermic Injections, p. 136.   † Op. cit., p. 136.
‡ Bull. Gén. de Thérapeutique, Oct. 15, 1871, p. 299, et seq.

taneous use of the extract of Calabar bean (physostigma), or of woorara, is much more effective in the treatment of tetanus.

The sufferings of the patient affected with *hydrophobia* may be much diminished by the hypodermatic injection of morphia, but I am aware of no case in which the fatal termination has been averted.

Local Muscular Cramp and Spasm.—Eulenberg has used the subcutaneous injection of morphia in the muscle-spasm succeeding amputation of the thigh. I have obtained the greatest advantage from this method of treatment in the painful jactitations of the muscles which occur in cases of fracture. In a case of fracture of the femur on the paralyzed side of a hemiplegic patient, the injection procured instant relief to the very violent and persistent muscular spasms which occurred in a few hours after the injury. As is well known, Dr. Marshall Hall was the first to point out the fact that in paralysis of cerebral origin the muscular irritability is not lost, and may indeed be greater than normal; afterward confirmed by Duchenne de Boulogne, and now universally admitted. In the patient to whom I refer the muscular irritability existed in an exaggerated degree. Besides the pain which the violent spasm produced, union of the fractured femur would have been impossible if no means had existed for terminating the muscular spasms.

Neuralgia.—The greatest triumphs of the hypodermatic method have been achieved in the treatment of neuralgia. As Dr. Anstie, in the able article already referred to, remarks, " The advantages of morphia, hypodermatically administered, over opiate medication by the stomach, are such as would be *a priori* incredible, nor can they as yet be fully explained. In particular, it is impossible to account for the far greater *permanence* of its action in relieving nerve-pain, which is so marked that its discovery has initiated quite a new era in the treatment of severe neuralgias." *

Following the classification of Valleix, the neuralgias are divisible into two classes :

I. Superficial Neuralgias.

II. Visceral Neuralgias.

The first class is subdivisible into the following :

Trifacial.

Cervico-occipital.

Cervico-brachial.

Intercostal.

Lumbo-abdominal.

Crural.

Sciatic.

The second class will be more conveniently referred to in connection with internal diseases.

---

* Op. cit.

8*

It would be unprofitable to devote space to a special consideration of nerve-pain according to its anatomical seat, for the principles of treatment are the same. I propose to make observations on the most important varieties, to illustrate the hypodermatic treatment in all.

Neuralgia of the fifth nerve, or trifacial, is the most important of the whole group. It occurs more frequently, is more painful, and is more difficult to cure. But from the lightest case of facial pain, due to irritation of decayed teeth or cold, up to the atrocious and incurable epileptiform tic, there are numerous gradations in respect to severity and curability.

In *toothache* the hypodermatic injection of morphia is often immediately curative. It is, of course, less permanently beneficial when caries exists, but even in this case it affords great relief. It may also be used to diminish the pain of extraction. The facial neuralgia of pregnancy is promptly cured by it, as I have repeatedly ascertained by trial. This fact was first pointed out, I believe, by Dr. H. R. Storer, of Boston, the eminent gynæcologist of that city. These cases, as is well known, are extremely obstinate under the old methods of treatment, and those who have suffered from them on former occasions are exceedingly grateful for the relief so promptly and permanently afforded by the hypodermatic method.

The attacks of neuralgic pain experienced in

any portion of the distribution of the fifth are readily relieved by the same means. This remark is true of *migraine, hemicrania, clavus hystericus,* and other forms of neuralgic headache. I need hardly remind the reader that this method of treatment is not proper in that form of headache which often ·precedes and is a symptom of cerebral hemorrhage. That severe and obstinate neuralgia of the fifth known as *tic douloureux* is generally curable by the hypodermatic injection of morphia, and if not curable, is always much ameliorated by this means. A single or two or three injections may not suffice, but the persevering use of full doses may at length be successful. In obstinate cases the dose may be raised from one-fourth to one grain twice a day. Even that intractable form of *tic douloureux* described by Trousseau,* under the name "epileptiform neuralgia," may be much ameliorated by this means, and the existence of the patient elevated from a condition of abject misery to comparative comfort. The extent of the curative influence exerted by the hypodermatic injection in cases of *tic douloureux* will depend upon the age of the patient and upon the presence or absence of structural changes in the nerve or in the brain. Certainly the injection, properly used, will render unnecessary those severe surgical measures sometimes practised (section of the

---

* Clinique Médicale, tome ii. p. 100, et seq.

nerve) for temporary relief to the agony which
the patient endures. I cannot too strongly in-
sist that for decided relief of these severe cases
very large doses are necessary—one grain twice
a day. It is quite common to hear that hypodermatic injections have been tried in a certain
case and have failed; but upon inquiry it will be
found that they have not been properly made,
or that a sufficient quantity of morphia has not
been used. In a case of severe epileptiform tic
now in my charge, a hypodermatic injection had
been used by another practitioner without avail,
but in my hands a half-grain of morphia does
not fail to induce sound and refreshing sleep for
the whole night, and great comfort and freedom
from pain for some hours on the following day.
What is equally gratifying in this case, the epileptiform convulsions have been rendered notably milder.

Cervico-occipital and *cervico-brachial neuralgia* are
more amenable to treatment than *tic douloureux.*
A few injections of morphia will generally suffice
to cure them.

I have had most gratifying success in the treatment of *herpes zoster* by this means. The hypodermatic injection at once suspends the severe
pain and burning (intercostal neuralgia) which
accompany this disease, and cuts short the duration of the eruption.

Next to the severer forms of tic, the most
troublesome neuralgic disorder with which we

have to deal is *sciatica.* I may affirm with regard to this what Dr. Anstie has remarked about epileptiform tic, that the hypodermatic method has inaugurated quite a new era in its remedial management.

In severe and protracted cases, in which changes in the nerve and in the nutrition of the limb have taken place, permanent relief cannot always be guaranteed to the patient; but the injections steadily continued in the maximum doses will in a great majority of cases effect a cure finally. When morphia fails, atropia may be tried, and *vice versa;* or both, as is preferable in my experience, may be employed together.

Dr. Lawson,* who has had an unfortunate personal experience with this painful and troublesome malady, and has also had a number of cases under treatment, concludes that the hypodermatic injection of morphia *" is almost the only remedy for sciatica."* He advises the injection to be made into the thigh, four inches below the hip-joint, and over the course of the nerve. Although I can coincide in judgment with Dr. Lawson in respect to the utility of the subcutaneous injection of morphia in the treatment of acute or recent cases of sciatica, I must demur as to chronic or old cases. In these relief to pain and amelioration of the condition may be

---

* The Medical Times and Gazette, Nov. 12, 1870, p. 650, and also, Sciatica, Lumbago, and Brachialgia, London, 1872.

certainly effected by the morphia injections, but curative results less certainly. We have in the deep injection of chloroform a more decidedly curative agent, and to the article on this subject the reader is now referred.

Notwithstanding the exceeding utility of hypodermatic injections of morphia in the treatment of neuralgia, no judicious physician will rely on them exclusively in the management of severe cases. A suitable dietary and regimen must be enforced; constipation and other reflex sources of nervous disturbance must be corrected, and anæmia relieved by iron, cod-liver oil, the hypophosphites, etc. The part which cachexias —syphilitic, plumbic, mercurial, and paludal— may play must not be overlooked in the selection of remedies. Even where curative results are not attained, where relief to pain only is the result, the existence of the patient may be rendered tolerable.

Is it necessary to confine the injections to the "painful points," or to the site where pain is felt? I have already indicated my belief that the position of Mr. Charles Hunter is in the main correct, and that "localization" of the injection is not necessary. There is by no means a unanimity of opinion on this point. Dr. Wood, the discoverer of the method, Béhier, Erlenmeyer, Lorent, Eulenberg, and Mitchell, Morehouse, and Keen, think that better results are obtained by injection into the painful spot.

Dr. Anstie, although believing that remote injection is in general as effective, maintains that exceptions are occasionally met with. Eulenberg bases his opinion on the fact that tactile and pain sensibility are diminished at the site of the injection. This point is disputed. Immediately after the injection is practised, the neighborhood of the puncture is more sensitive to impressions, but after a time a decline in sensibility occurs. Repeated injection, if followed by inflammatory action, increases the local sensitiveness, but, otherwise, division of the nerves in the skin by the needle lessens the sense of pain.

When the neuralgia is seated deeply in the trunk, the injection must necessarily be practised at some remote point. When the neuralgia is superficial, the nerve accessible, it is an easy task to inject the fluid into the tissues adjacent. This practice—the injecting into the neighborhood of the nerve—is more efficient than remote injection in cases of sciatica, herpes zoster, and other superficial neuralgic affections, especially in cases of long standing, in which we may suppose the sheath of the nerve or the nerve itself has become altered. For it has been found that under such circumstances, the neuralgic pain being local and produced by lesions of the nerve, as, for example, in many cases of sciatica, the injection of various irritant substances into the vicinity of the diseased nerve will often be followed by a notable diminution of the pain and sometimes by a cure. This important fact has been demonstrated by Luton,* Bertin,† and Ruppaner.‡ It is probable that in this way local injections sometimes succeed when remote injections fail.

Diseases of the Respiratory and Circulatory Systems.

There are various neuroses of the respiratory tract quickly relieved by the subcutaneous use of morphia, and certain inflammatory affections modified to a remarkable extent. The first named, merely functional disorders, will be considered first.

Laryngismus Stridulus.—This reflex spasm of the laryngeal muscles is quickly relieved by the hypodermatic injection of morphia. As simple attacks occurring in children are readily cured by less powerful measures, this method should be reserved for the more important cases. In adults the same condition of the laryngeal muscles may be due to the pressure of an aneurism or other tumor on the recurrent laryngeal nerve, and is quickly arrested by the morphia injection. *Hysterical aphonia* may be immediately removed by one injection, but I must urge the injunction that morphia must be given with great circumspection to hysterical and nervous subjects gen-

---

* Archives Générales, 1867, p. 506.　　† Ibid.
‡ Hypodermic Injections, op. cit.

erally, since they quickly fall into the morphia habit.

Cough.—Cough maintained by habit—for example, the cough succeeding to whooping-cough —is quickly improved by this treatment; sometimes a few injections effect a cure, but if not, decided amelioration. *Whooping-cough* in the spasmodic stage is greatly benefited by the injection of minute quantities of morphia and atropia in combination: $\frac{1}{60}$ to $\frac{1}{20}$ grain of morphia and $\frac{1}{350}$ to $\frac{1}{150}$ grain of atropia. The cough of bronchitis, of phthisis, of aneurism, etc., is often surprisingly relieved by very small doses of morphia thus administered.

Asthma.—For the relief of an asthmatic paroxysm there is no means now known comparable to the hypodermatic injection of morphia, or of morphia and atropia. This fact I have maintained for many years—in the first and subsequent editions of this work. Within a few years past there have been frequent allusions in periodical medical literature to the good effect of morphia subcutaneously in spasmodic difficulty of breathing, notably in asthma. Prof. Sée has especially been prominent in urging this method of treatment, and Prof. Hirtz declares it produces "marvellous results." The following are the effects to be expected in ordinary cases:

It promptly relieves the paroxysm and enables the sufferer to lie down and sleep quietly; it lengthens the interval between the seizures and

renders succeeding paroxysms milder. Usually
I combine atropia with morphia, to give larger
doses with safety, for in this as in some other
neuroses the maximum doses are sometimes required to give relief. Although the relief afforded
is most grateful and surprising, it cannot be al-
leged, I think, that any cases are cured, but that
decided amelioration has been obtained in many
who have been subjected to the treatment for
some time, is a well-assured fact.

The dose necessary will vary with the susceptibility and habit. Those unaccustomed to the
subcutaneous use of morphia and susceptible
may be relieved by one-twelfth of a grain. This
will be a sufficient dose to begin the treatment
in any subject, but habit will lessen the power
and diminish the relief, so that increasing doses
will be necessary. There is always danger of
the morphia habit forming in these cases. The
relief afforded is so prompt and grateful that
patients wish to have the syringe in their own
hands. The remedy is soon abused and an incurable habit formed. Moderation is the condition of benefit, for if the patient is allowed to
pursue his own inclination and consume an enormous quantity of morphia, a state of the nervous
system is soon reached in which the remedy is
constantly necessary.

Emphysema.—The hypodermatic injection of
morphia gives more relief to the paroxysmal difficulty of breathing in emphysema than any other

remedy. Judiciously used, and not permitted to become a habit, it is a precious resource. Even more apt is the subcutaneous use of morphia to become a habit in emphysema than in asthma, and with even more disastrous results. Having witnessed several unfortunate examples of the morphia habit in such subjects, I desire to impress on my readers the necessity for caution in the use of this remedy.

Hiccough.—Usually the hypodermatic injection of morphia gives prompt relief in this neurosis. It is not effective when hiccough comes on in the course of abdominal—chiefly hepatic—diseases, for the treatment of which morphia has been employed. It is effective the more nearly the disease approaches the neurotic form, and is less effective the more serious the lesions of which hiccough is a symptom.

Acute Inflammatory Affections of the Respiratory Organs.—An acute catarrh of the nares, pharynx, larynx, and bronchi—*a common cold*—may be aborted by the timely administration of a minute quantity ($\frac{1}{16}$ to $\frac{1}{8}$ gr.) of morphia subcutaneously. It is probably the most effective treatment which we can employ in the treatment of this disease throughout its course, if the initial stage has passed. It is equally effective in the initial stage of *bronchitis*, and throughout its subsequent stages. An attack of *pneumonia* may be prevented by a full dose of morphia at the formative stage. I make this statement with full knowledge of its importance, and because I have seen cases which appeared to me to have so resulted by this treatment. It is difficult to decide on the affirmative of this proposition, for if a case supposed to be the beginning of pneumonia is stopped as it begins, how shall its true character be determined? To be successful it is essential that a full dose ($\frac{1}{4}$ to $\frac{1}{2}$ gr.) be given just as the preliminary congestion is developing. I am the more inclined to maintain this ground since Prof. A. L. Loomis has recently (1881) strongly advocated the treatment of the first stage of pneumonia by the hypodermatic injection of morphia. When so skilful a diagnostician and therapeutist as Dr. Loomis maintains the superiority of this plan of treatment I am strongly inclined to adopt it, the more especially as my own observations have in a measure prepared me for it.

There can be no two opinions in regard to the success of the treatment of *pleuritis* by the subcutaneous injection of morphia. Here, as in the maladies above referred to, it is possible by a timely use of the remedy to abort an attack of pleurisy. If the disease has passed the initial stage, the same treatment is the best up to the occurrence of exudations.

The Cardiac Neuroses.—I have had very satisfactory results from this method in the treatment of that form of *angina pectoris* which consists essentially in a neuralgic affection of the cardiac nerves. It is also recommended by Bamberger in the same disease, and by Erlenmeyer, Lorent, Eulenberg,* and other authorities. In the so-called "restraint neuroses" of the heart, a few cases of which have fallen under my observation, the very formidable symptoms were quickly removed by the morphia injection. Whether the symptoms are dependent on irritation of the pneumogastric or reflex irritation through the sympathetic, the good effects of the injection are equally evident. As Handfield Jones† asserts,—an opinion in which my own experience coincides,—the inhibitory action is frequently exerted through the gastric nerves. Rheumatic, malarial, and saturnine affections of the nervous apparatus unquestionably exert an influence in the production of cardiac neuroses.‡ These agree in producing pain, anxiety, breathlessness, and great depression of the heart's action, and are quickly relieved by the hypodermatic injection of morphia. Of course permanent relief will be obtained from suitable treatment for the cachexia on which these neuroses are dependent.

Violent and irregular action of the heart, when a functional trouble merely, is quickly relieved by this treatment. Usually a minute dose suffices.

---

* Die hypodermatischen Injection, op. cit.

† Functional Nervous Disorders, p. 215, Am. ed.

‡ Ibid., p. 218.

When palpitation and irregularity are due to narrowing and obstruction at the aortic orifice, the hypodermatic injection of morphia seems to me very questionable, if not positively unsafe, practice.   There is, however, a condition of the heart in which this treatment does most conspicuous good : in the case of dilated right cavities, with cough, difficult breathing, low state of the vascular tension, ischæmia of the arteries, general œdema, dry skin, and scanty urine.   Frequently, under these circumstances, the appetite is lost, the stomach intolerant, and the medicines used for relief, notably digitalis, increase the existing distress and are rejected by vomiting. The good effected by the injection of $\frac{1}{12}$ gr. to $\frac{1}{6}$ gr. of morphia is most striking : the cough lessens, the breathing becomes easy, the arterial pulse grows stronger and fuller, the skin perspires freely, the kidneys act more energetically, and the stomach becomes quiet, so that food is taken with some relish.   Beside these good effects in the changed state of the functions, others are experienced from remedies, especially digitalis, which can now be taken.

Diseases of the Digestive Apparatus.

The late Dr. Anstie formulated the following point of practice : Whenever opium or morphia is indicated in any case of disease, and anorexia or vomiting or obvious gastric disturbance exists, the remedy should be administered by subcutaneous injection. Although morphia, when exhibited in suitable doses by hypodermatic injection, is less apt to produce nausea and vomiting than when administered by the stomach, this rule is by no means of constant application.

Dyspepsia.—Dr. Clifford Allbutt, of Leeds, England, advocates the hypodermatic use of morphia in nervous dyspepsia with intolerance of food.* There can be no doubt of its utility. Not only is the stomach rendered more tolerant of food, but an appetite is created, and hence the effects are peculiarly grateful. Here, again, I must interpose a caution : nervous subjects are so lifted up out of the Slough of Despond by morphia that a craving is quickly established. The symptom *gastralgia* is usually quickly relieved by this remedy, as also the pain of *gastric ulcer ;* but it does more. By allaying pain and arresting vomiting waste is stopped and the strength nurtured. In the treatment of *acute gastritis* the subcutaneous use of morphia is invaluable, for it relieves the pain and vomiting, checks the inflammation, and obviates the necessity for disturbing the organ by drugs.

One-fourth of a grain is a sufficient quantity to be injected daily in cases of dyspepsia, gastralgia, and ulcer. In acute gastritis, this quantity may be necessary every four or six hours. The site of the injection is of little consequence,

---

* The Practitioner, vol. ii., 1869, p. 341.

but patients generally prefer the epigastric region.

Scirrhus.—In cases of *scirrhus* of any portion of the digestive tract, especially of the stomach, no palliative is comparable to the hypodermatic injection of morphia. The existence of a patient afflicted with scirrhus of stomach is not only prolonged, but is rendered comparatively peaceful and calm, by this treatment, for it diminishes or arrests the vomiting, enables the food to be assimilated, gives freedom from pain, promotes sleep, and thus saves the strength.

Cholera.—The most instantaneous and striking relief is afforded by the hypodermatic injection of morphia in *sporadic cholera*. It is indicated in this disorder after the irritant cause, whatever it may be, is evacuated from the intestinal canal. From one-sixth to one-half a grain, according to the severity and violence of the attack, may be injected into the epigastrium. The subcutaneous injection is strongly indicated in *epidemic* or *Asiatic cholera*. In this disease, the gastro-intestinal mucous membrane is not in a condition to appropriate remedies; hence the subcutaneous method is eminently rational.

Dr. Patterson,* of the British Seamen's Hospital, Constantinople, has employed the hypodermatic injection of morphia in a recent cholera epidemic. Of 10 cases " treated in the usual manner,"

---

* Medical Times and Gazette, Jan. 27, 1872.

9 died and 1 recovered. Of 42 cases treated by morphia subcutaneously, 22 recovered and 20 died. Of these 42 cases, 8 were *in articulo mortis* when admitted, 1 had a severe disease of the liver, 1 was far advanced in consumption, 1 was sixty years of age, 1 was near her confinement, and 3 were intemperate. Dr. Asche* treated two cases of cholera by this method successfully. According to the author's experience, for the first symptoms in cholera, the morphia injection is the most serviceable remedy, but when cramps occur and collapse is imminent, morphia must be supplemented by chloral. A combination of these agents possesses peculiar curative power in true cholera, as the author has ascertained by actual trial.

The Vomiting of Pregnancy has been relieved by the hypodermatic injection when all other means had failed. For the milder cases this treatment is unnecessary and improper; but in those severe cases in which life is reduced to the lowest ebb by the continual vomiting, and in which forced abortion has hitherto seemed the appropriate remedy, it is eminently successful. In all severe cases in which the ordinary remedies fail to give relief, recourse should be had to the hypodermatic method. A daily morning injection ($\frac{1}{12}$ to $\frac{1}{4}$ grain) administered during the period of great-

---

* Schmidt's Jahrbücher der Gesammten Medicin, Band 125, s. 331–7.

est difficulty, will enable gestation to proceed without danger to the mother, and without the necessity of adopting that serious alternative—abortion.

Colic.—It is the present practice to employ this method for relieving the pain and spasm of colic.   In most of these cases, of course, further treatment is necessary: constipation must be relieved; obstructions be overcome; the saturnine cachexia be removed; but the injection, by relieving spasm of the muscular layer of the bowel, permits these objects to be accomplished much more easily and speedily than would otherwise be possible.   Cases of hepatic colic, within the range of my observation, have been quickly relieved by the hypodermatic injection of morphia, where opium internally failed to produce the least mitigation of the pain, and where the inhalation of chloroform procured only the most temporary respite.   When pain is very excessive, the reader should remember small doses may not suffice, but one-fourth and even one-half a grain may be necessary, repeated according to circumstances.

The same observations are applicable to *nephritic* and *uterine* colic.

Peritonitis.—Opium being the remedy *par excellence* for inflammation of serous membranes, the hypodermatic injection of morphia should be employed in all cases in which promptness and completeness of effect may be desired.   This is especially the case in peritonitis, whether primary or secondary. Moreover, as in many cases of this disease the alimentation is of prime importance, and as nausea and vomiting are frequently present, the stomach administration should be deprecated, and the hypodermatic be preferred.

Neuralgia.—In the various forms of neuralgic pain which affect the abdominal organs, whether *gastralgia*, *enteralgia*, *hepatalgia*, *nephralgia*, etc., no remedy procures so prompt and, in many cases, complete relief as the hypodermatic injection of morphia.

Constipation.—In many cases of colic due simply to constipation, the injection not only relieves the pain but overcomes the constipation. It is true that in many cases the first injection temporarily suspends the peristaltic movements, but when habitually used this effect disappears, and the normal movements are not diminished, but promoted. Cases in which constipation existed have thus been corrected during a course of hypodermatic injections. A physiological fact which I have already noted throws light upon this: in a few seconds after the injection borborygmi and distinct intestinal movements are observed. If, then, constipation exist in cases in which it may be desirable to use the hypodermatic injection of morphia, this circumstance need not be considered a contra-indication.

Diseases of the Genito-urinary Organs.

I have already indicated the utility of the hypodermatic injection of morphia in nephralgia and nephritic colic. Lorent* refers to its use in parenchymatous nephritis to relieve the headache of uræmic intoxication. To this experience must be added the remarkable observations of Loomis in respect to the exceptional utility of morphia injections in uræmic convulsions. When, however, the action of the kidneys is deficient, excretion lessened, or elimination checked, morphia is contra-indicated.

Affections of the Bladder and Urethra.—In cases of chronic cystitis I have given great relief by the hypodermatic injection. It suspends those violent expulsive efforts which occasion the principal suffering. In *acute cystitis* the injection, by procuring quiet to the organ and by diminishing the irritability of the mucous membrane, will directly contribute to the cure. The sufferings of the patient afflicted with *calculus* may be thus prevented until operative measures can relieve him permanently. *Spasm of the bladder* is quickly relieved by the same means; as also that painful but obscure affection, " the bar," which sometimes succeeds too violent and prolonged sexual intercourse. The hypodermatic injection may

---

* Die hypodermatischen Injectionen, op. cit.

also be used to relieve *spasmodic stricture*, but for this purpose it is by no means equal in my experience to chloroform. It is convenient to blunt the sensibility preliminary to the operation of catheterism, and is a capital means for relieving *chordee* and prolonged and teasing erections. But to prevent unpleasant erections and nocturnal losses, the use of morphia and atropia together is preferable to morphia alone. For information on this subject I refer the reader to the chapter on " Morphia and Atropia."

The hypodermatic injection of morphia is capable of a variety of important uses in obstetric practice. It promptly arrests those *false and irregular pains* at the beginning of labor, which annoy the woman without advancing the case. In primiparæ it has been used to diminish the sufferings of labor. It is much better than morphia by the stomach to procure rest and sleep during a prolonged first stage. No remedy is equal to the hypodermatic injection of morphia for the relief of *after-pains*. In all of these circumstances no fear need be entertained that the judicious use of the injection will interfere with regular uterine contractions. The quantity to be administered will vary from one-sixth to one-fourth of a grain; the latter amount need rarely be exceeded.

The pain of *dysmenorrhœa* can be promptly relieved by subcutaneous injection of morphia; but for all pelvic pain, as Dr. Anstie has remarked, atropia is the best remedy. As a palliative in *scirrhus of the uterus* and of the *mammæ* the hypodermatic injection of morphia is much superior, in respect of economy and effectiveness, to the stomach administration of the same drug. Lastly, on this topic, in all cases of severe pain involving any of these organs the hypodermatic injection of morphia is indicated.

Diseases of Constitutional or Specific Origin.—Dr. William Henry Fuller writes enthusiastically of the great value of the hypodermatic injection of morphia for relieving the pain of acute rheumatism. I shall have some remarks to make in a succeeding chapter upon the use of morphia and atropia in that disease, and will not now anticipate. I have used with great advantage the hypodermatic injection of morphia to relieve the *nocturnal pains of tertiary syphilis*. Besides the complete and permanent relief to the pain which I have procured by persistence in the injections, I have observed also remarkable improvement in the lesions of bones and muscles. Not only in syphilitic but other forms of disease in which pain precedes, and in which an altered condition of the nerves produces structural changes, I have observed that relief to the pain is followed by cessation of the morbid process in the part. This fact is well shown in zoster, an affection of the skin dependent upon some functional disturbance of its sensory nerves, which disappears very promptly after relief of the hyperæsthesia.

Of course, in syphilitic neuralgia, the hypodermatic injection should not be used to the exclusion of the iodide of potassium. In the cases in which I have employed it the pain persisted notwithstanding repeated use of large doses of the iodide,—a condition of things not unfrequently encountered, for long use of this remedy and to the point of saturation—to borrow a term from the chemists—induces a tolerance fatal to therapeutical efficiency.

In Certain Surgical Diseases and Operations.—To prevent shock, and to relieve pain after operations and injuries, the hypodermatic injection of morphia is not as much used as it should be. No means affords such relief as this in the first few hours after *fracture* or *dislocation*. The reduction of dislocations may be facilitated and the pain prevented by the injection, in cases where it is undesirable or impracticable to use chloroform. It has recently been shown * that the *reduction of strangulated hernia* is much facilitated by the same means. In all operations requiring the knife, to prevent the after-pain, to sustain the vital powers, and to maintain the necessary quietude of wounded parts, the hypodermatic injection of morphia should be used.

To aid Chloroform Narcosis.—Bernard † made

---

* The Practitioner, August, 1869.

† Bulletin Général de Thérapeutique, vol. lxxvii. p. 241, et seq.

the important discovery that the use of morphia subcutaneously, previously to the inhalation of chloroform, aided materially in the production of anæsthesia, and with a much smaller quantity of chloroform, and prolonged the stage of narcosis so that continued inhalation was not required. Nussbaum, the distinguished surgeon of Munich, soon after made a similar observation independently. Bernard advised the subcutaneous use of morphia before commencing the inhalation; Nussbaum, after the condition of analgesia had been induced. Prof. William Warren Greene, M.D., then of Pittsfield, Mass., some time afterward announced the same fact, without being aware, apparently, of the recommendation of Bernard and the practical application of the discovery to surgical practice by Nussbaum. The practice of the injection before beginning the inhalation diminishes the irritation of the air-passages, prevents the coughing and struggling, and, doubtless, also removes the danger of cardiac paralysis, which in some rather rare cases takes place with the first action of the anæsthetic on the cardiac ganglia. In many subjects protracted vomiting and great depression of the vital powers occur on recovery from the anæsthetic state: a morphia injection will prevent these results. It appears in a high degree probable that the subcutaneous injection of morphia will obviate the tendency to death by cardiac or respiratory failure in the anæsthetic state.

As it does prolong the anæsthetic stage with a lessened quantity of chloroform, it seems incredible that surgeons will neglect so important an addition to their resources.

As a Physiological Antagonist.—The antagonism existing between morphia and atropia has been abundantly proved by clinical facts. The nature of this antagonism and the practice based on it will be considered in the section devoted to this subject. Morphia has been used successfully as an antagonist in poisoning by *gelsemium*, and by *veratrum viride*. In a case of poisoning by gelsemium, narrated by Dr. Courtwright,* the symptoms were promptly relieved by the subcutaneous injection of morphia. Two grains of morphia sulphate were required to antagonize a tablespoonful of the saturated tincture, about equal in strength to the official fluid extract. Several cases of successful treatment of opium-poisoning by veratrum viride have been reported, and in many cases an alarming degree of depression caused by veratrum viride has been removed by the administration of tincture of opium. The clinical experience has been confirmed by trials on animals.†

---

* Cincinnati Lancet and Observer, vol. xxxvii., 1876, p. 961.

† Cartwright Lectures for 1880, "On the Antagonism between Medicines and between Remedies and Diseases." New York, 1881, p. 77.

CODEIA AND ITS SALTS.

THE PREPARATION.—The only salt of codeia readily procurable is the sulphate. As the strength of this alkaloid is barely one-half that of morphia, the dose for hypodermatic injection is from one-eighth to one-half—even to one grain. As, however, commercial codeia is apt to contain morphia, large doses ought not to be given until the strength of the specimen used is ascertained. Extemporaneous solutions should be prepared from powders of the strength required.

PHYSIOLOGICAL EFFECTS.—The actions of codeia are similar to those of morphia. It is less nauseant and more hypnotic. It probably, also, has less effect in restraining the intestinal movements, and in lessening the irritability of the bladder. The various secretions and excretions are less affected by codeia than by morphia. Codeia has also less pain-relieving power. Whilst thus, in the whole range of the action, codeia is less powerful than morphia, it has more distinctly a hypnotic action and less nauseating and constipating effects. When the usual medicinal dose—one-fourth to one-half a grain—is administered subcutaneously, the same local effects are produced by codeia as by morphia. The systemic action is as prompt, but is less decided; the stage of stimulation is less pronounced and shorter in duration, and the action of the heart and the arterial tension are less elevated than is the case with morphia. From these actions it may be inferred that codeia is possessed of valuable qualities which might be utilized in preference to morphia in various morbid states.

THERAPY.—Codeia may be used in the various maladies in which morphia is now administered hypodermatically, but it presents no advantages except in those cases in which a special hypnotic action is desired,—in *mania, hypochondria,* and *delirium tremens,* with the limitations already enjoined in the case of morphia. In *diabetes* it has been employed with distinct advantage by the stomach, and will probably be found more effective by the subcutaneous areolar tissue. In the *neuroses of the respiratory organs* codeia will probably prove more advantageous than morphia.

NARCEINE has been used subcutaneously, but without any advantage,* and morphia and narceine combined have been employed hypodermatically by Lubinski.†

EXTRACTUM OPII and LIQUOR OPII COMPOSITUS (Squibb's) have also been administered by the hypodermatic method, but they are greatly inferior to morphia.

---

* Eulenberg, Allg. Therapie—Percutane, Intracutane und Subcutane Arznei-Application, p. 82.

† Ibid.

THE OPIUM OR MORPHIA HABIT AND ITS TREATMENT.

THE introduction of the hypodermatic syringe has placed in the hands of man a means of intoxication more seductive than any which has heretofore contributed to his craving for narcotic stimulation. So common now are the instances of its habitual use, and so enslaving is the habit when indulged in by this mode, that a lover of his kind must regard the future of society with no little apprehension. It may well be questioned whether the world has been the gainer or the loser by the discovery of subcutaneous medication. For every remote village has its slave, and not unfrequently several, to the hypodermatic syringe, and in the larger cities men in business and in the professions, women condemned to a life of constant invalidism, and ladies immersed in the gayeties of social life, are alike bound to a habit which they loathe, but whose bonds they are powerless to break. Lamentable examples are daily encountered of men and women, regardful only of the morphia intoxication and indifferent to all the duties and obligations of life, reduced to a state of mental and moral weakness most pitiable to behold.

Usually the habit is formed in consequence of the legitimate use of the hypodermatic syringe in the treatment of disease. Employed in chronic painful maladies for a long period, it is discovered, when an attempt is made to discontinue the injections, that the patient cannot or will not bear the disagreeable, even painful, sensations which now occur. More frequently, when the injections are to be used for a long time, the patient is unwisely intrusted with the instrument, and taught all the mysteries of the solutions and the mode of administration. Under these circumstances, there being no restrictions on the sale of the drug, the patient rapidly increases the dose, and presently comes to use a quantity of morphia which may seem almost incredible. Twenty, forty, sixty grains of morphia daily the author has known to be consumed by persons who have come under his observation, and Levinstein* records cases in which, in a short time, 1 gramme (15 grs.) was the daily allowance. To maintain a constant effect on the organism there must be a material increase in the amount administered every few days, and ultimately in most subjects a condition of the nervous system is brought about in which the new dose simply relieves the horrors and bodily depression left by the preceding quantity. Slaves to a vice beyond their control, they no longer

---

* Die Morphiumsucht. Berlin, 1877.

experience the feeling of well-being, the exhilaration, the intoxication, which were produced at first. There are very obvious differences in the physical and mental effects of moderate doses used for a comparatively short period and large doses administered for years. It will conduce to a clearer conception of the subject to treat of these two classes of morphiamaniacs in separate paragraphs.

1. *Small Doses for a Short Period.*—If the injection have been administered in a moderate quantity—half to a grain several times a day for six months—and at a fixed hour, the patient begins to experience characteristic nervous sensations as the time for the injection approaches; he becomes uneasy, restless, "fidgety;" he is wakeful, his senses are abnormally acute, and he has more or less headache and vertigo; his feelings are easily touched; a globus rises in the throat; nausea and troublesome borborygmi, with some intestinal pain, occur; general malaise, a sensation of fatigue, accompanied with muscular pains and decided inability for physical exertion, with depression and a cold sweat, are felt. These are the sensations, in less or greater degree, according to the time which has intervened, that inform the individual of the need of a new dose. Marvellous, indeed, is the change when the injection is practised. All the disagreeable, even painful, sensations and the dreadful unrest, which had but a moment before

caused an indescribable discomfort, have now vanished, and in their stead are present a feeling of perfect comfort, and an active state of body and mind equal to any effort. How grateful is the patient for the feeling of relief, and how impossible to forego the use of a drug which so transforms his feelings and imparts a glow to the world about him!

If the injections are suspended suddenly and entirely, very severe nervous disturbances are induced. An obstinate headache, vertigo, tinnitus; wakefulness, coming on after a short period of somnolence, interspersed with snatches of sleep disturbed by horrible dreams; during the waking moments an inexpressible anxiety and gloom and depression; unappeasable restlessness, with an overpowering sense of fatigue and a deep-seated aching in the members; nausea, vomiting, repugnance to ·food, intestinal pain, diarrhœa, sometimes of a colliquative character; very great depression of the powers of life, a weak, small pulse, becoming rapid and thready on exertion; coldness of the surface, a cold, clammy sweat, are the formidable symptoms developed by the sudden withdrawal of morphia, when used for some months in moderate quantity.

2. *Large Doses for a Long Period.*—The symptoms already detailed are present in these cases, but are more pronounced. The physiognomy of the morphiamaniac is peculiar: his face is pallid,

eyes dull and glazed, pupil small and sluggish, countenance strange and weird, expression unearthly. His skin has an earthy, sallow tint, the nutrition impaired either in the direction of an increased accumulation of fat, the tissues being soft and watery, the muscles small and wanting in contractile energy, or in the way of general emaciation. Whether gaining or losing in weight, feebleness is a characteristic of the bodily state. The least exertion causes a rapid pulse and accelerates the breathing. The appetite is poor and digestion is feeble. Great repugnance is felt to animal food, and, indeed, towards all the more substantial articles of diet, and fluids and fruits are almost wholly used. This abnormal taste is in part due to the dry mouth and cracked tongue, —physical conditions unfavorable to the sense of taste,—and in part to the poor digestion. The secretions of the intestinal canal and of its annexed organs, notably the liver, are so diminished in amount as to affect digestion seriously, hence the stools are dry, hard, scybala-like, yellow or grayish in color, and coated with tough mucus. So insensible does the mucous membrane become that the· fæces are retained for lengthened periods, hemorrhoids form, and an obstinate eczematous eruption appears at the margin of the anus. After a time, the retained fæces set up a high degree of irritation, an acute gastro-intestinal catarrh is produced, and an attack of cholera morbus occurs, with sometimes

very serious depression of the powers of life.
In some individuals, it is true, the hypodermatic
use of morphia does not impair the appetite and
the digestive power, and does not interfere with
the normal and regular action of the intestines;
but these cases are exceptional. Gastro-intestinal
attacks, such as I have described, occur in some
morphiamaniacs every few weeks; in others
every few months,—several times, certainly, during the course of the year. The effect of the
capricious and *bizarre* appetite, of the lessened digestive power, and of the diminished absorption,
is to impair the quality of the blood,—to induce
a serious kind of anæmia. None of the organs
of the body can perform their functions properly
under these circumstances; hence the mental and
physical feebleness of the morphiamaniac. There
is a function, however, which suffers especially,—
the reproductive. The first effect of the use of
morphia to a moderate extent is to increase the
sexual feelings, but a considerable dose administered for the first time will depress or suspend
the power of erection. Victims of the subcutaneous use of morphia soon lose all sexual feeling,
and are deprived of the power of erection and
the production of semen. During the continuance of the habit no semen whatever is secreted,
and no nocturnal losses occur; when the habit
ceases, the secretion of semen is resumed and
involuntary evacuations again take place. Morphia suspends the function without otherwise

impairing it, for we find that these subjects possess the same virility after the cessation of the morphia habit that they possessed before. The same result occurs in women. When the morphia habit is established, the menstrual function ceases and the sexual life is entirely suspended, and the woman is as absolutely without all of those feelings and instincts pertaining to her sexual relations as if they had never existed. As in man, this suspension of the sexual life is co-existent with the morphia habit, for the natural order is restored when the vice ceases.

Levinstein emphasizes the occurrence of albuminuria and diabetes in cases of morphia habit. I have made many urinary examinations in these cases, and have as yet met with no instances of these maladies. It is true, in a few examples of considerable hepatic disturbance, I have noted the presence of sugar in the urine, but it was not permanent, and they could not, therefore, be regarded as cases of diabetes. Without presuming to call in question Levinstein's accuracy, it may be affirmed of cases met with in this country, that they are not due to the subcutaneous use of morphia.

The frequent use of the syringe, often the hasty introduction of the needle, and the use of a rusty and dirty needle, the injection of badly-prepared solutions, the repeated injection into certain localities, have a disastrous effect. Large, hard nodules form, which slowly suppurate, ex-

tensive sloughing may take place, and septicæ-
mia and pyæmia sometimes occur with a fatal
result. In a large proportion of these morphiamaniacs, suppuration, abscesses of considerable
size, and ulcers are produced. I have seen the
arms, the abdomen, the thighs and legs, a mass
of ulcers, of abscesses in various stages of formation, and of cicatrices.

Dujardin-Beaumetz* narrates a case in which
the injuries thus produced resulted in death. M.
Calvel† has collected many cases of abscesses,
traumatic fever, and other accidents produced
by the injections, but he rightly enough refers
them to the causes above mentioned,—the state
of the needle, improperly-prepared solutions, and
the cachexia induced by the morphia habit.
Braithwaite‡ reports a most instructive case of
morphia habit of six years' duration, in which
there occurred numerous abortions. In a new
pregnancy at six months, a vast abscess formed
in the thigh, from which erysipelas developed,
and a high degree of constitutional disturbance
arose. Nevertheless, delivery occurred at term,
and an attempt was then made to stop the morphia suddenly, but most serious troubles resulted,
the erysipelas reappeared, and the attempt had
to be abandoned. On the other hand, some

---

* Bulletin Général de Thérapeutique, Jan. 1879, p. 87.
† Thèse de Paris.
‡ Lancet, 1878, p. 874.

escape these accidents entirely. One of the most inveterate subjects I have ever encountered was a man living in the wilds of Texas, who used a glass hypodermatic syringe that had been broken many times and mended with successive deposits of sealing-wax, until only the rusty old needle remained in view, and yet escaped all accidents. Several instances have been reported—one already quoted—in which death was produced by the suppuration and the systemic condition thereby induced. That there is a special state of the tissues induced by morphia, to which the formation of abscesses is due, is hardly admissible. The causes mentioned above are quite sufficient to account for them.

After a time the repetition of the injection does not induce any pleasurable sensations. For a few minutes after the insertion of the morphia the patient experiences mental sensations of a most depressing kind, but gradually a condition of well-being follows, consisting chiefly in relief from the horrible mental and physical agony which comes on as the morphia influence declines.

The morphiamaniac never has sound and refreshing sleep. Although, after a period of wakefulness due to the stimulant action of the narcotic, he lapses into a condition of somnolence more or less profound, it is disturbed by dreams and visions of the most horrifying aspect, entirely without the range of human experiences. If the individual awake in the midst of these weird dreams, some time elapses before he can realize his situation, and then comes over him, like a flood, a dreadful sense of the position in which the morphia has placed him. Doubtless the visions of the English Opium-Eater, which are not realized in the experiences of those who take opium as a test experiment, were actually present during sleep or the half-waking state. It results from this condition of the brain during sleep that the organ is not adequately rested, hence the sense of fatigue of mind which is felt on awaking, and which is removed only by the narcotic. In many subjects, ultimately, sound sleep is never produced, and a certain proportion pass into that condition of obstinate wakefulness known as *coma vigil.* The action of morphia must then be supplemented by the bromides, chloral, etc., for this condition is one of imminent danger to the mind. In spite of all the means which can be used, some of these cases pass into a busy, active, and trembling delirium,—*delirium tremens,*—or into acute mania or acute melancholia, with strong suicidal impulses.*

In the more severe cases of morphia habit, attacks of fever similar to ordinary intermittents take place irregularly. In my experience these attacks are usually associated with an acute gastro-intestinal catarrh, and are preceded by

---

* Leidesdorf, London Medical Record, Nov. 15, 1876.

constipation and a much overloaded colon. They occur more usually in the summer and fall, rarely in the winter, and they may appear in regular order for several days as quotidian intermittent, or assume the remittent type, terminating in two or three days in a profuse sweat. When the paroxysms are quotidian, they are identical with quotidian ague,—there is a chill, followed by fever and a sweat. Although they may be regular, they are usually irregular, and are not amenable to quinia, but do readily yield to an increased quantity of morphia. Very great depression of the powers of life may occur in some of these cases when a chill is coincident with a severe attack of cholera morbus. I have known instances in which the objective phenomena of a seizure were similar to those of a " pernicious intermittent."

Besides the immediate results of the morphia habit by hypodermatic use, the unfortunate morphiamaniac is assailed by dangers accidental and contingent, but nevertheless of high importance. A sudden illness, the performance of a surgical operation, may be seriously complicated if the physician or surgeon in attendance is not aware of the existence of the habit and the extent to which it is indulged. Still more serious are cases of sudden insensibility or impairment of the language faculty, for then the patient cannot communicate the fact of the habit.

Sufficient data do not exist as yet to permit an

exact statement of the anatomical changes occurring in the morphiamaniac, except the anæmia or cachexia; but experiments on animals indicate that slow changes occur, similar to those in chronic alcoholismus.

When, in the old and confirmed cases of morphia habit, an attempt is made to withdraw the morphia suddenly, the most serious symptoms are produced. As soon as the effect of the last dose taken has passed off, they describe various uneasy sensations,—of creeping and crawling in the skin; tingling in the hairy scalp, in the hands and feet, and other places; a more or less profuse, often very profuse, perspiration breaks out over the body; the nose runs freely with a watery mucus, and sneezing comes on in paroxysms; nausea is experienced, and after a time vomiting occurs; the bowels become relaxed, and soon an exhausting watery diarrhœa comes on; the pulse grows quick and the action of the heart excitable and more feeble as the waste goes on by vomiting and purging; the urine may be albuminous or contain sugar, as affirmed by Levinstein, and the nervous system falls into a very unstable condition. As these symptoms progress, the mind is disturbed by horrible depression during the waking moments, and by strange, fantastic, weird dreams during the brief snatches of sleep. Great depression of the vital powers comes on as the case progresses, and in old morphiamaniacs a condition of collapse ensues. Having had one experience of this kind, I shall not be again induced to repeat it, if for no other, for strictly humanitarian reasons, since the mental and physical sufferings are truly horrible. Levinstein advocates this method and succeeds, but one may accomplish results in an asylum not attainable in ordinary practice, where the patient possesses entire liberty of action. But Levinstein's experience is not agreeable to any humanitarian. Although the details are brief, it is obvious that his patients suffer severely and are in danger of death. He describes two degrees of collapse,—the mild and the severe, —in which the patients pass into the condition of the algid stage of cholera, and may require, to save them from death, a hypodermatic injection of morphia. The only permanent cures are, in the experience of the author, those in whom the reduction was gradual. I do not deny that by the immediate withdrawal a cure may be effected in a few days or weeks, but such cures are not permanent. The time in which they are effected does not relieve the system of the terrible unrest, the wakefulness, and the longing, which persist for months after the withdrawal of morphia. On the other hand, by the slow, almost insensible diminution of the daily amount, the nervous system has the opportunity to adapt itself to the change, and hence the unrest and the longing die out.

TREATMENT OF THE MORPHIA HABIT.—The

amount of difficulty in the treatment of any case will depend on sex, constitutional peculiarities, the length of time the habit has continued, and the *per diem* quantity which has been administered. When the physician or an attendant has administered the injections and the patient has not acquired the method, the task is comparatively easy. I have usually succeeded by following these rules:

Never stop the injections suddenly.

Diminish the dose very gradually, without the knowledge of the patient.

Never use morphia alone for a lengthened period, but with atropia.

As the morphia is diminished, increase the proportional quantity of atropia until the effects of the latter preponderate.

When the effects of the atropia are fully experienced, the patient will generally begin to complain that the injection has lost its peculiar influence, has become unpleasant, and will desire that it be discontinued.

But the difficulty of breaking up the morphia habit is vastly greater in the case of confirmed subjects who have used the syringe themselves for years. What method must be pursued in these cases? I am firmly of the opinion that the morphia should be very gradually diminished, —so gradually as to make but little demand on the moral strength and the self-control. If the patient is required to suffer the horrible sensations produced by the want of morphia, the treatment will fail, for he will prefer indulgence though it lead to death. The patient's co-operation must be secured, and he must decide for himself that the attempt shall be made. Strangely enough, the morphiamaniac's impatience must be held in check. When under the influence of the morphia they have great confidence in their self-control, and they demand that a large reduction shall be at once made. It is never safe to yield to these importunities, for when the flood of desire comes rolling in they are powerless to resist, and when cheating begins the attempt is a failure. It is a fundamental rule,—*reduce the morphia by insensible degrees.*

The patient must give up the custody and use of the syringe to some one else, and must have the quantity necessary to make him comfortable at certain regular intervals, and without failure. If the daily quantity used is not large,—say four grains,—the syringe should be given up at once, and the morphia be administered by the stomach in proportional quantity,—*i.e.*, about three times as much. Thus, if four grains was the daily allowance subcutaneously, at least twelve grains will be needed by the stomach. The rule may be formulated as follows: *Give by the stomach a sufficient quantity to make and keep the patient comfortable.* It is a most important advantage gained to exchange the subcutaneous mode of administration for the stomachal,—for, although the effect is slower in the latter, it is better maintained, and the patient experiences less sudden and severe changes in his feelings. What is even more important, the chain of morbid associations connected with the hypodermatic syringe is broken up, and the patient feels hopeful, and anticipates release from his bondage because already freed from the necessity of puncturing his skin.

When the *per diem* allowance of morphia hypodermatically is from one scruple to a drachm, considerable reduction must take place before the syringe can be abandoned, but it should be dropped at the earliest moment.

The rate of reduction should not be more rapid than one-sixteenth of a grain hypodermatically, and one-fifth of a grain by the stomach, each three to eight days. The necessary time must be given to it, though a year or more may be required. Haste on the part of the physician and impatience on the part of the subject will defeat the purpose in view, and when the bounds are once broken the work must be begun again. *Festina lente* is the proper rule to follow, and a wise and firm patience is the highest attribute of the physician.

Are there any aids to treatment? Is there not some drug which may destroy the appetite for the narcotic? These questions are constantly asked, and they may be answered in the affirmative, but not in accordance with popular notions.

The success of the plan proposed may be facilitated by several expedients. It is of the first importance to correct the abnormal condition of the digestive functions. One or two compound cathartic pills at night will change the character of the evacuations, and induce a more healthy state of the intestines. As a stomachic and nerve tonic, a solution of strychnia in a mineral acid is highly useful:

> ℞ Strychniæ, gr. i;
> Acid. muriatic. dil., ℥ij. M.
> Sig.—Ten minims in a tablespoonful of water three times a day, before meals.

If the stomach is irritable and the hepatic function torpid, the following prescription is serviceable:

> ℞ Acid. carbolic.,
> Tinct. iodinii, āā ʒss. M.
> Sig.—One drop in water three times a day, before meals.

If there is merely an atonic condition of the digestive functions, the tincture of nux vomica, in doses of ten to fifteen drops three times a day, may be very useful. Under the same circumstances, quinine is indicated, especially in solution with a mineral acid; or the quinine may be given in combination with iron, as in the elixir of phosphate of iron, quinia, and strychnia; or the tinctures of cinchona, with the other bitters, may be prescribed in combination. The fluid extract of cuca or coca (*Erythroxylon Coca*) has been used with distinct advantage in many cases as a tonic and restorative. According to some experienced observers, it has an effect on the nervous system which entitles it to be regarded as supplying a need or a craving.

The most important point in the management of these cases is the alimentation. If the morphiamaniac can take food and digest it, the difficulty in the treatment is reduced one-half. It is, in fact, a useless effort to give tonics if the food-supply is wanting, or inappropriate, or undigested. Milk, egg-nog, animal broths, should be given freely, and as soon as possible steak, chops, and other substantial food. Their digestion may be aided by the simultaneous administration of pepsin, pancreatine, and mineral acids. If the stomach refuses everything else, it will probably take milk, or milk and lime-water. If but little food enters the stomach, it may be supplemented by rectal alimentation,—notably by injections of defibrinated blood, on the plan of Dr. Smith, of New York. If food can be taken in a small quantity only, it should be taken frequently,—every three hours. The supreme point is to renovate the blood, so that all the organs shall functionate properly. With an improved state of the cerebral nutrition there will come a more manly feeling, a firmer will, and a higher moral sense.

The use of alcohol is a highly important question. When the nervous system is losing the loved morphia impression, it will take kindly to alcohol. There is a loss rather than a gain in the substitution of alcohol for morphia, and, unfortunately, this is an exchange which has not unfrequently been made. Levinstein refers to cases, and I have known the trade to be made in both ways. Although alcohol in any of its forms must be used with caution, it is undeniably serviceable. A whiskey toddy at bed-hour may induce quiet and refreshing sleep; wine at dinner in moderation will promote digestion. But I especially warn the practitioner against a procedure which the patient will be inclined to adopt, that is, to take sufficient alcohol to cause a distinct impression on the nervous system, in place of the morphia impression. This must result disastrously, for when the alcohol influence expires there will occur such a condition of depression that more alcohol or more morphia will be necessary.

To procure quiet and refreshing sleep is essential in these cases. When the morphia is very gradually diminished, the function of sleep may not be disturbed, and if proper care is used will not be. When, however, the morphia is decreased rapidly, or is suddenly stopped, the most agonizing feeling of unrest is felt all over the body, but especially in the members, conjoined with the most absolute wakefulness. Under these circumstances chloral is extremely useful, indispensable, indeed, for by procuring sound and refreshing sleep life even may be saved. During the course of treatment chloral will be necessary now and then, but the utmost circumspection is required to prevent the substitution of a chloral for a morphia habit. The patient is always clamorous for some agent as a substitute.

Occupation is an important adjunct to the treatment, for every disagreeable sensation increases with the attention given to it. The occupation should give employment to both mind and body, and should be engrossing but not harassing. Depressing news, the ordinary annoyances of life, and especially anxiety of every kind and degree, should be removed from these patients, that there may be no excuse for the smallest departure from the prescribed course. Travel may be serviceable, but there are so many contingencies as to involve risk of failure in the treatment. Furthermore, there are the fewest number in a pecuniary condition to justify the attendance and the largely increased expenditure. But change of scene, in so far that the individual is removed from the associations connected with his habit, is always desirable.

ATROPIA.

Tᴜᴇ Sᴏʟᴜᴛɪᴏɴ.—The sulphate is the salt chiefly employed for hypodermatic use. This supplies all the conditions: it is readily soluble in water; the solution is free from irritating qualities. The formula which I employ is the following:

℞ Atropiæ sulphat., gr. ij;
Aquæ destil., ʒi. M.

Five minims of this solution represent one-forty-eighth of a grain. A much stronger solution may be used, as the following:

℞ Atropiæ sulphat., gr. i;
Aquæ destil., ʒi. M.

A minim of this represents one-sixtieth of a grain. Or the following may be preferred:

℞ Atropiæ sulphat., gr. i;
Aquæ destil., ʒij. M.

A minim of this contains one-one-hundred-and-twentieth of a grain. I prefer the first solution for these reasons:

It is sometimes desirable to inject very minute quantities in susceptible subjects, and this cannot be done when the solution is very concentrated.

140

The dose may be much more varied in a weak solution.

I have elsewhere stated the general objections to strong solutions, which apply to atropia.

A *penicilium* develops very rapidly in an atropia solution, and at the expense of the atropia; the more concentrated the solution the greater the loss.

On account of the rapid growth of the *penicilium*, the solution of atropia should not be kept too long, but should be prepared in small quantity frequently during warm weather. Filtration will, of course, free the solution from visible impurities, but considerable loss of strength will be noticeable each time.

DOSE.—Extraordinary discrepancies are to be found in the statements of various authorities as to the quantity of atropia which may be used subcutaneously. Dr. Anstie * notes with surprise the large quantity advised by Trousseau,—$\frac{1}{12}$ to $\frac{1}{6}$ of a grain,—a quantity sufficient to produce most serious toxic symptoms. Dr. Ruppaner † gives the dose at $\frac{1}{60}$ to $\frac{1}{30}$ of a grain, Lorent ‡ at $\frac{1}{25}$ of a grain, and Courty employed as much as $\frac{1}{6}$ of a grain at a single operation. Five minims of the solution which I recommend to the reader, or $\frac{1}{48}$ of a grain, is the largest amount desirable to use

---

* The Practitioner, op. cit.
† Hypodermic Injections, op. cit.
‡ Die hypoder. Inject., l. c.

in most cases. Very great differences in the
susceptibility to the atropia influence are found
to exist.   Children bear a much larger proportional amount than adults. Women are much
more susceptible than men. Persons having a
light complexion are much more easily influenced
by it than those having a dark complexion. A
delicate female, having light-blue eyes and flaxen
hair, possesses, according to my observation, the
maximum susceptibility. For such subjects two
minims of my solution, or $\frac{1}{120}$ of a grain, is a
sufficient dose to commence with, and even this
amount may occasion serious symptoms. To
produce a curative effect in many severe cases of
neuralgia, *e.g.*, sciatica, much larger doses than I
have recommended may be necessary. It will
rarely be required, however, to inject more than
$\frac{1}{40}$ of a grain at one time.

Physiological Effects.—The local symptoms
at the point of puncture are the same as those I
have described for morphia.

A peculiar dryness and pallor of the lower lip
is the first systemic effect to be observed. The
dryness quickly invades the mucous membrane
of the mouth, fauces, and larynx, rendering deglutition somewhat difficult, and the voice husky.
At the same time the pupil begins to dilate,
reaching its maximum dilatation in about thirty
minutes. With the dilatation of the pupil there
occur also deranged accommodation—the vision
being presbyopic—and dimness of vision, the

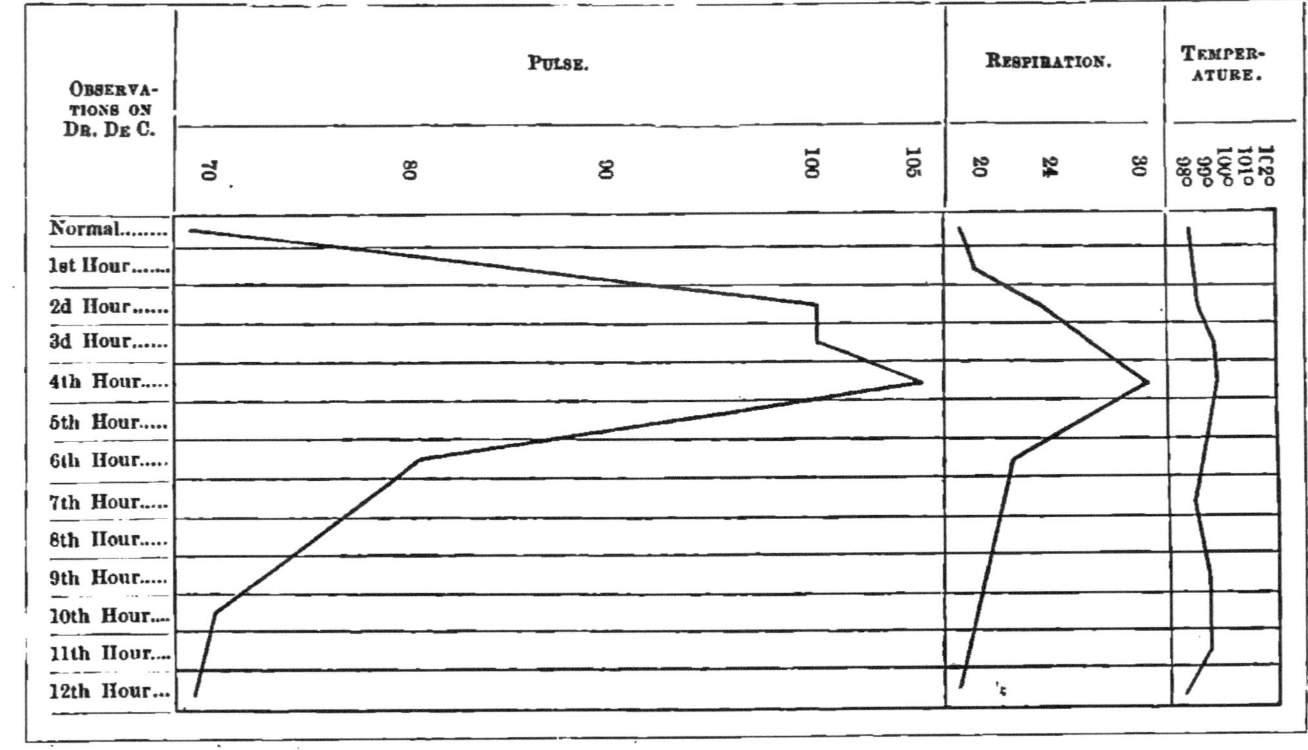
OBSERVATIONS ON DR. DE C.
PULSE.
RESPIRATION.
TEMPERATURE.
70
80
90
100
105
20
24
30
102°
101°
100°
99°
98°
Normal
1st Hour
2d Hour
3d Hour
4th Hour
5th Hour
6th Hour
7th Hour
8th Hour
9th Hour
10th Hour
11th Hour
12th Hour

outlines of objects being blurred and indistinct.
Flushing of the face, more or less deep according to the temperament of the patient, fulness of
the head with supraorbital pain and sense of
distention, and giddiness, are now experienced.
With the development of these effects we observe
increased action of the heart and rise in the bodily temperature. The pulse rises in a few minutes
to nearly twice the normal number of beats, and
the thermometer exhibits elevation of temperature; but the correspondence between pulse-rate
and temperature characteristic of fever does not
exist. In the diagram, page 143, the influence of
atropia upon the pulse and respiration movements, and upon the temperature, is exhibited.
I subjoin also a sphygmographic tracing showing the influence of atropia on the arterial tension. This must be compared with the first
tracing on page 68, which is the normal tracing
of Dr. Drake, upon whom the observation was
made.

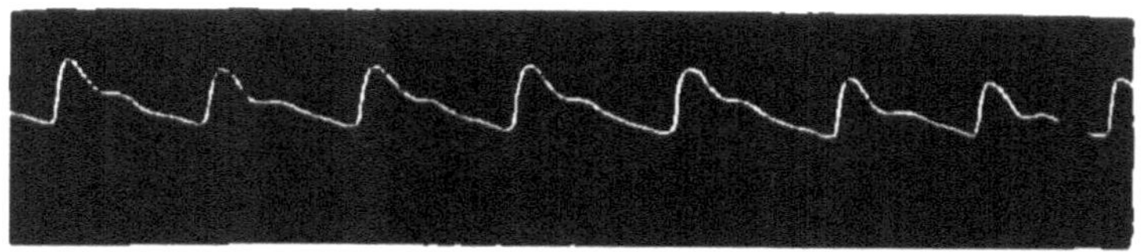

At this period the subjective sensations of the
patient, as well as the objective phenomena, are
those of fever; the skin is hot and burning, and
dry; the pulse full and bounding; the face
flushed; the eyes injected; the head aches; the

ears ring; the mouth is dry and hot; the voluntary movements are disordered in consequence of the vertigo and of the impairment of the muscular sensibility; objects appear confused, and distances cannot be correctly appreciated; hallucinations and illusions occur; when sleep takes place it is disturbed by vivid dreams, sometimes frightful, sometimes pleasing, the patient awaking and holding conversation with imaginary persons. Sometimes a somnambulistic state is produced, in which the patient walks about as if engaged in his usual avocations, talks with the objects of his visions, and quarrels and struggles with those who would oppose and restrain him.

Sometimes the face and forehead are of a vivid red hue, resembling in color the eruption of scarlatina; the fauces are also red and injected, and, to complete the resemblance to this eruptive fever, a whitish fur covers the tongue, through which the red and enlarged papillæ project.

The dryness of the mouth, after some hours, is replaced by a moist condition, in which a viscid, sticky, and somewhat odorous secretion makes its appearance. Corresponding to this change in the mucous membrane of the mouth some increase in the peristaltic movements of the intestines is to be observed, the evacuations being somewhat loose.

Frequent desire to evacuate the bladder is now experienced, with diminished power, the emission of urine taking place slowly and with difficulty, and sometimes, indeed, only after repeated efforts does the flow occur.

The mental effects, generally such as I have described, are sometimes of a character to awaken grave anxiety. Great depression of mind, a melancholic state, with a suicidal tendency, at night horrible dreams and visions, leading to acts of violence, have been noted by me in some exceptional cases. I mention this so that the reader will ascertain what peculiar mental effects, if any, have followed the atropia injection, and avoid repeating it if the sensations' above described have been experienced by the patient.

Such, in general, are the effects produced by the hypodermatic injection of a full medicinal dose. These effects continue about twenty hours; the dilatation of the pupil, the disorders of vision, and the slowness and difficulty of micturition being the last symptoms to disappear.

Atropia cannot be considered very actively toxic. The symptoms which it produces afford ample warning of danger before the life of the individual is really placed in jeopardy. The sensations which accompany the full manifestation of its physiological effects are so unpleasant that the patient early seeks relief, and the symptoms are so characteristic that a mistaken diagnosis is hardly possible.

When a fatal dose is received, all the effects which I have described exist in an exaggerated degree. The pulse finally becomes small and

thready, the action of the heart weak, and coldness of the surface succeeds to the unnatural
warmth.　This change in the symptoms indicates that the "irritability" of the organic muscular fibre is exhausted.

In order to a thorough comprehension of its
therapeutical action, we must form some exact
notions of the mode in which these physiological
effects are produced.*

The facts to be investigated are these:

The dilatation of the pupil.

The dryness of the mouth (arrest of secretion).

The increased action of the heart and lungs.

The rise of body heat.

The influence on sensibility and motility.

Several opinions have prevailed as to the mechanism by which the dilatation of the pupil is accomplished.

This effect, as well as the presbyopia, is now
known to be produced through the influence of
atropia on the organic muscular fibre.　By contraction of the radiating fibres of the iris, which
are innervated by the sympathetic, the pupil
dilates; by a similar action on the muscle of
accommodation, the lens is elongated, its diameter diminished, and the subject becomes presby-

---

* I have examined this whole question in my Prize Essay
of the American Medical Association for 1869, on Atropia
its Physiological Effects and Therapeutical Uses, to which
the reader is referred for full information.

opic. It is probable, also, that this effect is facilitated by the paralyzing action of atropia on the oculo-motor nerve.

A number of experiments have been made to determine the character of the influence exerted by atropia upon the heart and lungs. The part that paralysis of the pneumogastric plays; the part that direct stimulation of the cardiac portion of the sympathetic takes in the production of the phenomena, have been earnestly discussed. The inhibiting influence of the pneumogastric on the action of the heart is well understood: if the terminal filaments of this nerve are paralyzed, the action of the heart increases. It has been found, however, by Lemattre,* that the action of the heart is increased by atropia, notwithstanding division of the pneumogastric: this agent must, therefore, exert an immediate stimulant action on the cardiac ganglia of the sympathetic. This same effect is witnessed on the organic muscular fibre of the arterioles, as demonstrated by Lemattre in the vessels of the frog's foot and confirmed by myself. I have demonstrated another fact: the contraction of the vessels after a time ceases, and relaxation takes place. This change is coincident with a weakened action of the heart; in other words, the atropia finally exhausts the irritability of the organic muscular fibre. This is a capital fact, which must not be

* Archives Générales, 1864.

forgotten in our therapeutical employment of atropia.

The rise in body-heat is a product of increased oxidation due to the greater activity of the circulation. The redness of the skin and mucous membrane is due to the larger amount of blood pumped into the capillaries and the increased arterial tension. The increased oxidation finds expression in a much greater excretion of urea and the urates.

There are several physiological facts which explain the action of atropia in arresting secretion of the pulmonary and intestinal mucous membrane. Prevost * has demonstrated that ablation of the spheno-palatine ganglion is followed by greatly increased secretion from the Schneiderian mucous membrane. The action which atropia exerts on the ganglia of the sympathetic must be the opposite of this.

Patients brought fully under the influence of atropia generally experience considerable disorder of voluntary movement. This effect is compounded of vertigo, diminished sensibility of the sensory nerves, loss of co-ordinating power, and paresis of the muscular system of animal life.

A very curious phenomenon was observed by Frazer † in frogs paralyzed by atropia many

---

* Archives de Physiologie Normale et Pathologique, vol. i.

† Previously Undescribed Tetanic Symptoms produced by Atropia in Cold-blooded Animals. From Transactions of the Royal Society of Edinburgh. Edinburgh, 1869.

hours. When they lay limp and motionless, completely paralyzed and apparently dead, it was found that cutaneous irritation immediately excited tetanic spasms. I had noted previously (Prize Essay) that during the combined action of atropia and physostigma these convulsant and tetanic spasms could be excited at once. This remarkable fact serves to show the close relationship in action of those agents which belong to the two groups respectively of paralyzers and tetanizers.

THERAPY.—It will be convenient to arrange the subjects under this head in the same way as in the section on the therapeutical applications of morphia.

Diseases of the Brain and Nervous System.

Cerebral Diseases.—The subcutaneous injection of atropia is contra-indicated in inflammatory affections of the brain and meninges, for a constant result of the toxic effect of this remedy is hyperæmia of these organs. I have seemed to produce some good results, and certainly have relieved the referred pains of the extremities in cases of general paralysis. The "*late rigidity*" which comes on in many cases of hemiplegia, and which is often accompanied by severe pain in the affected limbs, has been much benefited by the hypodermatic injection of atropia. The pains of *progressive locomotor ataxia,* and that annoying disturbance of the sensory nerves, " *the fidgets*," which so constantly attends upon this disorder, may be relieved by this means. It has seemed to me that the subcutaneous injection of atropia exercised some influence also in retarding the progress of this disorder. Lorent has used the injection of atropia with advantage for relieving the pains which accompany *chronic meningitis* and *myelitis*. According to the views of Brown-Séquard, who holds that belladonna, by producing contraction of the arterioles, diminishes the supply of blood to the cord, the hypodermatic injection of atropia ought to be very serviceable in myelitis. But it is now known that the increased action of the heart, and the greater arterial tension produced by atropia, favor hyperæmia of these parts.

The hypodermatic injection of atropia is serviceable in certain cases of *delirium tremens*. The indications for its use are these:

Obstinate insomnia with great restlessness.

Weakened action of the heart; coldness of the surface; clammy sweat.

Failure of nutrients, bromide of potassium, chloral, and hypodermatic injections of morphia, to quiet the delirium and induce sleep.

In similar conditions in the *psychical disorders* the subcutaneous injection of atropia is serviceable. This method of treating these disorders has the sanction of the eminent authority of Graefe. My own observation entitles me to in-

sist on this caution : the use of atropia is unsuited to cases in which there is hyperæmia of
the nervous centres, or in cases of excitement
with power. Moreover, it is not suited to cases
of melancholia, for the reason already stated,
that in many persons it produces great despond-
ency of mind.

Certain cases of *mania*, characterized by restlessness, motor activity, and mental as well, with
hallucinations and incoherent rambling, the physical state being that of weakness and relaxation,
are sometimes remarkably benefited by atropia.
Ringer * describes such a case, and shows that
atropia is nearly if not quite as useful as hyoscyamia has been in analogous cases.

In *puerperal mania*, the general system being
in the condition of weakness and depression,
atropia is often successful in securing sleep and
improving the mental state.

Atropia cannot be considered a *hypnotic* in the
true sense of that term. It is sometimes said to
produce this effect indirectly; by allaying pain,
it is believed to render sleep possible. This, in
the opinion of the author, is not a correct statement of the ground of its utility in certain cases.
It is sometimes very useful as a hypnotic in cases
of wakefulness and coma-vigil, dependent upon
cerebral anæmia.

Neuralgia. — The subcutaneous injection of

---

* The Practitioner, vol. xviii. p. 166.

atropia is not as effective in the treatment of the
neuralgias in general as morphia by the same
method. The systemic effects of atropia are
also more unpleasant. For these reasons morphia is generally preferred. Nevertheless, when
morphia fails to produce the desired result, or
disagrees with the patient, as is sometimes the
case, atropia may be used. In certain neuralgias,
it must be admitted also, atropia is to be preferred to morphia, *e.g.*, in pelvic pain, in which
Dr. Anstie considers it superior to morphia, in
sciatica, and in certain cases of *tic douloureux*. In
the pain of the various forms of *dysmenorrhœa*,
in *ovarian neuralgia*, and in the pelvic pain experienced a few days after delivery, and due to the
pressure of the womb on certain nerves, atropia
by subcutaneous injection is most serviceable.

The principal triumphs of atropia over neuralgia have been in cases of *sciatica*. It is now admitted that atropia is one of the best remedies
for this disease. First proposed and used by
Mr. Hunter, it was afterward employed by Béhier, Courty, Oppolzer, Lorent, and others. It
has been found, however, that distant injection,
and even injection into the subcutaneous tissue
of the affected thigh, do not produce such good
results as throwing the fluid deeply into the
neighborhood of the affected nerve. More frequently, indeed, than in any other form of neuralgia, except the most obstinate and protracted
cases of tic douloureux, the nerve itself, or its

sheath, has undergone structural alteration; the limb is often diminished in size, its temperature and sensibility lowered, and the power of its muscles impaired. Under these circumstances more advantage is to be derived from local than from distant injection, just as Luton, Bertin, and Ruppaner have cured such cases by the injection of irritants into the affected parts.

In severe cases of sciatica and tic douloureux one-fortieth of a grain of sulphate of atropia may be injected; but it should not be forgotten that this quantity will excite very severe symptoms in susceptible subjects. Generally, five minims of my solution, or one-forty-eighth of a grain, will produce decided atropinism. Cessation of the pain is not immediate upon the systemic effects, as Mr. Hunter originally pointed out; indeed, the pain is often at first increased, but improvement takes place after a variable interval, and is often more permanent than after the morphia injection.

Tetanus and Hydrophobia.—In tetanus, atropia has been used in numerous cases, but without success. Recovery has undoubtedly occurred in certain chronic cases, and in idiopathic tetanus; but it does not appear that the result was fairly attributable to the subcutaneous injection of atropia. Within the sphere of my observation, it has been freely used in cases of tetanus and hydrophobia, but without permanent benefit.

Epilepsy.—Brown-Séquard proposed the subcutaneous use of atropia in epilepsy, but he combined it with morphia. Erlenmeyer used it, but with a negative result. My own experience with atropia in this disease is as combined with morphia. The subcutaneous injection of atropia may be employed, instead of the internal use of belladonna, on the method of Trousseau.* Recent experience at Leidesdorf's clinic has demonstrated that atropia has remarkable curative power in epilepsy. Its administration was based on the property possessed by it of reducing the reflex function in small doses. Large doses, as is well known, have the opposite effect on the reflex faculty. A number of cases have been reported cured. The daily use of $\frac{1}{120}$ grain subcutaneously is probably a suitable amount.

Diseases of the Respiratory and Circulatory Organs.

The subcutaneous injection of atropia is applicable to the treatment of certain neuroses of the thoracic viscera.

Asthma.—Courty was the first to employ atropia subcutaneously for the relief of asthma. He injected the solution over the pneumogastric nerve. Belladonna, in large doses, is now held to be the best remedy by Hyde Salter, Prof. Sée, and others.† Prof. Sée recommends belladonna because it is a " vascular and cardiac" agent, and

---

* Clinique Médicale, tome ii.
† The Practitioner, July, 1869.

" because the means of modifying respiration is to be found in the power to alter the pulmonary circulation." The hypodermatic injection of atropia is preferable to the internal use of belladonna for the following reasons:

The effect is more speedy and certain.

The relief which it affords is greater and more lasting.

In my experience cases of emphysema and spasmodic breathing, due to dilatation of the right cavities of the heart, are not so much benefited by atropia as asthma. I think it prudent to add a caution here: as atropia exhausts the irritability of the sympathetic ganglia, it is not proper to push the use of this agent in cases in which the muscular tissue of the heart is weakened by dilatation or fatty degeneration.

In order to procure the greatest relief to the asthmatic paroxysm, the injection should be made promptly at the beginning of the attack. The dose will vary from $\frac{1}{96}$ to $\frac{1}{48}$ of a grain. It may be inserted at any convenient situation. Succeeding attacks should be anticipated if possible, the injection being made when the first warnings are felt by the patient. As the effect of the atropine injection reaches its maximum in about a half-hour, it will at this time be perceived whether a sufficient quantity has been administered.

This method of administering belladonna is much to be preferred to the stomach administration, or to the methods of fumigation, pulverization, or inhalation, notwithstanding fumigation is strongly urged by Prof. Sée* in some lectures on the subject of asthma.

The administration of atropia may occasion much distress in the case of those asthmatics who suffer from dryness of the bronchial mucous membrane, and who experience relief when the secretion of mucus becomes abundant. I have known most alarming dyspnœa produced by the use of atropia in such subjects, and I therefore record a warning for the benefit of the inexperienced.

Harley †—influenced by the fact that great increase of the heart's action follows the administration of atropia, a fact, indeed, previously much insisted on by V. Bezold—recommends this agent as a cardiac stimulant in conditions of great depression of this organ. It is certainly exceedingly useful in those restraint neuroses in which the inhibitive action is exerted through the pneumogastric, for by paralyzing the terminal filaments of this nerve and stimulating the cardiac ganglia of the sympathetic, the action of the heart is quickly improved and the depression overcome. It is in this action, according to Prof. Sée, that we have an explanation of the utility of atropia in asthma.

---

* Bulletin Général de Thérapeutique, 15 Août, 1869.
† Gulstonian Lectures, also Vegetable Neurotics.

Diseases of the Digestive Apparatus.

Atropia, it will be remembered, first arrests secretions of the intestinal mucous membrane, but in the reaction which ensues from this state increased secretion takes place. It promotes peristaltic movements by its action on the circular fibres of the intestinal tube.

Vomiting.—Sea-sickness and the vomiting of pregnancy are both relieved by subcutaneous injection of a small quantity—$\frac{1}{200}$ to $\frac{1}{120}$ of a grain—of atropia. But the good effects are not constant, and, when successful, diminished by repetition.

Colic.—The various forms of colic may be relieved by this agent, but it is not so effective in most of them as morphia. It is adapted to cases of colic dependent upon constipation or upon lead-poisoning, but the most desirable resultsare obtained by the conjoined administration of morphia and atropia.

Cholera.—In the algid stage of cholera, during the last epidemic in the Southwest, the subcutaneous use of atropia appeared to bring on reaction in some very unfavorable cases. It is desirable to give the agent further trial in any succeeding epidemic.

Diseases of the Urinary and Genital Organs.

For all varieties of pelvic pain, as Dr. Anstie has informed us, the subcutaneous injection of atropia is the best agent. I need not repeat here what has already been said on this topic.

Bladder Diseases.—In *dysuria* and *enuresis* it is often most effectual. Belladonna has long had a deserved pre-eminence in the treatment of nocturnal incontinence of urine. Atropia by subcutaneous injection is the most effective way of administering it.

Irritation of the bladder, when arising from a nervous erythism, may be relieved in the same way. That troublesome disorder, *spermatorrhœa*, is most successfully treated by the hypodermatic injection of atropia. Two indications are to be supplied in many of these cases: the erotic sensations which originate during the sleeping state are to be suppressed; the reflex act of emission to be prevented. No agent accomplishes this more successfully than the subcutaneous injection of atropia at bedtime and at such intervals as observation has shown to be necessary.

Constitutional Diseases.

Remarkable relief to the pain and soreness of *acute rheumatism* has been obtained by Lorent from the subcutaneous injection of atropia. This treatment has been suggested by Harley as if it were an original idea with himself. He recommends that the atropia be injected in the neighborhood of the inflamed joint. I have followed this practice with great relief to the patient. One injection of $\frac{1}{48}$ of a grain daily will generally be sufficient to quiet the pain ; but morphia may be combined with it advantageously, if the patient be wakeful. It has seemed to me to exercise no little influence over the severity and duration of the disorder.

As a Physiological Antagonist.—The subject of the antagonism of morphia and atropia will be discussed in the next chapter.

The subcutaneous injection of atropia may be used against the toxic symptoms of certain vascular agents, as aconite, veratrum viride, tartar emetic, digitalis, which produce great depression of the heart's action. It has been proposed, also on insufficient grounds, for relief of poisoning by hydrocyanic acid. In my prize essay on atropia I have shown that hydrocyanic acid in toxic doses acts too speedily for atropia to influence the result, and that animals fully under the effects of atropia are quickly poisoned by an ordinary toxic dose of the acid.

Atropia is the antagonist to pilocarpine, muscarine, and physostigmine (eserine), and may be used to overcome and remove the lethal symptoms caused by either of these agents. The following observations, taken from my Cartwright Lectures, are appropriately reproduced here.

ANTAGONISM OF ATROPIA AND PHYSOSTIGMA.

HISTORY.—For the first time, in 1864, Kleinwächter treated a case of poisoning by atropia by the internal administration of physostigma, the symptoms being relieved to a great extent. In 1867, Bourneville, in a thesis on the treatment of tetanus by physostigma, related a single experiment in which the effects produced by a quantity of the powdered kernel, introduced into the stomach of a cabiai, were overcome by the subcutaneous injection of atropia. In 1868 I made a number of experiments proving the existence of the antagonism. The most important research was that of Professor Thomas R. Fraser, of Edinburgh, in 1869, who performed a great variety of experiments, and introduced new principles for the guidance of future researches of the same kind.* This investigation was followed by the report of the Committee of the British Medical Association, Dr. J. Hughes Bennett, Chairman.†

ANTAGONISM.—Before proceeding to the analysis of the published facts and experiments, we must have a definite conception of the actions of the two agents. In what respect do atropia and

---

* "On the Antagonism between the Actions of Physostigma and Atropia." From the Trans. of the Roy. Soc. of Edinburgh, vol. xxvi.

† Brit. Med. Jour. for 1874.

physostigma differ ? I have already described the
deliriant effect of atropia, its power to dilate the
pupil, to stimulate the heart and the respiration,
to arrest secretion, to flush and at the same time
dry the skin. Physostigma does not affect the
cerebral functions; it contracts the pupil, paralyzes the voluntary muscles, but does not impair
sensibility, increases secretion, energizes the heart-
beats and raises the arterial tension, and causes
death by paralysis of the respiratory muscles.
Placed in opposition, we find that the points of
difference are : on the brain, atropia causing delirious excitement, with hallucinations and illusions,—physostigma not affecting this organ at
all; on the pupil, atropia causing dilatation by
stimulating the radiating fibres innervated by
the sympathetic,—physostigma causing contraction by paralyzing the radiating fibres, thus leaving the third nerve unopposed; on the respiration, atropia stimulating the respiratory centre,—
physostigma paralyzing the muscles of respiration; on the heart, atropia increasing the rate of
movement without adding to the power,—physostigma increasing the power without hastening
the movements of the heart; on secretion, atropia
drying the mouth and the secretions of the intestinal tube,—physostigma increasing the salivary
flow and the secretions of the whole intestinal
canal; on the voluntary muscular system, atropia
causing paralysis of the motor nerves,—physostigma producing spinal paralysis. As regards

the lethal effects, the tendency to death by paralysis of the respiratory muscles, produced by physostigma, is overcome by atropia. Or, as it is expressed by Professor Fraser, " atropia prevents the fatal effect of a lethal dose of physostigma by so influencing the functions of certain structures as to prevent such modifications from being produced in them by physostigma as would result in death. The one substance counteracts the action of the other, and the result is a physiological antagonism so remarkable and decided that the fatal effects, even of three and a half times the minimum lethal dose of physostigma, may be prevented by atropia."

The first reported example of atropia-poisoning treated by physostigma proved a success. The first experiment made with the definite purpose of ascertaining whether an antagonism existed, also, apparently proved the point. But the first sustained and sufficiently extended experiments made to test the antagonism were those undertaken by myself in 1868, before the published observation of Bourneville. While acknowledging the superiority in every way of the research undertaken by Fraser, I respectfully submit that my investigations, as published in my prize essay* of the American Medical Association, clearly preceded his by a year. Claims of priority are, however, ungracious, and I do

---

* Trans. of the Am. Med. Assoc. for 1869.

not therefore urge mine. In his historical review, Professor Fraser has not sufficiently, I think, put my claim on its proper basis. Quoting from my essay, he takes a sentence or two from the general conclusions, which do not adequately convey the whole meaning of my researches. Thus, he says, "Dr. Bartholow deduces a number of general conclusions regarding the mutual counteraction of the two substances on several of the structures and functions modified by them. The following quotation contains an epitome of his views: 'Atropia is not a physiological antagonist to physostigma, except in regard to their action on the organic nervous system. It would be improper, then, to use atropia against poisoning by Calabar bean.'" As I shall presently show, my conclusions have been confirmed by subsequent investigations,—the antagonism existing in the actions on the nervous system of organic life, as I had demonstrated. After the detail of some typical cases, out of a large number of similar experiments, I came to the following conclusions:

"Atropia and physostigma are antagonistic as to their influence over the respiratory movements, —atropia increasing and physostigma retarding them.

"They are antagonistic in their action on the heart,—atropia producing excitation of the cardiac ganglia, and physostigma paralyzing them.

"They are opposed in respect to their action

on the sympathetic,—atropia causing increased action, and physostigma paralyzing this system.

"They have opposite effects on the pupil in virtue of opposite effects on the sympathetic,—atropia dilating the pupil by its action on the radiating fibres of the iris, and physostigma contracting the pupil by paralyzing the radiating fibres."

My conclusions of 1868 have not been invalidated by the subsequent investigations, and hence the experimental data must have been accurate. I therefore venture to submit that Professor Fraser's quotation from my essay does not adequately represent my opinions. Apparently without investigating on his own account, and accepting a very restricted excerpt from my paper, Dr. II. C. Wood* says, "In 1869, Professor Roberts Bartholow, of Cincinnati, on the strength of a few really indecisive experiments, arrived at a conclusion opposite to that of Bourneville." Dr. Wood has absolutely no warrant for this positive assertion. So far from coming to a conclusion opposed to that of Bourneville, it was to the same purport, and based on a number of really decisive experiments. I have dwelt on my own views longer probably than they deserve, but historical accuracy is of some moment, and no man wishes his proper opinions mangled and distorted by others.

---

* Therapeutics, Materia Medica, and Toxicology, 3d ed., p. 320.

The quotation I have made from Fraser's paper indicates his belief in the existence of an antagonism in the lethal effects of atropia and physostigma of wide range, and his experiments, which were very numerous and carefully made, certainly support his opinion.   The Committee of the British Medical Association hold this antagonism in less favor; although they admit its existence, they find it is more limited in range than Dr. Fraser had supposed.   Their general conclusion is: "sulphate of atropia antagonizes to a certain extent the fatal action of Calabar bean," yet they maintain that, "for all practical purposes, atropia as an antidote to Calabar bean is useless, and not to be compared with the effects of chloral hydrate." In the first part of this strong statement, the Committee confirm the conclusion to which I had come, several years before, in respect to the use of atropia as an antagonist to the toxic effects of physostigma.

The special points of antagonism have been elaborately studied by various observers.   As respects the heart, atropia first causes a rise of the blood-pressure, but this is followed by the opposite condition, or diminution of blood-pressure, while the action of the heart continues accelerated. Physostigma slows the movement by lengthening the diastolic pause, and increases the vigor of the contraction, and also raises the arterial tension. By Arnstein and Sustschinsky,* the excitability

* Centralbl. f. d. med. Wiss., No. 40, 1867.

of the cardiac branches of the vagi was found to
be increased by physostigma, and lessened by
atropia. The experiments of Rossbach and Fröhlich, in all respects remarkable and novel,* seem
not to confirm these observations. Köhler† and
Harnack and Wilkowski‡ found that physostigma
lessened the pulse-rate, after the peripheral filaments of the vagi were completely paralyzed by
atropia. Harnack,§ in a polemical paper strongly
characterized by the *fortiter in re*, controverts the
views put forth by Rossbach and Frölich, and by
Rossbach alone, in respect to the action of atropia on the heart and on the pupil. Köhler holds
that physostigma slows the heart by paralyzing
the accelerator nerve. It had already been shown
that atropia stimulated the accelerator nerve (Bezold and Blocbaum). Tachau‖ and Roeber¶
maintain that the retardation of the heart is due
to a paralyzing action of physostigma on the cardiac ganglia, but Laschkewich** shows that this
retardation is due to stimulation of the inhibitory
apparatus. The rise of arterial tension produced
by physostigma is probably due to contraction of
the constrictor fibres of the arterioles, since strong

---

* Pharmacol. Untersuchungen, Würzburg, 1873, p. 77.

† Archiv f. exper. Pathol. u. Pharmacol., i. p. 277.

‡ Ibid., v. p. 204.   § Ibid., iv., 1875, p. 146.

‖ Archiv d. Heilkunde, vi. 69.

¶ Hermann's Lehrbuch der experiment. Toxicologie, p. 339.

** "Beobachtungen über die physiol. Wirkungen der Cala-
barbohne," Virchow's Archiv, xxxv. p. 291.

local contractions of the intestine are produced by this agent when it is thrown into an artery supplying a small part of the bowel (Bauer).* How much soever the explanations differ, the fact remains that atropia and physostigma act in an opposed manner on the heart. As respects the respiration, there are fewer differences of opinion. That physostigma causes death by paralysis of respiration, the heart continuing in action after respiration has ceased, seems abundantly established.† On the other hand, it is generally conceded that atropia stimulates the respiratory function. Physostigma suspends, ultimately, reflex excitability, and is a spinal paralyzer; hence the function of respiration is only affected (Laschkewich, Tachau). On the other hand, the respiratory centre is stimulated by atropia, an acceleration of breathing takes place when the vagi have been divided (Bezold and Bloebaum). It is, therefore, clear that these agents are opposed in their actions on the function of respiration.

The point of opposition most conspicuous, and that which first suggested the existence of the antagonism, is the effect on the pupil—eserine causing contraction, and atropia dilatation of the pupil. Marked differences of·opinion exist as to the mechanism of the antagonism. By some the contraction of the pupil caused by eserine is referred to a paralyzing action on the dilator

---

* Hermann, op. cit. † Hermann, op. cit., p. 341.

fibres (Fraser, Hirschmann *), and by others to a spasm of the sphincter fibres (Grünhagen and Rogow,† Bezold and Goetz). That the latter view is correct seems supported by the fact that the effect of physostigma on the muscular layer of the intestine is to induce tetanic contraction or spasm. Further, when the pupil is contracted by eserine the contraction is readily overcome by atropia, but the atropinized pupil resists the action of eserine.

The delirium, hallucinations, and illusions caused by atropia are in no respect affected by physostigma. In all of the instances of poisoning by Calabar bean reported, the mind remained unaffected until near the end, when, carbonic-acid poisoning coming on, stupor and drowsiness supervened. All respiratory poisons, pure and simple, are accompanied at the close of life by the carbonic narcosis due merely to the suspension of hæmatosis. Carbonic-acid narcosis is an important element in the morbid complexus of atropia-poisoning. These agents do not, therefore, have an antagonistic action on the cerebrum.

In the spinal effects of atropia and physostigma there are obvious differences. They are both paralyzers, but atropia causes, in cold-blooded animals, a subsequent tetanic condition.

* Archiv f. Anat. u. Physiol., 1863, p. 309.
† Centralbl. f. d. med. Wissensch., 1863 p 577

When atropia and physostigma are administered simultaneously, this tetanic condition occurs at once,—a fact which I was the first to demonstrate; and so exalted is the reflex function of the spinal cord, that a slight tap on the surface of the body causes a tetanic spasm, the condition in the intervals being that of relaxation. In several of the cases of atropia-poisoning, trismus was a marked symptom. Atropia affects the spinal cord, Ringer and Murrell have shown;* and the paralysis induced by it, they maintain, is largely spinal, although it does impair the irritability of the motor-nerve trunks. According to the experiments of Dr. Mary Putnam Jacobi, the sensibility of the sensory nerves is impaired by atropia. Physostigma, on the other hand, increases the irritability of the sensory nerves and is a spinal paralyzer, leaving the motor nerves and the muscles intact. These agents, therefore, agree on more points than they differ in their action on the spinal cord.

As respects the function of secretion, there is an obvious difference in action between physostigma and atropia. An increased flow of saliva, of the intestinal juices, of the tears, and of the sweat, is a constant result of the action of physostigma, and is due, according to Heidenhain,† to a central excitation of the secretory nerves.

---

* Jour. of Anat. and Physiol., xi., Part xi.

† Arch. f. d. ges. Physiol., v. p. 40: quoted by Hermann.

This conclusion seems established by the fact that the increased secretion of saliva failed to occur when the chorda tympani was divided near the submaxillary gland. The action of atropia is the opposite of this—it suspends secretion, most probably by paralyzing the end organs of the nerves in the gland, for, as Schiff has shown, arrest of the secretion of the submaxillary gland follows division of the chorda tympani. Increased outpouring of saliva takes place when the divided extremity of the nerve is galvanized; whence it may be concluded that physostigma stimulates the secretory centres.

On the motor functions, and on the muscles, atropia and physostigma act differently. I have already emphasized the tetanizing action of atropia on cold-blooded animals, and the trismus which occurs in so many cases of poisoning. Botkin* was the first to show that atropia paralyzed the motor-nerve trunks, and Laschkewich† and Fraser proved that, in poisoning by Calabar bean, the irritability of the motor nerves and the contractility of the muscles were unaffected. The action on the motor functions is therefore different and not opposed.

In summing up the results of the various researches, it may be regarded as established: 1. That physostigma, or eserine, and atropia are antagonistic in their effects on the pupil. 2. That

---

* Virchow's Archiv, xxiv. p. 85.   † Ibid., loc. cit.

they act differently, but probably not antagonistically, on the heart, unless we accept the views of Köhler and Bezold and Bloebaum,—the former maintaining that physostigma paralyzes the accelerator nerves of the heart, and the latter that atropia stimulates these nerves. 3. That they are opposed in their action on respiration, physostigma paralyzing, and atropia stimulating the respiratory function. 4. That they are not opposed in their action on the cerebrum, atropia producing delirium, and physostigma having no effect on the cerebral functions, while both cause more or less carbonic-acid narcosis. 5. That they act differently and not in an opposed manner on the spinal cord and nerves, both producing paralysis, but atropia does, and physostigma does not impair the irritability of motor nerves. As regards the sensory nerves, physostigma augments their irritability, while atropia seems rather to lessen it, if any effect is produced. 6. That they act oppositely on secretion, physostigma stimulating and atropia arresting the secretions in general.

It follows from these considerations that the lethal effects of physostigma, due to paralysis of respiration, are overcome by atropia by sustaining the respiratory function. The Committee of the British Medical Association assert that " the antagonism exists within very narrow limits," but this happens to be sufficient to avert death when doses little more than lethal have been administered; still, the use of physostigma against the lethal effects of atropia is of doubtful propriety. The paralyzing effect of physostigma on respiration may, doubtless, be successfully overcome by the suitable application of atropia.

ATROPIA AND PILOCARPINE.

The antagonism of action between belladonna and pilocarpus, or atropia and pilocarpine, is one of the most interesting, as it is one of the most exact, in the whole series of antagonisms of medicinal agents. The functional disturbance produced by atropia has been sufficiently elaborated in the preceding sections. Our task is now chiefly concerned with the peculiar powers and attributes of pilocarpine. The history of jaborandi affords us a capital illustration of the benefit of physiological research as applied to the study of remedies. When it was first introduced, a great many observers in all parts of the world set about the study of its actions. In an almost incredibly short time we were put in possession of its actions, and the range of its uses was at once indicated. All has been abundantly confirmed by trials on man, and the first conclusions arrived at have only been supported by subsequent investigations. The literature of pilocarpus is already vast. I will call your attention only to the subject of its antagonistic action. We must first form a definite conception of what pilocarpine does.

In a few minutes after the alkaloid pilocarpine
has been injected subcutaneously, or taken into
the stomach, the action of the heart increases,
the face flushes, and a subjective sense of heat is
felt throughout the body, but especially about
the face. The increased action of the heart does
not take place when very large doses are administered, and the increase from small doses is
not maintained after the characteristic sweating.
The pupil contracts, spasm of the accommodation occurs, and recession of the near point takes
place. More or less headache is experienced,
and there are present a feeling of frontal tension
and transient vertigo. Soon after the flushing
of the face and the subjective sense of heat are
experienced, perspiration begins, first on the
forehead usually, and then over the whole body,
and presently the sweating is enormous, the
skin literally pouring out water. Simultaneously
with, or often before, the sweating, the salivary
glands become active, and presently mouthful
after mouthful of saliva is discharged, so that the
quantity may be measured by ounces, even pints.
In some instances the one secretion seems to be
substituted for the other. Thus, when the salivary
flow is great, the sweat is less, and *vice versa*, but
the usual experience is that both secretions are
enormously increased. With the full development of the salivary and sudoral discharge, the
pulse declines in force, in volume, and in the
number of beats, the face becomes pale, the

strength diminishes, and a feeling of exhaustion is experienced. The temperature, which was slightly or not at all increased during the stage of excitement, descends somewhat below normal after the sweating. The secretion of urine is rather less than normal, but the bladder is irritable and the desire to micturate is frequent. The surface of the body is cool, and a sense of chilliness is experienced. Drowsiness comes on, as a result of the exhaustion, and is not a direct effect of the remedy on the brain. When the preparations of pilocarpus are taken into the stomach, and, to a much less extent, when the active principle is thrown in under the skin, more or less nausea, even vomiting, is produced, and not unfrequently a watery diarrhœa.

The opposition of actions, between an agent causing such functional disturbances as I have just described and atropia, is apparent at a glance. Let me briefly indicate the main points as a preliminary to the study of the mechanism of the antagonism. The first increase in the cardiac movements caused by pilocarpine is of very short duration, and is followed by feebleness of the heart and diminished arterial tension; atropia induces and maintains a quickened heart-beat and a high arterial tension during at least the whole duration of the action of pilocarpine. A subjective sensation of heat and flushing of the face is caused by both, but is very transient in the case of pilocarpine. Contraction of the pupil is produced by pilocarpine, dilatation by atropine. Dryness of the mouth and of the skin results from atropia, profuse secretion from pilocarpine. Both of these agents tend to cause nausea and vomiting, and a watery diarrhœa. Both render the bladder more or less irritable, and atropia increases the urinary secretion a little, while pilocarpine diminishes it. As regards the nervous system of animal life, no antagonism exists. Pilocarpine does not affect the cerebral functions directly, while atropia causes delirium. Pilocarpine induces weakness of the muscular system, but atropia brings on a tetanic condition by stimulation of the cord, and paralysis by an action both on the cord and on the peripheral motor nerves. In all those actions involving the functions of the organic nervous system there is very complete antagonism, but in respect to the nervous system of animal life no antagonism is possible.

The only examples of application of the antagonism to the treatment of poisoning, which I have been able to find, are two cases of poisoning by belladonna liniment, received into University College Hospital in charge of Dr. Sydney Ringer.* Pilocarpine was injected subcutaneously in both, without any obvious influence over either. The experience in the more important of the two cases demonstrated that one

---

* Lancet, March 4, 1876.

grain and a third of pilocarpine failed to excite perspiration, when one-third of a grain of the same sample caused in healthy persons most profuse sweating. It is obvious that belladonna is relatively more intense, as it is more prolonged, in its effects.

The first experiments to determine the antagonism of atropia and pilocarpine were those of Vulpian,* and were confined to the salivary and sweat secretions. When the saliva and sweat are pouring out in a stream from the action of pilocarpine, the flow of secretion is almost instantly arrested by the administration of atropia. The mechanism of this antagonism has been thoroughly investigated by Vulpian,† Langley,‡ Marmé,§ Petrina,|| and numerous other investigators. Pilocarpine stimulates the nerve ends in the glands, and, as Heidenhain long ago proved, atropia paralyzes the end organs of these nerves. The chorda tympani and the sympathetic filaments distributed to the submaxillary gland being divided, pilocarpine still has power to cause increased secretion, as Langley has shown, thus proving that this agent also stimulates the gland cells. In this respect, also, it is probable that atropia has an antagonistic action. The experi-

---

* Gaz. Hebdom., 1875–76, p. 81. † Loc. cit.
‡ Jour. of Anat. and Physiol., xi. Part 1, pp. 173, et seq.
§ Virchow u. Hirsch, Jahresbericht, 1878, p. 173.
|| Deutsch. Arch. f. klin. Med., xxi. p. 258.

ments of Langley on this point have been confirmed by Nawrocki,* Fuchsinger,† and the other observers just named.

The increase of secretion caused by pilocarpine is not limited to the skin and salivary glands, but extends to the mucous membrane of the nose, bronchi, and intestinal canal, although to a less extent. The arrest of these secretions by atropia is not less prompt and decided. The increased secretion caused by the subcutaneous injection of one-fourth of a grain of pilocarpine muriate or sulphate is arrested by $\frac{1}{100}$ grain of atropia. In a personal trial of this quantity of pilocarpine, I found that the salivary flow began in three minutes, and in five minutes I was drenched by perspiration, the flush of the face and sense of warmth had ceased, the surface felt cold, and a condition of extreme bodily depression came on. A marvellous change was wrought by the subcutaneous injection of $\frac{1}{100}$ grain of atropia. In three minutes the sense of depression began to decline, in five minutes the surface grew warm again and the flow of sweat and saliva ceased, so that by the end of ten minutes the disturbances caused by each had disappeared and I was in the same condition as if neither had been taken.

The first effect of pilocarpine on the heart is to

---

* Centralbl. f. d. med. Wissensch., vi. p. 97.
† Pflüger's Archiv, xv. p. 483.

increase its action. This is coincident with flushing of the face. Belladonna, after a very brief preliminary slowing, greatly increases the action of the heart, and also flushes the face. The increased action due to pilocarpine is brief, and is followed by slowing and feebleness of movement. The resemblance in action is only apparent. The increased movement produced by atropia may be explained, as we have seen, in either of two modes,—by paralysis of inhibition, or by stimulation of the accelerator fibres. The increased action due to pilocarpine is a result of the dilatation of the arterioles. It is just here that the antagonism exists. The manometric observations of Kahler and Soyka,* the experiments of Langley, Hardenhewer,† and Robin,‡ alike demonstrate that pilocarpine lowers the vascular tension by a paralyzing action, causing dilatation of the arterioles. The sudden withdrawal of the blood to the peripheral vessels necessarily causes increased action of the heart. Belladonna exactly antagonizes these effects : it raises the arterial tension by inducing contraction of the arterioles. The depression in the heart's action, and irregularity of rhythm, due to the action of pilocarpine on the motor apparatus, and which suc-

---

* "Kymographische Versuche über Jaborandi," Arch. f. exper. Path. u. Pharmacol., vii. p. 435.

† Berlin. klin. Woch., No. 10, 1877.

‡ "Étude Physiologique et Thérapeutique sur la Jaborandi," Jour. de Thérap., various numbers for 1875.

ceed to the preliminary increased movement, are antagonized by atropia (Service).*

The temperature variations observed by all who have carefully investigated this point are explained by the circulatory disturbance. According to Robin, just before sweating begins, and when it is going on actively, the temperature rises, but this does not appear to be a constant result. When the sweating has reached its maximum the temperature begins to fall, the decline reaching from 0.5° to 2° F., and this reduction of body heat persists for several hours,—it may be for twenty-four hours (Robin, Curschmann,† Weber,‡ Ringer and Gould,§ *et al.*). The decline of temperature caused by pilocarpine is antagonized and prevented by atropia. By raising the vascular tonus, and arresting or preventing the profuse discharge of saliva and sweat, atropia restores the normal equilibrium, and consequently the fall of temperature is prevented.

Extending our investigation now to the eye, we find that the most exact opposition of actions exists in the effects of pilocarpine and atropine on this organ. Myosis, spasm of accommodation, and recession of the near point are produced by pilocarpine; and the exactly opposite effects—

---

* Jour. of Anat. and Physiol., April, 1879.
† Berlin. klin. Woch., June 18, 1877.
‡ Centralbl. f. d. med. Wissensch., No. 44, 1877.
§ Lancet, Jan. 30, 1875.

dilatation of the pupil, paralysis of the accommodation, and removal of the distant point—are produced by belladonna (Königshofer, Tweedy,* Galezowski,† *et al.*).

That pilocarpine directly affects the brain is doubtful. It is true, headache, vertigo, tinnitus aurium, etc., have been observed from considerable doses; and drowsiness, even sleep, accompanies the state of languor and depression caused by the profuse salivary and sudoral discharge and the lowered vascular tonus. These secondary results of the action of pilocarpine are not antagonistic to the delirium, hallucinations, and illusions of atropia. In the cases narrated by Dr. Ringer the delirious excitement of belladonna-poisoning was not modified by the action of pilocarpine,—so that, viewed from either the theoretical or the practical stand-point, the existence of an antagonism on the brain must be denied.

The nausea and vomiting caused by pilocarpine are probably not affected, or are increased, by atropia. When the action of the drug ceases, the stomachal distress occasioned by it ceases also,—hence, in this indirect mode, atropia may prevent or arrest it.

I have already indicated some points of similarity of action between pilocarpine and atropia,— the quickened heart and flushed face,—but these,

---

* Lancet, Jan. 30, 1875.
† Med. Times and Gaz., 1877, ii. p. 358.

as has been shown, are apparent, and not real. They both agree, however, in the insusceptibility of children to their action. The observations of Ringer and Gould are very precise in regard to this insusceptibility of children to the action of jaborandi. They found that the quantity which sufficed to produce profuse sweating in adults affected children very slightly or not at all. Children are equally insusceptible to the effects of belladonna.

To sum up the results of the investigation, we find that belladonna and pilocarpus are antagonistic in their action : 1. On the secretions, especially of sweat and saliva, pilocarpus promoting and belladonna arresting them. 2. On the heart and arterial system, pilocarpus slowing and enfeebling the heart and depressing the vascular tonus, belladonna stimulating the cardiac movements and raising the arterial tension. 3. On the eye, pilocarpus contracting the pupil, inducing spasm of accommodation, and approximating the nearest and most remote points of vision, belladonna dilating the pupil, paralyzing accommodation, and making the vision presbyopic.

On the brain there is no real antagonism. The excitement, the delirium with hallucinations and illusions, and the subsequent coma, caused by atropia, are not affected by any of the actions of pilocarpine. The soporose state brought on by the latter, as I have pointed out, is a secondary effect, the result of exhaustion and cerebral anæmia.

Continuing the subject of the antagonistic relations of atropia, we have next to consider the mutual interactions of

ATROPIA AND MUSCARIA.

As muscaria, or muscarine, is comparatively little known, it may be useful to make a preliminary statement of its history and characteristics. It is obtained from amanita muscaria, the fly fungus. We owe to Schmiedeberg and Koppe the discovery of the alkaloid, and to Schmiedeberg and his pupils the full and accurate information now in our possession in regard to its physiological actions.* Muscarine has strong alkaline and basic properties, uniting with acids to form salts. It is a colorless substance having the consistence of syrup, is readily soluble in water, and its salts deliquesce rapidly on exposure to air. It seems to be actively toxic,—$\frac{1}{30}$ grain producing in the human subject very decided symptoms. The effects, taking a general view, are as follows: Considerable gastro-intestinal disturbance, nausea, vomiting, and diarrhœa, and violent colic, due to a tetanic contraction of the muscular layer of the bowel, are produced by it. An active and rather pleasurable delirium, rambling, and incoherence, not unlike that of

---

* Das Muscarin, das giftige Alkaloid des Fliegenpilzes, etc., Leipzig, 1869; also, Arch. f. exper. Pathol. u. Pharmacol., iv. and vi. Hermann, op. cit.

alcohol, are caused by the fungus, so that it is used as an intoxicant by some of the inhabitants of Eastern Asia. In toxic doses the excitement is followed by more or less profound stupor, epileptiform attacks, trismus, and abolition of all reflex movements. During the stage of pleasurable intoxication the pupil is contracted, vision is dim, objects are seen as through a mist, and also probably double. The action of the heart is weakened and finally arrested in the diastole, the respiration is labored and stertorous, the salivary secretion is increased, the surface of the body becomes cold, and death ensues from failure of the heart.

On the brain, it is probable that muscaria acts in two modes, directly and indirectly; it first excites the cells of the gray matter, and ultimately paralyzes them; the heart being weakened, less blood passes to the brain, and hence this organ is in a condition of anæmia. On the eye muscarine produces peculiar effects. It causes spasm of the accommodation and a marked degree of myosis, by stimulation of the motor oculi. The vision is disturbed, therefore, by the spasm of the accommodative apparatus and by the myosis, which limits the amount of light admitted to the retina.

The secretions generally are increased by muscarine, but it especially stimulates the salivary secretion. According to Prévost,* the bile and

---

* Gaz. Méd. de Paris, 1870, iii. p. 243.

the pancreatic and urinary secretions are increased. It promotes the salivary secretion by stimulating the end organs of the nerves, and this is independent of a centric influence, for it takes place after the trunks of the nerves have been divided.* It is probable, if Prévost's view is correct, that the increase of the other secretions is due to the same mode of action.

A slight and momentary increase in the cardiac movements is first produced by muscarine, but this is followed by retardation. Direct application of this agent arrests the heart in the diastole, but mechanical, chemical, or electrical irritation will induce contraction. Section of the vagi does not prevent this effect. It may therefore be concluded that muscarine acts on the motor ganglia in the substance of the heart, and not on the muscle, nor on the apparatus of inhibition. A very considerable decline in the blood-pressure is a constant result, after a short preliminary rise. The walls of the vessels relax, as Bogosslowsky† has shown, and, as the action of the heart is at the same time depressed, it is obvious that the vascular tension must be reduced. During the stage of delirious excitement, the respiration is rather hurried, but when the subsequent depression comes on, the respiration

---

* F. A. Falck, Der Antagonismus d. Gifte. Volkmann's Samml. klin. Vortr., No. 159, 1879.

† Centralbl. f. d. med. Wissensch., 97, 1870.

becomes slower and shallower, this result being
due to a paralyzing action of muscarine on the
respiratory centres.

When we come to compare these disturbances
of function caused by muscaria with those produced by atropia, we must admit, with Schmiedeberg, that no example of physiological antagonism
could be more exact. On the brain, the intoxication, with cerebral anæmia, of muscarine is
opposed by the active delirium and cerebral hyperæmia of atropia. On the eye, the contracted
pupil of muscaria, due to stimulation of the circular fibres innervated by the third nerve, is
opposed by the dilated pupil of atropia, produced
by stimulation of the radiating fibres, innervated
by the sympathetic. The effect of atropia on the
eye is relatively more powerful, for, when the
pupil is contracted by muscarine, it can be dilated
by atropine, but, when dilated by atropia, it cannot then be contracted by muscarine. On the
function of secretion the antagonism is not less
striking. Muscarine promotes the salivary secretion by stimulating the end organs of the nerves
in the gland, and atropia arrests this secretion
by paralyzing these nerves.* But atropia is
relatively more powerful here, also, for, when
the salivary secretion is arrested by atropia,

---

* Luchsinger, "Die Wirkungen von Muscarin u. Atropin
auf d. Schweissdrüsen d. Katze," etc., Archiv f. d. ges. Phys.,
18, 1878, p. 501.

muscaria cannot re-establish it, yet the secretion caused by the latter is promptly arrested by the former. This opposing mechanism probably extends to the hepatic and pancreatic secretions as well. The intestinal cramp caused by muscarine is removed by atropine. On the heart, nothing can be more perfect than the opposing actions of these agents. This fact is frequently adduced by physiologists as a striking exemplification of the doctrine of antagonism. If the heart is arrested in the diastole by muscarine, it is started again by atropia. If an animal is first brought under the influence of atropia, the heart is not stopped by muscarine, notwithstanding it is so readily poisoned by this agent. The antagonism is equally exerted on the respiratory function,— muscarine lessens the respiratory movements and finally arrests them, while atropia stimulates this function.

Thus, viewed from all sides, these agents are exactly antagonistic. Is a function disturbed by one agent in a particular mode, it is also disturbed by the other agent in an opposite mode. In fact, we should search in vain for an illustration of the law of antagonisms more perfect than that subsisting between atropia and muscaria.

ATROPIA AND QUINIA.

The only systematic experimental investigation of the antagonism between atropia and quinia which I have been able to find is that of Pantelejeff.* Clinical experience on this point is abundant enough, but we are not now concerned with this aspect of the question. Pantelejeff has ascertained that quinia arrests the heart in diastole, and that the subsequent administration of atropia causes the heart to resume its contractions. This result was observed both in frogs and in rabbits. In the latter animals, when the action of the heart was resumed after the suspension of its movements, the auricles began to contract before the ventricles. Examination of the web of the frog's foot disclosed the interesting fact that, after the subcutaneous injection of quinia, the calibre of the arterioles was lessened by contraction of their walls, while the opposite effect, or dilatation, followed the administration of atropia. Quinia causes a rise in the blood-pressure, after a brief preliminary fall, and atropia retards it.

BROMAL HYDRATE AND ATROPIA.

One of the subjects undertaken by the Committee of the British Medical Association, to whose important labors I have so often to refer, was the investigation of the antagonism of bromal hydrate and atropia. This research was especially in charge of Professor McKendrick, and the scope of it was limited to the lethal effects. All of the facts are comprehended in

---

* Lancet, July 31, 1880, p. 176.

the conclusions to which he was conducted by his experiments, as follows :

" 1. There is a distinct physiological antagonism between bromal hydrate and atropia. 2. After a fatal dose of bromal hydrate, the introduction of atropia arrests excessive secretion from the salivary glands and mucous surfaces of the lungs, and thus obviates the tendency to death from asphyxia caused by the accumulation of fluids in the air-passages. Atropia also causes contraction of the blood-vessels, and thus antagonizes the action of bromal hydrate, which causes dilatation of these vessels by paralysis of the sympathetic nerve. 3. While atropia may save life after a fatal dose of bromal hydrate, the converse apparently does not hold good, as we never have succeeded in saving life after a fatal dose of atropia by the subsequent injection of bromal hydrate."

ATROPIA AND ACONITE.

The last application of the physiological antagonism of atropia is that with aconite, for which we are indebted to Dr. J. Milner Fothergill.* These researches are not extensive, but they probably represent the actual state of the antagonism. *A priori*, a very perfect and extended opposition of actions would be presumed to ex-

---

* The Antagonism of Therapeutic Agents. Philadelphia, 1878, p. 41.

ist. Aconite, a respiratory and cardiac depressant, ought to be neutralized by atropia, a respiratory and cardiac stimulant. The facts in the main support this supposition. "Thus, to a rabbit weighing two pounds six ounces, I gave," says Dr. Fothergill, "three grains of atropia, and six minutes afterward $\frac{1}{300}$ grain of aconitine; the animal survived. A week afterward the same rabbit had the aconitine alone, and died in two hours and a half." Small doses of atropia he found had very striking effects on animals to which lethal doses of aconitine had previously been administered. The animals all recovered from doses of aconitine which subsequently killed them all when administered without the atropia. "It was found, however, that if the administration of the atropia was delayed beyond sixteen minutes, it was powerless to arrest the lethal action of aconitine."

HOMOTROPINE.

A new alkaloid has been obtained from atropia by chemical means. The first step consists in splitting up atropia into *tropine* and *tropic acid.* *Tropeins* are produced by the action of dilute hydrochloric acid on the salts of tropine. From the amygdalate of tropine is thus produced *homotropine*, an alkaloid of much promise.

The effects of homotropine are similar to, but milder and of shorter duration than those of atropia. The tetanizing effect of atropia, which in cold-blooded animals follows after twenty-four to seventy-two hours, occurs at once from the use of homotropine. The action of the heart is increased by homotropine by a paralyzing action on the intra-cardiac inhibitory apparatus. In man homotropine retards and renders irregular the heart-beat. It acts very quickly on the iris, dilating the pupil widely in fifteen to twenty minutes, and affects the accommodative apparatus equally rapidly. The ocular effects subside comparatively quickly, and in twenty-four hours the accommodation is restored. In these respects homotropine presents marked advantages over atropia. It deserves trial in the treatment of various diseases.

So numerous and important are the uses of these agents when administered together that a consideration of the combination in a separate chapter seems necessary and desirable. The two agents are used together in varying proportions, and much depends on an accurate adjustment of the quantities to the powers respectively. A *penicilium* develops in the solution, and slowly diminishes its activity by growing at the expense of the alkaloids.

A permanent solution may be prepared as follows :

R Morphiæ sulphatis, gr. xvi ;
Atropiæ sulphatis, gr. ss ;
Acidi carbolici, gr. viij ;
Aquæ lauro-cerasi, ℥i.   M.

Sig.—Five minims contain $\frac{1}{6}$ grain of morphia and $\frac{1}{192}$ grain of atropia.

Powders for extemporaneous solutions may be prepared as follows :

R Morphiæ sulphatis, ϶i ;
Atropiæ sulphatis, gr. ss.   M.
Fiat pulv. No. cxx.

Sig.—Each powder contains $\frac{1}{6}$ grain of morphia and $\frac{1}{240}$ grain of atropia.

192

On the whole, these are to be preferred : they are convenient to handle, readily soluble, accurate, and therefore satisfactory. The relative proportions of morphia and atropia in the solutions, as in the powders of the mixed alkaloids, will be governed by the character of the cases for which they are administered.

HISTORY.—The following historical review of the subject of the physiological antagonism existing between morphia and atropia is reproduced here from my Cartwright course of lectures.

By the year 1810 considerable experience of an empirical kind had accumulated in regard to the antagonism of opium and belladonna; for we find that in this year Joseph Lipp published an inaugural thesis on the toxic effects of belladonna berries, and on the curative powers of opium. We owe to Graves, the great Dublin clinician, the first really scientific suggestion of an antagonism. He supposed that the state of the pupil would afford an indication in fevers of the need of opium or belladonna—the former to be given when the pupil was dilated, the latter when it was contracted. Acting on this suggestion, Dr. Thomas Anderson,* of Edinburgh, employed belladonna against opium-poisoning—a mydriatic against a myositic—with success. Two years sub-

---

* Braithwaite's Retrospect, 1855, Part xxx. p. 301.

sequently, Dr. William H. Mussey,* of Cincinnati, seeing the account of Dr. Anderson's cases, tried the same expedient successfully in a case of attempted suicide with laudanum. In July, 1859, Mr. Benjamin Bell,† of Edinburgh, published an account of two cases, in which symptoms of poisoning produced by the subcutaneous injection of atropia were removed by considerable doses of morphia. Influenced by these results of Mr. Bell, in December of the same year Mr. Seaton,‡ of Leeds, treated eight cases of poisoning by belladonna berries with opium,—seven of the eight cases recovering. In January, 1862, Dr. C. C. Lee,§ of Philadelphia, reported two cases, one of opium-poisoning treated by belladonna, and one of belladonna-poisoning treated by opium, the result a success in each case. Dr. Lee also entered into some detail on the literature of the subject, referring to the experiences of Anderson, Mussey, and Seaton, and to the adverse experiments of Brown-Séquard. During the same year (1862), the most important paper which had hitherto been published made its appearance from the pen of Dr. William F. Norris.‖ In this paper the cases illustrating an antagonism of action

---

* Cincinnati Med. Observer, vol. i., 1856, p. 70. There were but two volumes issued of this periodical, when it was united with the Lancet.

† Edinburgh Med. Jour., vol. iv., 1859, p. 1.

‡ Med. Times and Gaz., Dec. 3, 1859, p. 551.

§ Am. Jour. of the Med. Sci., vol. xlii.   ‖ Ibid., vol. xliv.

between opium and belladonna, which had been previously published, were tabulated ; and a full historical account of the subject, from which subsequent writers have drawn their information, and to which I am much indebted, is there given. In 1865 an admirable paper, based on clinical and experimental observations made at the military hospital for wounds and injuries of the nerves, and embodying the results of an immense experience, was published by Drs. Mitchell, Morehouse, and Keen.* In the following year (1866) Dr. Constantin Paul† published a monograph, supporting the view of the existence of such antagonism. Since this time the cases, papers, and monographs have so greatly multiplied that it would be impracticable to name them all in this historical review. I have collected all the published cases for statistical study, and will refer to the more important papers and monographs hereafter. The cases thus far collected by me number one hundred and sixty of opium and belladonna-poisoning, in which the one drug was used to counterbalance the effects of the other.

The history of this subject would not be complete without some reference to the opinions of

---

* Am. Jour. of the Med. Sci., July, 1865, vol. l. p. 67. "On the Antagonism of Atropia and Morphia. Founded on Observations and Experiments made at the United States Hospital for Injuries and Diseases of the Nervous System."

† De l'Antagonisme en Pathologie et en Thérapeutique, 1866, pp. 92–115.

those who doubt the existence of the antagonism,
or disbelieve in it utterly. The opposition to the
generally accepted view is based chiefly upon researches on animals. The most influential of
these experimentalists is Brown-Séquard.* His
observations have been made for the most part on
guinea-pigs and rabbits. Bois † studied the effects
of these agents on cats. He regards the following experiments as conclusive against the view
that an antagonism exists. To a cat he gave a
dose of morphia just less than sufficient to cause
death; when entirely recovered from the effects
of this quantity, he gave to the same cat a dose
of atropia having effects just short of lethal.
When a sufficient time had elapsed to insure complete recovery from that dose, he administered
those quantities together, when the result was
fatal. Camus ‡ investigated the action of the alkaloids of opium, and the antagonism of atropia
and morphia, using cats and pigeons, while On-
sum § conducted his researches on frogs. In what
mode soever, or on what animals, the investigations were conducted, the results were uniformly
opposed to the existence of an antagonism. I
may now anticipate so far as to say that the methods of investigation pursued were not free from

* Jour. de la Physiol., etc., tome iii., 1860, p. 726.
† Gaz. des Hôp., 71, 1865.
‡ Gaz. Hebdom., 2 sér., xii. 32, 1865.
§ Schmidt's Jahrbücher, Band 128, p. 288, abstract.

sources of fallacy, and that the results obtained were largely vitiated. The most elaborate series of experiments on this topic, embracing animals and men, were those of Harley,* but his facts admit of a different interpretation from that which he has given them. His fundamental error consists in regarding as examples of antagonism only those in which the opposition of actions exists throughout the whole range of effects, which, as I have already stated, is hardly true of any known examples.

In 1870, Dr. Köning† published a dissertation on the supposed antagonism of morphia and atropia, his research being conducted on animals. As had his predecessors in this inquiry, Köning decided adversely to the existence of this antagonism, although he noted the antagonizing influence of these agents on the pupil, the respiration, and the action of the heart. In 1873, Fröhlich,‡ of Würzburg, experimented with these agents on frogs and cats. His experiments rather indicated the existence of points of opposition, but not sufficient to prevent death from a lethal dose of both agents. In 1874 § appeared the report of the committee appointed by the British Medical Association, Professor J. Hughes Ben-

---

* The Old Vegetable Neurotics, p. 280, and p. 291.

† Schmidt's Jarbücher, vol. cxlix. p. 18.

‡ Pharmakologische Untersuchungen, 1873, pp. 224 and 231.

§ Brit. Med. Jour., 1874, vol. ii., various numbers.

nett, M.D., of Edinburgh, Chairman. In making the report on this division of the subject—the antagonism of morphia and atropia—the reporter says: " Extraordinary pains were taken to determine the question whether or not morphia and atropia were antagonistic of one another; and the researches now to be described will be found to add largely to our precise and exact knowledge as compared with the unfounded and contradictory opinions which have hitherto prevailed. The conclusions at which they arrived, after experiments on the rabbit chiefly, are as follows:

" 1. Sulphate of atropia is physiologically antagonistic to the meconate of morphia within a limited area. 2. Meconate of morphia does not act beneficially after a large dose of sulphate of atropia, for in these cases the tendency to death is greater than if a large dose of either substance had been given alone. 3. Meconate of morphia is not specifically antagonistic to the action of sulphate of atropia on the vaso-inhibitory nerves of the heart; and, 4, the beneficial effect of sulphate of atropia after the administration of large doses of meconate of morphia is probably due to the action sulphate of atropia exercises on the blood-vessels. . . . It may also assist up to a certain point, not precisely fixed in these experiments, by stimulating the action of the heart through the sympathetic, and obviating the tendency to death from deficient respiration observed after large doses of morphia."

In 1876 the same investigation was undertaken by Corona, dogs and cats being the animals employed. He arrived at the singular conclusion that a partial physiological antagonism existed between morphia and atropia, but not a therapeutical antagonism,—for whilst morphia is useful in atropia-poisoning, in poisoning by morphia the effects are not removed by atropia. In this opinion Corona stands quite alone. In the following year (1877), Dr. Hans Heubach reviewed the literature of the subject, and undertook a new investigation of the supposed antagonism, confining his experimental research to animals. These investigations, carried on at Binz's laboratory at Bonn, support the view of a limited antagonism in the cardiac and respiratory organs but not in general.

PHYSIOLOGICAL EFFECTS.—Although much has been said in the preceding pages upon the physiological effects of morphia and atropia, when separately administered, it is necessary now to show the influence which they reciprocally exert when administered together. Their so-called "physiological antagonism" may be most conspicuously exhibited by a comparison of their individual with their combined action on the different parts of the body.

1. *On the Nervous System.*—Both act upon the brain,—atropia producing delirium, hallucinations, and disturbed sleep; morphia causing, generally, somnolence. Both relieve pain, but this

effect is much more decidedly the property of morphia. Both produce disorders of motility, staggering, difficulty of co-ordinating muscular movements, vertigo, confusion of mind, and headache. When given together, these effects are curiously modified.

Morphia corrects the hallucinations and phantasms of atropia.

Atropia in small doses—$\frac{1}{90}$ of a grain—increases the hypnotic power of morphia; but if the quantity of atropia be sufficient, it overpowers the effects of morphia on the cerebrum, causing wakefulness or disturbed sleep, phantasms, and illusions.

The pain-relieving power of morphia is increased by atropia.

The disorders of motility, and the vertigo, are not diminished when the two agents are used together, but the after-headache and confusion of mind are much less.

When toxic doses are used, the narcotism of morphia is overcome by atropia, and *vice versa.* In a case which occurred to myself, and which I have already referred to, serious symptoms produced by 1 grain of morphia were relieved by $\frac{1}{24}$ of a grain of atropia. As, however, the effects of atropia are much more prolonged than morphia, it is not easy to exactly counterbalance the effects of one by the other. The cases of morphia-poisoning, in which atropia was used as an antidote, that have fallen under my observation, received too much atropia, the toxic symptoms of the latter remaining long after the narcotism of the morphia had disappeared.

Upon the organic nervous system these agents seem exactly to antagonize each other.

Morphia produces contraction of the pupil, and a tetanic condition, according to Graefe, of the muscle of accommodation; atropia produces dilatation of the pupil, and contraction of the ciliary muscle. When used together, these effects may be precisely balanced. It takes, however, but a minute quantity of atropia to overcome the action of morphia on the pupil. When these effects on the pupil are balanced, it does not follow that the muscle of accommodation is in a condition to act in a normal manner, for visual defects frequently remain.

Morphia and atropia antagonize each other's action on organic muscular fibre. Morphia prevents the contraction of the arterioles produced by atropia, and, as a consequence of this action, prevents the subsequent relaxation of the muscular fibre. They antagonize each other, therefore, as respects their action on the arterial tension.

On Circulation and Respiration.—Morphia depresses the action of the heart; atropia is a powerful cardiac stimulant. Morphia produces pallor of the surface, and reduces the external temperature; atropia causes redness and injection of the skin and elevation of the body-heat.

17*

The extent to which they modify each other's action is well exhibited in the annexed diagram. It will be seen that the antagonism between them does not extend to the respiratory function; for, whilst morphia administered alone depressed the respiration from 17 to 12 per minute, morphia and atropia combined reduced the number from 18 to 10. When Dr. De Courcey received the morphia alone, he experienced much less soporific effect than when both agents were injected together; and to this 'quiescent state of the cerebral functions is to be attributed the slower respiratory movements. The morphia exercises a marked influence over the increase of body-heat produced by atropia. Notwithstanding this, the flushing of the face and the strong subjective sense of heat are experienced by the patient almost as fully when morphia is administered with atropia as when atropia is given alone.

In the experiment represented on the diagram, the quantity of atropia was not sufficient to produce the full degree of antagonism, otherwise the pulse-line would have continued on the same plane. In so far as the atropia influence preponderates, a progressive rise in the pulse-rate is noted.

3. *On the Digestive Apparatus.*—As regards dryness of the mucous membrane of the mouth, fauces, larynx, etc., there is no antagonism, but both agents produce this state and exalt it when

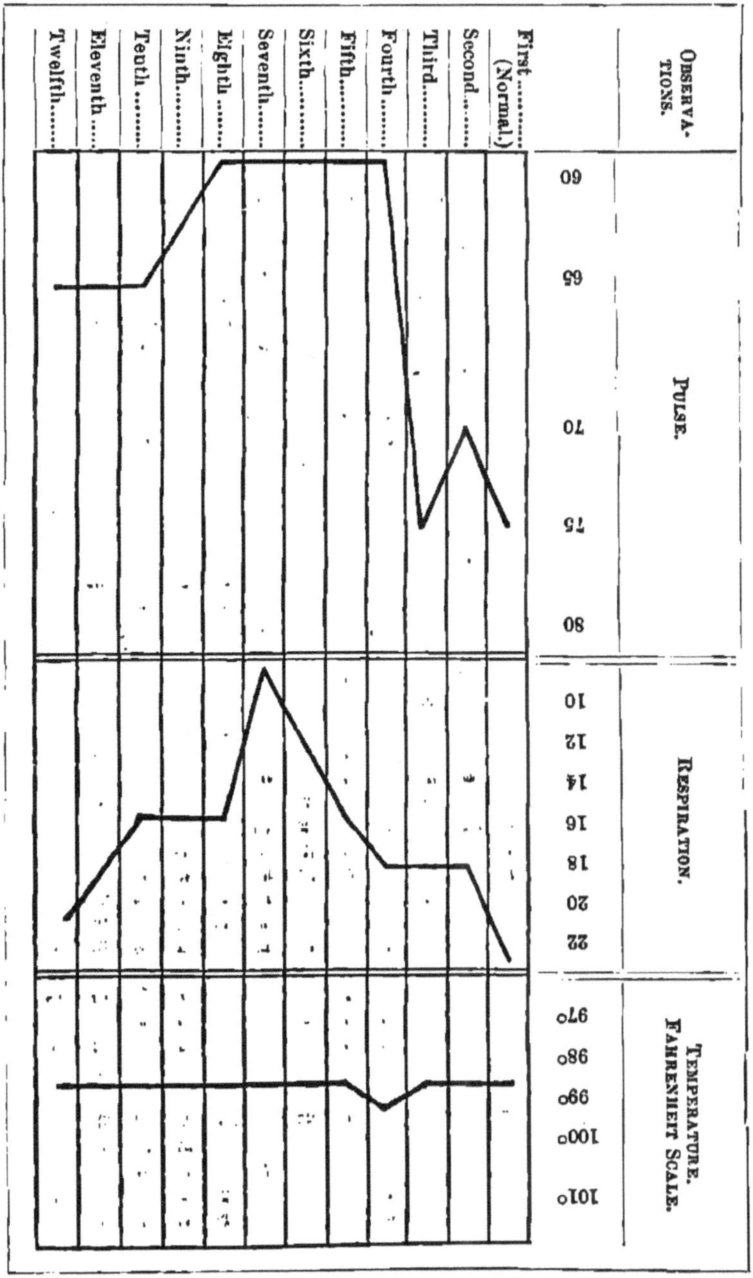

OBSERVATIONS.
First (Normal.)
Second
Third
Fourth
Fifth
Sixth
Seventh
Eighth
Ninth
Tenth
Eleventh
Twelfth
PULSE.
60
65
70
75
80
RESPIRATION.
10
12
14
16
18
20
22
TEMPERATURE. FAHRENHEIT SCALE.
97°
98°
99°
100°
101°

administered together. Morphia tends to produce constipation; atropia relaxes the bowels. When administered together, they produce almost immediately intestinal movements, frequently borborygmi, and sometimes sharp pain, and the bowels are kept in a soluble state. The sickness and nausea, and the not uncommon great depression of the vital powers caused by morphia are opposed by atropia. These agents may therefore be given together in cases in which morphia cannot be borne alone. The after stomachal effects of morphia—indigestion, loss of appetite, a pasty tongue—are much diminished by the atropia, but are not absolutely prevented. Atropia itself is capable of producing these stomach disorders when used in considerable doses; hence, to produce the result which I have described, the proportion of morphia and atropia should be as follows:

Morphia, $\frac{1}{4}$ of a grain;

Atropia, $\frac{1}{120}$ of a grain.

4. *On the Genito-urinary Organs.*—These agents are antagonistic as to their effects on the kidneys and the urinary excretion. Morphia suspends and atropia promotes the functional activity of the kidneys. By inducing congestion of the Malpighian tufts, and increasing the *vis a tergo*, atropia acts as a diuretic, and with the additional water there strains off from the blood the larger amount of urates produced in the more rapid metamorphosis of tissue. Morphia increases

the action of the sudoriparous glands, and atropia diminishes it, thereby in the one case lowering, in the other case exalting, the functional activity of the kidneys.

Both produce dysuria, but this result comes of a different action in each case. Morphia impairs the contractile power of the muscular coat of the bladder, so that it contracts with difficulty, the emission of urine taking place slowly; atropia maintains steady tonic contraction of the sphincter, so that it dilates slowly under the voluntary effort, when the desire to micturate is experienced.

Both morphia and atropia impair the sexual appetite; atropia at once, and morphia when long used.

A comparison of the actions on man shows that opium and belladonna act oppositely, or in an opposite manner, *on the brain, on the pupil, on the circulation, on the lungs, on the stomach, and on the skin.* Opium, with the exceptions named, causes somnolence and stupor; belladonna, excitement, hallucinations, and delirium. When administered jointly and in the proper proportions, sopor, closely approximating natural sleep, is the result. This was well exhibited in the case of Dr. Legg,* whose patient, a boy of five years, drank by mistake a mixture of equal parts of liniment of opium and liniment of belladonna.

---

* Med. Times and Gaz., Nov. 3, 1866, p. 474.

The effects of the belladonna, owing to its more rapid action, first dominated the situation, when there was delirium with hallucinations, the boy driving sheep and picking up money from the bed; but then drowsiness supervened and heavy sleep, when he was not forced awake and kept walking. The violence of this ambulatory treatment was wholly unnecessary, and indeed injurious, for, if he had been permitted to sleep, the antagonism on the respiration and circulation would have sufficed to save life. Facts of the same kind were observed in a case jointly cared for by Dr. Mussey, of Cincinnati, and myself. A boy of eight years, the son of a physician of Cincinnati, was given internally by mistake an anodyne application for earache, containing two grains of morphia and one grain and a half of atropia. When the toxic symptoms were well advanced the mistake was discovered, and Dr. Mussey and myself were summoned. We found the pupils fully dilated, the face flushed, and an active delirium, in which the boy fought and struggled violently against imaginary enemies. After an hour or two of this excitement, a soporose state came on, and was very profound for a number of hours. As, however, the respiration was full, strong, and rhythmical, the pulse regular and of good volume, we decided to await the result of the antagonism. Dr. Mussey had published one of the first cases of opium-poisoning illustrating the antagonistic action of belladonna, and I had seen several cases, so that we were perfectly agreed as to the proper course, and the result justified our decision. Another case in which the simultaneous administration of opium and belladonna was due to accident was reported by Dr. Cotter.* A young lady swallowed a liniment composed of opium and belladonna, the amount taken being equivalent to twenty-five grains of the extract of belladonna and twelve grains of opium. At first the symptoms of belladonna-poisoning were largely in excess; after some hours she appeared like one helplessly drunk, and was so drowsy as to be kept awake with great difficulty; then another period of excitement came on, and this was followed by a period of profound sleep, from which she awoke relieved. Such are the facts as taught us by these accidental experiments on man. What is the clinical experience available for further study of the problem?

As a result of large observation and experience of the effects of these agents on man, Drs. Mitchell, Morehouse, and Keen conclude that "the headache and phantasms of atropia are certainly thus controlled [*i.e.*, by morphia], as well as the partial deafness and visual defects which in high doses it occasions. On the other hand, when morphia has been fully used, the drowsiness and stupor which are the best tests of its power

---

* Am. Jour. of the Med. Sci., vol. l. p. 67, et seq.

disappear before the influence of atropia. . . .
Perhaps the most peculiar cerebral symptom of
atropia is its tendency to cause phantasms and
illusions. We found under doses of $\frac{1}{25}$ of a
grain these were common, and in some men
could always be brought on. Usually they were
absent so long as the eyes remained open, but
arose at once on closing them. This condition
was singularly subdued by morphia. Drowsiness caused by morphia was as surely lessened
or destroyed by the counter agency of atropia;
and, in fact, atropia given alone and in full
doses is very apt to cause a restless night to follow, so that it is assuredly in no sense a hypnotic."

Harley strongly insists on the modifying influence of morphia over the cerebral effects of atropia. "The influence of opium in converting the
insomnia of belladonna into sleep, and the influence of belladonna in determining not only sleep,
but narcotism in individuals under the influence
of opium, are illustrated in several examples.
Some of the cases," he further says, "serve to
give greater force to these observations, and teach
us that we must be careful how we employ opium
as a means of converting the restlessness and insomnia following excessive doses of belladonna
into quiet sleep." Harley, strangely enough, does
not regard these different cerebral effects as due
to an antagonistic action, but as synergistic. It
is, nevertheless, evident enough that his observa-

tions are confirmatory of those of Mitchell, Morehouse, and Keen, who state with more precision
the exact features of the reciprocal influence. In
fact, at the present time professional opinion is
no longer divided on this point, and morphia and
atropia, and opium and belladonna, are constantly
prescribed together to secure an hypnotic effect,
not attainable by the exhibition of either remedy
alone. Clinical experience on man has been confirmed by observations on animals, so far as the
facts are applicable. Thus, Erlenmayer[*] shows
that the exciting effect of atropia on the brain is
lessened by the narcosis of morphia. Harley's
experiments on dogs were similar in results: "The
cerebral effects of atropia are," he says, "intensified and prolonged,—the insomnia which results
from excessive doses is converted into narcotism,
or a mixture of narcotism and delirium." Heubach,[†] whose researches were carried on in Binz's
laboratory, was led to similar conclusions. Obviously, the actions of such agents on the brains of
animals can be compared only according to the
extent of development, for, the brain of man being more complex in structure and more highly
specialized, must be affected both with less severity and in a greater variety of manifestations.
In animals the effect of the narcotic is necessarily

---

[*] Berlin. klin. Woch., loc. cit.

[†] Arch. f. experiment. Pathol. u. Pharmakol., 1878, Band
viii. p. 31. "Antagonismus zwischen Morphin u. Atropin.

limited to the cephalic organs possessed by them, whereas in man, not only to those, but to the higher special organs he is possessed of, is the influence distributed. In animals the narcotic more affects the motor centres and the centres of respiration and circulation, while in man its effects are exerted not only upon these centres, but upon the higher centres and upon the mental sphere. Do we not have in this difference in development the reason of the much greater toxic power in animals of morphia and atropia when administered simultaneously? Bernard* has signalized this important point in his introduction to the study of experimental medicine. After declaring that observations on animals, in respect to the functions of the cerebro-spinal nerves, and the vaso-motors and secretors of the sympathetic, and on circulation and digestion, hygiene and toxicology, are perfectly and at all points applicable to man, he indicates conditions under which the observations on animals are not thus applicable. For example: "From the physiological point of view, the experimental study of the organs of sense and of the cerebral functions must be made on man necessarily, because on the one hand man is above the animals in respect to those faculties of which they are not possessed, and, on the other, animals are unable to indicate the

---

* Introduction à l'Étude de la Médecine Expérimentelle." Paris, 1865, p. 219.

nature of those sensations of which they may become conscious."

My conclusion, after the examination of the experimental and clinical evidence, therefore, is, that, as respects the brain, opium and belladonna exert opposing actions. The illusions, hallucinations, and busy delirium caused by belladonna are counteracted by opium. The result of their conjoined action is sopor, deepening into coma when the quantity of both is large. When administered simultaneously, if the effects of atropia preponderate, there will occur periods of excitement and delirium, interspersed with relatively shorter periods of sopor and coma. The more decidedly opium preponderates, the less there will be of delirium, and the more of sopor. When opium is in excess, the tendency is to coma and stertorous breathing, after a period of sopor.

There are some highly important points in regard to the antagonistic action of morphia and atropia on the pupil. Graves, as is well known, first proposed to make use of this antagonism as a guide to treatment. There can be no doubt that this antagonism exists,—that opium contracts and belladonna dilates the pupil; opium weakening and belladonna stimulating the radiating fibres of the iris. There are, however, occasional exceptions. As the state of the pupil is usually regarded as a guide to the use of the antagonist in cases of poisoning, it becomes in a high degree important to know if this indication can or can not be depended on, and to what extent. In Case XIV. of a list of unsuccessful cases, we find that a very large quantity of morphia was given to counteract the effects of some belladonna liniment taken by accident, and that, notwithstanding the apparent preponderance in the action of the morphia, the pupil continued dilated. In one of the successful cases of joint administration of opium and belladonna, in which the symptoms produced by the latter much preponderated, the pupil was minutely contracted. It has been observed occasionally, in cases of opium-poisoning, that at a certain stage in the narcosis the pupil dilated. On the other hand, in profound belladonna narcosis, the largely dilated pupil has suddenly contracted in some occasional cases. These are exceptional manifestations, it is true, but, as there are two examples in 120 cases, the value of the indication afforded by the state of the pupil is correspondingly weakened. The antagonism between morphia and atropia may be exerted without the contraction caused by the former, or the dilatation by the latter, being entirely overcome. No fewer than twenty cases illustrate this proposition. The rate at which these agents act on the pupil varies greatly. Atropia acts both more promptly and for a much longer time. Atropia has, also, a more powerful action,—for, of the twenty cases which show that the size of the pupil may not be much affected by the antagonist, sixteen were examples of preponderating dilatation. From these facts, it must be concluded that the state of the pupil cannot always serve as a guide for the further administration of the antagonist.

The next point for consideration is—the antagonistic influence of opium and belladonna on the heart. That opium, in full doses, acting alone, slows the heart, and that belladonna quickens it, are unquestionable facts. Observers are by no means agreed as to the influence reciprocally exerted by these agents when administered simultaneously. Mitchell, Morehouse, and Keen find that " morphia has no power to prevent atropia thus influencing the pulse, so that as regards the circulation they do not counteract one another." Harley maintains that morphia, here as elsewhere, increases the effect of atropia. " If, however," he says, " the dose of atropia is small, and the morphia produce considerable derangement of the vagus, the rapidity of pulse is not greater than when the atropia is administered alone. In my own observations I have invariably seen that the acceleration of pulse produced by atropia is lessened by morphia, and *vice versa*, and this is the conclusion derived from a study of the reported cases of poisoning. The effect of the atropia, however, preponderates. The result of the combined effect is not the mean of the two, but is nearer the standard of atropia than of morphia. As wakefulness and active delirium increase the pulse-rate, and stupor with absolute repose lessens it, these factors must also be considered in estimating the relative share of opium and belladonna in the result. The experiments on animals have usually demonstrated an antagonistic action as regards the heart." Harley's experiments on dogs certainly show that the accelerating effect of atropia on the heart is remarkably lessened by combination with morphia. In the careful experiments of Heubach, the same result is shown; the increased pulsations caused by atropia are diminished by morphia, but the general level of effect is above the mean considerably. We must, therefore, conclude that the effects of morphia are antagonistic to those of atropia on the heart to a limited extent, but that the effects of atropia preponderate, and, hence, the result of the combined effects is a rate of movement greater than the mean.

Without doubt, the most important point in the whole range of the antagonism of morphia and atropia is the opposed action on the respiratory function. Less difference of opinion exists on this than on any other point connected with the subject. In general terms, it may be said that opium is a respiratory depressant, and atropia a respiratory stimulant. The cause of death in opium narcosis is failure of respiration, the action of the heart ceasing after respiration. Atropia counteracts this tendency, and maintains the activity of the respiratory function. All the cases of poisoning teach this lesson. As the opium narcosis deepens, the respiratory acts become less and less frequent and more and more shallow; the quantity of oxygen admitted to the blood lessens, and the oxidation processes decline; the surface becomes cold, and, carbonic acid accumulating, carbonic-acid narcosis is added to the toxic coma. Atropia counterbalances these effects by raising the number and increasing the depth of the respiratory acts, hence more oxygen is admitted to the blood, the chemical interchanges are more extensive and speedy, and excretion is facilitated. The improvement is represented by a flushed face, a warm and dry skin, and a more active circulation generally.

Atropia proves fatal by exhausting the irritability of the motor ganglia of the heart and of the general vaso-motor system, and also of the respiratory centres. Morphia, by lessening the work of the heart and of the lungs, opposes these effects of atropia. The facts presented in the 120 cases of poisoning generally support this view of the antagonism. In some of the cases, it is true, the narcosis was too profound to permit any new impression to be made; but, in those suitable for the action of the antagonist, nothing could be more striking than its favorable influence on the respiration. Dr. Johnston, of Shanghai, whose experience of opium-poisoning has reached to hundreds of cases, says that the effect of the atropia is simply marvellous in stimulating the respiratory function and removing the carbonic-acid narcosis. In the fatal case of atropia-poisoning narrated by Dr. Gross, the injection of morphia induced stertor. I have already suggested that the more gradual introduction of the morphia influence would have prevented this accident, which seems to have been an idiosyncrasy, rather. In a case narrated by Dr. Fothergill,* the influence of the antagonist on the respiratory function is most conspicuous. A woman had taken, at 11 A.M., laudanum containing from 12 to 17 grains of opium. At 2 P.M. the respiration was almost gone, but the pulse, though small, was rhythmical and regular. One grain of sulphate of atropia was then injected subcutaneously. In a half-hour the respiration was becoming well established, and, in an hour and a half after the injection, was going on steadily, 13 to the minute, and long and deep. No further use of the antagonist was necessary to overcome the effects of the poison. It is probable, indeed, that the quantity of atropia used was rather in excess, as an emetic had caused the discharge of some opium, and the subsequent account shows a preponderating action of atropia. An equally instructive case, as showing the power of atropia to overcome the respiratory depression caused by morphia, is narrated by Dr. McGee.† A stout, muscular man of 40

---

* The Antagonism of Therapeutic Agents. Philadelphia, H. C. Lea, 1878, p. 132.

† Am. Jour. of the Med. Sci., July, 1869, p. 282.

years swallowed 30 grains of opium in 10 or 12 ounces of whiskey. He became profoundly comatose. In two hours an eighth of a grain of atropia was injected, and, this having no effect, in half an hour the same quantity was repeated. The respirations were then nearly suspended, the face being livid, but under the influence of the atropia the respirations increased greatly; the pulse rose to 140, the pupils became widely dilated, and consciousness was so far restored that the patient could be roused. He then slept profoundly for a number of hours, but his pulse continued at 81, with the respirations full and deep, and Dr. McGee, wisely trusting to the antagonistic action, did not exhaust his patient by ambulation, flagellation, artificial respiration, and other ingenious devices for keeping awake those who need the restorative effects of sleep and quiet. I might narrate many examples from the collection of cases made for this study, showing the importance of the antagonism exerted on the respiratory functions. There is no difference in the lesson taught us in the cases of opium narcosis. The cases of atropia-poisoning treated by morphia are not less instructive. Various examples come to us with the authority of such names as Graefe,* Schmidt,† Fronmüller,‡ Cohn,§ and others, oc-

---

* Schmidt's Jahrbücher, vol. cxxv. p. 350.
† Ibid., vol. cxxiv. p. 167.   ‡ Ibid., vol. cxxvi. p. 282.
§ Berlin. klin. Woch., 11, 16, 1865.

curring in ophthalmic practice. Some of these were probably not lethal, although characteristic and violent symptoms were produced; yet the antagonistic action of the morphia was not less conspicuously displayed.

If we now pass from the clinical evidence to the results of experimental research on man and on animals, we are greatly surprised with the differences in the conclusions drawn. Mitchell, Morehouse, and Keen conclude that " the influence of atropia on the pulse and respiration is in no way altered by the use of full doses of morphia, so that in this particular their supposed antagonism does not exist." In some experiments of my own, made on a medical student, I found that morphia modified to a considerable extent the effects of atropia on the pulse and respiration,—a fact clearly exhibited in the graphic representation of the results.* Harley expresses himself with decision against the supposed antagonism of these agents on the respiratory function, but he indicates conditions under which they may be used in opposition with advantage,—a singular contradiction between his facts and his opinions. " Belladonna is powerless to obviate the chief danger in opium-poisoning, viz., the depression in the respiratory function." But, in another place, he says, "in the treatment of belladonna-poisoning, our efforts must be directed to

---

* See the tracings on another page.

sustain the breathing. Opium must be used, not as an antidote, but as a means of calming the nervous agitation when it is excessive," etc. It is impossible to find any meaning in such explanations. Again, he says, "when the heart shows indications of failing power, the subcutaneous injection of $\frac{1}{96}$ grain of sulphate of atropia, at intervals of two hours, must be practised." The facts of Dr. Harley admit of very different interpretation from those which he has advanced; they prove that atropia exerts a distinct stimulant action on the respiratory organs, and are in conformity with clinical experience. We may now regard it as settled that atropia antagonizes the depression caused by morphia on the respiratory function, notwithstanding the adverse opinions just quoted.

The antagonistic action of atropia and morphia is further exhibited in the control of the former over the nausea, depression, and actual syncope caused by the latter. This antagonism is exhibited in ordinary medicinal doses, and clinical experience justifies the remark of Harley, that morphia should not be administered alone unless its action on the subject is known, but always with atropia. The explanation of the utility of atropia in preventing the nausea and depression caused by morphia consists in the counterbalancing action of these agents on the cerebrum. While the depression—ofttimes the syncope—is thus prevented, the nausea may occur, for atropia also excites nausea in some subjects. The coldness of the surface and the clammy sweat caused by morphia are removed by atropia. The importance of this fact is considerable. The first effect of morphia is to raise the arterial tension and to energize the cardiac movements, but this is followed by decline in the tension and by slowing of the movements. The peripheral vessels become relaxed, and the blood current becomes slow; the sweat glands act freely, and the functional interchanges between the blood and tissues are suspended. The action of atropia brings about an important change; the peripheral vessels contracting in their vermicular manner, and more blood being received from the heart, the surface grows warm and dry, and the function of metamorphosis of tissue is resumed. The effect of this resumption of activity at the periphery on the condition of the cerebrum is only less important than the renewal of hæmatosis at the lungs.

Atropia stimulates the action of the kidneys somewhat, and morphia checks the flow of urine. They both act to render the emission of urine more difficult, but it is an error to suppose that they act in the same way. Morphia dulls the sensibility of the mucous membrane and diminishes the contractile energy of the muscular coat of the bladder: atropia stimulates the sphincter to more energetic contraction, so that the voluntary efforts at relaxation are opposed.

Having now indicated the points of antagonism, and examined into the opinions for and against the belief in its existence, we are prepared to ascertain how a lethal dose of the one can overcome the effects of a corresponding dose of the other agent. It is evident that very rarely is a lethal dose of one agent counterbalanced by the other in animals. The reason apparently is the difference in the extent and variety of the cerebral structures in man, as· compared with the inferior animals. The physiological actions are the same in animals as in man, except the difference in degree, to employ the words of the illustrious Bernard, but when we reach the brain, we find that in animals the force of the poison is expended on a few comparatively simple organs, whereas in man it is diffused over much more extensive and complicated structures.

Experience has demonstrated that the quantity of poison which can be antagonized successfully and a fatal result averted is comparatively limited. Very considerable quantities, as we have seen, were taken in some of the successful cases, but they did not exceed a certain limit, and the stomach-pump and emetics were freely used, so that the actual amount entering the blood was far less than that taken into the stomach. What disposition of the poison is effected? There is no chemical union of the antagonist, to destroy the toxic power. It is simply opposed until elimination is accomplished. The tendency to destroy life by overwhelming the functions of particular organs is opposed and held in check, and gradually the poison is eliminated. Furthermore, the separation of the poison from the blood and its excretion by the usual channels are greatly promoted by the action of the antagonist in maintaining the functional activity of the organs depressed by the poison. The rate of elimination and the means of promoting it become, therefore, important elements in the management of these cases, and, I may also add, are usually wholly neglected. The principal route of excretion is by the kidney, but the skin and intestinal canal also convey off some of the poison. In a few minutes after the alkaloids are swallowed, traces of them are discoverable in the urine. Free action of the kidneys should therefore be maintained by the use of diluents. Another practical point of high importance is the removal of the urine as fast as it accumulates in the bladder. Brown-Séquard has shown that absorption of alkaloids takes place from the mucous membrane of the bladder, and he proposes to make use of this fact by injecting morphia solutions into this viscus. It is probable that alkaloids contained in the urine may diffuse into the blood again from the bladder. The action of the bowels should be free, and the skin should be stimulated,—in fact, all the channels of excretion should be kept freely at work.

No absolute rule can be laid down as to the quantity of the antagonist to be used. Taking morphia-poisoning as the type, the quantity of atropia must be determined by the effects. What are the guides? The pupils? No. For, although they may react in the usual way to the antagonist, it must be remembered that the action of atropia preponderates, and in some instances they do not react normally. The true guides are the state of the respiration and that of the circulation. If the breathing is deep and rhythmical, and the pulse is full and strong, the state of the pupil and the depth of the narcotism are of little moment. When the amount of the antagonist administered suffices to establish the respiration and circulation in their proper condition, the quantity is sufficient, whether or not it may be theoretically. As a rule, it is better to give the antagonist in small quantity, frequently repeated, until the amount required has been given. Large doses, as is evident in some of the cases, produce unpleasant effects, and may be in excess of the real requirements. In some actual trials, I found that $\frac{1}{20}$ grain of atropia was about equal in toxic power to a grain of morphia. In deciding on the dose of the antagonist, the amount of the poison probably eliminated must be taken into consideration.

THERAPY.—It would be a waste of space to repeat the therapeutical applications of morphia and atropia already given with considerable fulness in the preceding sections. Nevertheless, it is necessary to indicate the circumstances requiring or permitting their conjoined administration. A general rule may be formulated as follows :

Whenever the hypodermatic injection of morphia is proper and necessary, atropia should be combined with it unless contraindicated.

In the *psychical disorders*, in which power is in excess, the conjunctivæ injected, the temperature high, morphia should be used alone. When power is deficient, the tendency being to depression, atropia should be combined with it. This is the rule, also, for other *affections of the brain* in which the subcutaneous injection is indicated.

For the relief of *insomnia*, or to procure sleep, the combination of morphia and atropia is to be preferred. The reader should not forget that an excess of atropia, or an amount of atropia sufficient to antagonize the cerebral effects of the morphia, will prevent sleep. They should be used in the proportion of $\frac{1}{120}$ to $\frac{1}{90}$ grain of atropia to $\frac{1}{4}$ grain or $\frac{1}{2}$ grain of morphia. As the susceptibility to atropia varies immensely, the precise quantity to be employed in any case must be regulated accordingly.

In the treatment hypodermatically of the *various convulsive disorders*, morphia and atropia should be combined.

The *neuralgias* are best treated by the combined morphia and atropia solution. There are several reasons for this:

Much larger doses of morphia may in this way be injected without danger to the patient; and the larger the quantity, as Brown-Séquard has shown, the greater the curative power.

Morphia and atropia combined are more effective than either singly.

The systemic effects during the time of maximum narcosis, and also after the narcosis has disappeared, are much less unpleasant and depressing when the two agents are combined than when morphia is used alone.

Sometimes atropia is better borne than morphia, and *vice versa :* in this case the agent whose effects are least unpleasant should be in excess.

In *sciatica* atropia is often more effective than morphia: the proportions in which they should be used are as follows: $\frac{1}{48}$ to $\frac{1}{120}$ of a grain of atropia, $\frac{1}{4}$ to $\frac{1}{2}$ grain of morphia; here the physiological effects of atropia predominate, but the toxic effects are guarded by the morphia.

In *neuroses of the respiratory and circulatory organs* morphia and atropia should be used together. This is especially the case in *angina pectoris* and *asthma,* with the caution I have already given as to the use of atropia in certain diseases of the heart. Morphia alone is to be preferred in *pleuritis.*

In the *diseases of the digestive apparatus,* requiring

hypodermatic medication, morphia and atropia should be used together.

As a general rule, in *diseases of the urinary and genital organs*, the two agents should be combined. For some purposes atropia should be in excess, as in *spermatorrhœa*, when the more decided anaphrodisiac effect of this agent is indicated. In cases of *pelvic* and *uterine pain*, atropia should be proportionally in larger amount than morphia.

Acute rheumatism, rheumatic gout, muscular rheumatism, and *myalgia* are best relieved by a combination of morphia and atropia, the latter being in excess, as respects its physiological action, of the former. The injection of atropia, thus guarded by morphia, exerts in these diseases an action beyond the relief of pain, how desirable, soever, that may be: it modifies, in a way not now understood, the morbid process. The progress of research renders it more and more probable that rheumatism is an expression of disorder in the nervous system, rather than an affection *per se* of the fibrous structures. Besides relieving in some way this centric disturbance, atropia favors the excretion from the blood of products (the urates) representing the active but imperfect tissue-change occurring in these diseases.

In surgical disorders of various kinds, the combined use of morphia and atropia has most important and varied applications: *to prevent and relieve shock; to cure pain; to relax spasm; to facili-*

tate surgical operations. Whenever, in surgical practice, the hypodermatic injection of morphia and atropia is indicated, the following rule should regulate the relative proportion in which they are employed:

If the action of the heart be feeble, the surface cold, and the vital powers depressed, atropia should be in excess as respects the physiological effects.

TREATMENT OF TOXIC SYMPTOMS CAUSED BY MORPHIA OR ATROPIA.—I may assume, notwithstanding the objections of Harley and the results of experiments on animals by Brown-Séquard, that the physiological antagonism of morphia and atropia has been amply demonstrated by cases of poisoning occurring in man.

In treating cases, the difficulty of precisely regulating the amount necessary to overcome the toxic symptoms is not easily surmountable. I ascertained, in the case which occurred to myself, that one-twenty-fourth of a grain of atropia was equal in toxic power to one grain of morphia. The state of the pupil affords valuable but not unerring indications; atropia possesses more power, relatively, over the movements of the iris than morphia.

In a case of morphia-poisoning, subcutaneous injections of atropia should produce the following results:

Dilatation of the pupil.

Flushing of the face succeeding to pallor.

Dryness and warmth of the skin succeeding to a cold and clammy sweat.

Rise in the pulse-rate and temperature.

Return of reflex movements of eyelids and fauces.

The dilatation of the pupil should be slightly maintained, and should not be carried to the exaggerated degree sometimes thought necessary. The mistake should not be made of confounding the sopor produced by morphia and atropia with morphia coma. This caution is the more necessary because this sleep is often considered a condition of danger requiring renewed administration of the antidote, and the patient is at length poisoned by atropia. Sufficient atropia should be administered to maintain the action of the heart and the respiration. So long as these continue good, no danger is to be apprehended from *sleep* merely.

Atropia, relatively considered, does not equal morphia in toxic activity. Severe physiological effects do not necessarily imply a condition in which life is endangered. It is to be remembered that the toxic effects of atropia endure much longer than those of morphia, and hence repeated applications of the physiological antidote may be required.

DUBOISIA.

Duboisia is the alkaloid of Duboisia Myopo-roides, a member of the Solanaceæ.

The Solution.—The salts of the alkaloid, or active principle, are freely soluble in water, and hence the solutions for hypodermatic use are readily prepared. The following formula will be found useful:

R Duboisiæ muriat. vel sulph., gr. i ;
Aquæ destil., ʒi.   M.
Sig.—Eight minims contain $\frac{1}{80}$ of a grain.

The Dose.—The amount administered will depend on age, idiosyncrasies, habit, etc. For an adult the dose will range from $\frac{1}{100}$ to $\frac{1}{40}$ grain. Eight minims of the above-mentioned solution will produce characteristic physiological effects, · but a much larger quantity can be administered without causing dangerous symptoms.

Physiological Effects.—Dryness of the mouth and fauces, difficulty of deglutition, and a husky voice are experienced in a few minutes; simultaneously there is a sense of fulness in the head, tinnitus, and vertigo; the action of the heart is accelerated, the pulse gains in tension, the face flushes, the pupils dilate, and the vision for near objects is blurred and indistinct; the sense of fulness in the head is followed by headache, especially of the frontal region, the vertigo impairs the locomotion, and the voluntary muscles, especially of the lower limbs, become paretic. During the time of the maximum effect of a full medicinal dose there is considerable excitement of mind, an intense restlessness, but apparently no sensations of a pleasurable kind, but rather anxiety and dread. With the subsidence of the more active symptoms, notably the decline in the circulation and the diminished excitement, a more quiet condition of the mind, a feeling of somnolence, comes on, followed by sound sleep. Dreams and visions disturb the sleep somewhat. In animals (dogs) large doses produce a high degree of excitement, apparently hallucinations and delirium. No corresponding experiences have thus far occurred or been noted in man.

The effects of duboisia are very nearly the same as those of atropia. Instilled into the eye, the pupil dilates, but more readily than from atropia, and the dilatation ceases earlier. Duboisia is less irritating to the mucous membrane, hence it will probably supersede atropia in ophthalmic therapeutics. As duboisia seems to have more decided calmative and hypnotic effects than atropia, it will also probably supersede the latter in hypodermatic employment, if the quantity to be obtained and the price will justify the change.

THERAPY.—Duboisia may be substituted for

atropia in all the conditions of disease in which the latter is now employed. Duboisia is to be preferred probably in all cases; but recent experiences justify me in the expression of my conviction that it is much more effective in *psychical disorders* than atropia. The indications for the administration of these agents are the same.

HYOSCYAMIA.

THE alkaloid of commerce exists in two forms,
—as a brown, soft solid; as a white, crystallized
substance. Both found in the shops are, as a
rule, prepared by Merck, of Darmstadt. The
amorphous preparation is generally preferred,
owing to its comparative cheapness and to its
activity. A solution of this is made in the
proportion of one grain to twenty minims,—
eight minims of alcohol, six minims of ether,
and six minims of water (Prideaux). This may
be diluted by equal parts of alcohol and water.
A solution of the acetate may be formed ex-
temporaneously by dissolving one grain of the
amorphous hyoscyamia in two drachms of
water acidulated with thirty minims of acetic
acid. When solution is effected, it should be
carefully neutralized by ammonia, and afterwards filtered.

The crystallized alkaloid in the form of a salt
—the sulphate most usually—is more readily
prepared for hypodermatic use. When its isola-
tion shall be readily effected, we can hardly
doubt it will be found more uniform in its effects

and more active than the extract containing it.
The following is the formula proposed by Seguin :

  ℞ Hyoscyamiæ (Merck's cryst.), gr. ii ;
   Glycerinæ,
   Aquæ destil., āā, m̃c ;
   Acid. carbol., gr. ss. M.
   Filtra. ⁻
  Sig.—One minim contains $\frac{1}{100}$ grain.

The dose of hyoscyamia is variously stated,
and indeed ranges from $\frac{1}{100}$ grain to two or three
grains. As this extraordinary variation is plainly
due to differences in the quality of the preparation, care must be used. The specimens of soft
extract containing the alkaloid are not, in respect
to any two specimens, alike as to the quantity.
Some of them probably are not more active than
good specimens of the ordinary extract. It is
necessary to proceed with caution, since violent,
even dangerous symptoms have been noted by
Gill,* Empis,† and others. In using the crystallized alkaloid, the dose should not exceed one-
one-hundredth of a grain for the initial trial.
Gill had violent symptoms from $\frac{1}{60}$ grain. When
the strength of any given preparation is known,
the dose will be determined by the character of
the case and by the quantity needed to produce
physiological effects, which varies much in individuals and in diseases.

---

* The Practitioner, February, 1878, p. 84.

† Annuaire de Thérapeutique, 1881, p. 31, et seq.

PHYSIOLOGICAL EFFECTS.—Whilst hyoscyamia corresponds closely in action to atropia and duboisia, there are differences. Hyoscyamia is less excitant and deliriant, and more calmative and hypnotic. In respect to the mechanism of the action on the heart and circulatory system, on the respiration, on the pupil, and on the brain, there is no difference between these several alkaloids of the Solanaceæ.

THERAPY.—Within a few years past much clinical experience has been published showing the value of hyoscyamine in *mental disorders.* Prideaux* makes the important observation that it acts differently as respects promptness and efficiency under varying conditions of insanity. Thus, in *acute mania* characterized by depression, one-sixteenth grain will have a decided effect, whilst in the condition of excitement of *chronic mania* larger doses are necessary, reaching as high as one-tenth grain subcutaneously, which he regards the preferable mode of administration. In mania with intense motor excitement and destructive tendencies, Prideaux regards hyoscyamine as "the most rapid and reliable narcotic we possess." In *epileptic mania, delusional insanity,* and in *chronic dementia,* it does good in many cases.

Dr. C. Reinhard† has used hyoscyamine in

---

* The Lancet, 1879,—Sept. 27, Oct. 4 and 11.

† Archiv für Psych. und Nervenkrankheiten, Band xi.

fifteen insane and twelve epileptics. In eight of the insane it produced calmative effects and did good, and in five epileptics with maniacal attacks it diminished their number and severity. Mendel[*] has also used hyoscyamia in various psychoses with advantage, those improved being characterized by high motor excitement. In *active delirium* the crystallized alkaloid prepared by Merck has been used by Fronmüller[†] with good results. To these observations showing the value of this remedy in disorders of the mind may be added the reports of Pearse,[‡] Gill,[§] and Lawson,[||]—all confirming the utility of hyoscyamia in mania with high motor activity. More recently, Séguin[¶] has made an exhaustive study of the actions and uses of this agent. He finds that in mania it produces sleep more certainly even than chloral, and without bad after-effects. It has produced a positive cure in a case of delusions of persecution, and has done more than any other remedy in *paralysis agitans*, as respects relief to the trembling. In *chorea, mercurial trembling, senile trembling*, etc., in *spasmodic cough, laryngismus, hiccough*, etc., hyoscyamia has been used

---

[*] Allg. Zeitschr. f. Psych., xxxvi., 1879.

[†] Memorabilien. Quoted in Virchow u. Hirsch's Jahresbericht for 1877.

[‡] Lancet, Sept. 1876, p. 319.

[§] The Practitioner, Feb. 1878, p. 84.

[||] Ibid., Aug. 1878.

[¶] Archives of Medicine, June, 1881.

with success as a palliative in numerous instances,
occasionally with curative results. (Oulmont.*)

HYOSCINE.

Ladenburg has prepared from hyoscyamus
secondary alkaloids such as had been previously
obtained from atropia. *Hyoscine* was so derived.
A crystallizable salt is formed by combination of
hydriodic acid with hyoscine. Its physiological
effects correspond to those of hyoscyamia, but
are less powerful. It causes less dryness of the
mouth, and less disturbs accommodation, and is
more decidedly sedative. In the clinical trials,
one-half of the cases of whooping-cough were relieved, and it did good in all the cases of asthma,
six in number, in which it was used. Hyoscine
also relieved the pain of enteralgia. There is
much to be hoped from further experience with
this interesting remedy.

* Bull. Gén. de Thérap., vol. lxxxiii. p. 481.

STRYCHNIA.

HISTORY.—Strychnia was probably the first agent submitted to systematic examination by the physiological method. Magendie, having ascertained its properties, suggested that "medicine would perhaps derive great advantage from the knowledge of a substance whose property is to act on the spinal cord, for we know that many severe diseases have their seat in this part of the nervous system." Causing muscular rigidity, he supposed it might be used with good effects in the condition of paralysis, and it was not long before Fouquier subjected the suggestion to the test of experiment, and treated cases of paralysis successfully. The first application of strychnia hypodermatically in the treatment of disease was made by Dr. Béhier, of Paris, but the observations of Mr. Charles Hunter really initiated the clinical experience since continued so successfully.

THE SOLUTION.—The following solution is convenient:

> ℞ Strychniæ sulphatis, gr. i ;
> Acid. carbolic., gr. i ;
> Aquæ, ℥i. M.
> Sig.—Ten minims contain $\frac{1}{48}$ grain.

As a solution of strychnia will long remain free from a penicilium, the addition of carbolic acid is necessary only when the solution is intended to be kept several months. Although one grain will dissolve in an ounce of water entirely, at the ordinary temperature, it tends to crystallize out; hence before taking out the required amount the bottle should be placed in a vessel containing some hot water. The sulphate, in larger relative proportion, and other salts, as the nitrate, have been proposed, but from a mistaken notion of the solubility. The sulphate is the most soluble of the salts of strychnia, but not more freely than in the proportion of the above formula. By the aid of heat, two or more grains will dissolve in an ounce of water, but on cooling the surplus will crystallize out. On the other hand, the solution containing one grain to the ounce will remain a perfect solution for some time, and not until after several months will some minute crystals form on the glass.

The dose of strychnia subcutaneously has been variously given. Lorent employed from one-twenty-fifth to one-tenth of a grain, and Eulenberg has given up to one-eighth. Hunter administered from one-ninetieth to one-twenty-fourth of a grain. Echeverria produced toxic symptoms in a boy, which, however, were readily recovered from, by one-thirtieth of a grain. From five to ten minims of the solution recommended will be suitable quantities under the varying circumstances of cases. Half a grain is the smallest fatal dose recorded.

PHYSIOLOGICAL EFFECTS.—It is important to note the effects produced by the hypodermatic injection of medicinal doses. Unfortunately, until toxic symptoms are excited, the disturbance is too vague for characteristic description. Some facts can be stated, however, from clinical observation.

When a solution of strychnia of the usual strength is injected under the skin, a sensation of heat and smarting persists for some time in the part. The skin also becomes red in the neighborhood of the puncture; a subjective sensation of warmth is perceived in the limb, and an actual rise in temperature may be noted. At the same time erection of the hair-follicles (*cutis anserina*) takes place.

In a few seconds pain or distention is felt in the abdomen, intestinal movements and loud borborygmi occur, just as is the case so frequently after the hypodermatic injection of the narcotic alkaloids. Next the pupils dilate, deep-seated pain and throbbing are felt in the brain, and an unpleasant giddiness renders the erect posture painful, and standing or walking uncertain. Ringing in the ears, detonation, anxiety, a feeling of dread, and flashes of light before the eyes are also quite commonly experienced. The countenance of the patient affords some indication of the cerebral disturbance, appearing anxious and distressed.

The foregoing symptoms are more severe if larger doses be administered, and in addition there occur some stiffness of the jaws, jerking of the extensor muscles, and sharp pains like electric shocks shooting through the limbs. Dr. Echeverria has so well described these severe symptoms that I transcribe his account. My own observations supply no further experiences than those I have just detailed.

"I injected first the right thigh, and about two minutes after, the left. In two minutes more the boy commenced to sigh, and have a meaningless smile, with stiffness in the jaws, soon passing into real trismus. The pupils were largely dilated, the face congested, and tetanic spasms of the respiratory and cervical muscles followed. Every attempt to articulate a word awoke a spasm. He could neither speak nor be touched without being seized with a jerk, and the whole surface of the body was in a perspiration."* In another case Dr. Echeverria had similar experiences. He thus describes them: "In about eight minutes she complained of giddiness, and was soon seized with trismus and opisthotonos. The tetanic spasms were not violent, and were accompanied by general perspiration, congestion of the face, and enlargement of the pupil." Other impor-

---

* Treatment of Paralysis by Hypodermic Injections of Strychnine. Medical Communications of the Connecticut State Medical Society, 1868.

tant observations were made by Dr. Echeverria. "The temperature of the limbs was always raised after the injection. The frequency of the pulse was also augmented. The capillary circulation was rendered more active in the limbs, exhibiting large red patches, more intense in the vicinity of the punctured region. This condition would last three and even four days after the operation. The injections were attended with perspiration of the head and limbs, more profuse with the girl than with the boy. The pupils were always dilated, and gurgling of the bowels would persist some minutes after the puncture. Another very perceptible result was the fibrillar contractions, or twitching of the muscles in the limbs, lasting for a minute or two, and which I have found prolonged for more than an hour in other similar cases."

When we come to analyze the symptoms produced by the subcutaneous injection of strychnia in full medicinal doses, we observe that the effects are exerted on the nervous system of animal life, and to some extent on the sympathetic system.

In small quantity strychnia does not affect the irritability of the motor and sensory nerves, as Klapp* and Spitzka† have shown, but in large

---

* The Journal of Nervous and Mental Diseases, vol. v., 1878, p. 619.

† Ibid., vol. vi., 1879.

doses it does appear to have this effect, as Vulpian * and others have demonstrated. The opposing observations on this point are reconciled by the fact, discovered by Martin-Magron et Buisson, that the action of strychnia on the nerves is local, and therefore greatly influenced by the quantity reaching them.

Strychnia causes a rise in pressure of the blood by stimulating the vaso-motor centre in the medulla, and by inducing contraction of the arterioles, as has been experimentally demonstrated by Mayer,† Spitzka,‡ and others. It also, in medicinal doses, stimulates the intra-cardiac ganglia, thus increasing the heart's rate of movement. Clinical observation has seemed to be conclusive as to the power of strychnia to stimulate the respiratory organs and to increase the depth and force of inspiration.

In a lethal dose the effect follows immediately almost on the administration of the poison. The head feels powerfully distended; a shudder passes over the body, with a catch in the breathing; a pain deep in the epigastrium shooting to the spine occurs at the same time; the jaws are clinched; electric-like shocks fly through the limbs; the muscles of extension of the extremities and the muscles of the abdomen become rigid and start

---

* Archives de Physiologie Norm. et Path., 1870, p. 116, et seq.

† Archiv f. experiment. Pathologie u. Pharmacol., Band 11, p. 458.   ‡ *Supra.*

up in sudden strong contraction; the face is pale and distorted by a grim smile (*risus sardonicus*); the pupils are dilated; the pulse is quick; the breathing jerking. With the progress of the action the sensibility of the reflex centre becomes so acute that the minutest peripheral impression— a breath of air, a touch, a gleam from a mirror— will excite a spasm, in which general extension of the voluntary muscles takes place, the breathing is suspended, the hands are clinched, the toes incurvated, the head bent backward, and the body so arched that the heels and the occiput are the only points of support. During the paroxysm the face grows dusky, and the skin generally dark and perspiring. Death ensues by the fixation of the respiratory muscles, but rarely occurs in the first paroxysm, and may be delayed to the third or later. The mind is unaffected until carbonic-acid narcosis comes on. Much soreness is felt in the muscles after the paroxysm, but they are not rigid. The paroxysms increase in number and violence to the end, which occurs usually within two hours.

THERAPY.—The original suggestion of the use of strychnia in the treatment of *paralysis* was made, as has been shown, by Magendie, after his course of experiment demonstrating the nature of its actions. Dr. Béhier, of Paris, was, it appears, the first physician to employ strychnia by the hypodermatic method, and afterwards Prof. Courty, of Montpellier, used it with complete success in three cases of *facial paralysis.* Notwithstanding these, and some other authoritative statements regarding the curative effects of strychnia thus administered, it was not until Mr. Charles Hunter's paper—"On Strychnia Hypodermically administered in Paralytic Affections"*—appeared that professional attention was strongly directed to this subject. Echeverria's paper also revived the interest in this country, continued by cases occurring in the practice of Dr. Hammond, of New York, which were reported by Dr. Reuben A. Vance.† These were cases of hemiplegia, paraplegia, and local paralysis. As might have been expected, the local paralyses were most decidedly benefited, but all were improved in a marked degree. The forms of paralysis which have been treated in this way are the following:

Hemiplegia.	Infantile paralysis.
Paraplegia.	Local paralyses.

Progressive muscular atrophy.

Progressive locomotor ataxia.

Mr. Hunter reports three out of four cases of *hemiplegia* cured by the injections of strychnia. Two of the cases were respectively of six and two and a half years' duration. This statistical statement should not mislead the reader. Suc-

---

* British and Foreign Medico-Chirurgical Review, April, 1868.

† Journal of Psychological Medicine, vol. iv. p. 367, et seq.

cess like this cannot be expected in the treatment
of paralysis of cerebral origin; the cases of Mr.
Hunter were evidently very favorable cases for
treatment by this method. Nevertheless, the
hypodermatic injection of strychnia, in many
cases, is decidedly curative. As Dr. Echeverria
has well remarked, " the effects of strychnia are
widely different when administered hypodermatically or by the mouth. By the latter method
the quantity may be repeated and increased, un-
successfully, as manifested in the cases of Hunter, and in those here related; and yet a smaller
dose of the substance, exhibited hypodermatically, be capable of regenerating at once the lost
muscular power."

We should possess clear notions, then, as to
the circumstances in which it may be proper to
use the hypodermatic injection of strychnia in
hemiplegia, for, manifestly, a remedy of such
power may prove to be as harmful when indis-
creetly employed as it is unquestionably useful
in suitable cases.

It is contraindicated in recent hemiplegia.

In my own experience it has not been useful
in old cases characterized by contractions of the
palsied limbs.

It has been exceedingly useful in old cases of
hemiplegia in subjects not very advanced in life,
the paralysis being partial as to motility, and the
limbs not wasted.

The hypodermatic injection of strychnia has

been used in *spinal paraplegia* by Béhier, Courty, Ruppaner, Hunter, Echeverria, and others, with success. The rules for its administration are similar to those I have given for hemiplegia.

It is not proper in acute cases involving structural alterations of the spinal cord.

In cases of paraplegia due to softening or tumor in the spinal canal it will do harm.

It will be beneficial in cases of reflex paraplegia, in paraplegia due to anæmia of the cord, in hysterical paraplegia, and in those cases of paresis of the muscles of the inferior extremities due to concussion of the cord, but after the acute symptoms have subsided.

It is certainly true, however, that Mr. Hunter obtained advantage from it in a case the symptoms of which indicated myelitis. Dr. Echeverria's Case I. may be classed in the same category, —the patient complaining of formication and numbness, and being paralyzed both as to motion and sensation.

The hypodermatic injection of strychnia has proved an exceedingly valuable adjunct to the treatment of *infantile paralysis*. If the electromuscular contractility to the continuous or induced current be not lost, very beneficial results may be expected from this treatment. The injection promotes the capillary circulation, and increases the growth and power of the muscles.

In various *local paralyses* the hypodermatic injection of strychnia is even more decidedly

curative. Courty* cured *facial paralysis* by injecting strychnia over the course of the facial nerve. Pletzer, Lorent, Sacmann, and Eulenberg had good results from the same treatment.†
In a case of paralysis of the vocal cords with aphonia, Neudörfer failed, but in a similar case Waldenburg succeeded with the strychnia injection.

In the "drop wrist" of lead-poisoning—*paralysis of the extensors*—it is a very important addition to the other means of treatment of this very obstinate affection. It is more successful than any other agent in *writer's cramp*. Palsy of single muscles or groups of muscles, following cold or rheumatism, is generally curable by this means. The injection also increases much the contractile power in cases of palsy following injury of nerve trunks.

Paralysis of the bladder, with dribbling of urine, and *paralysis of the sphincter ani* not due to myelitis, are much benefited and frequently cured by this means.

In *progressive muscular atrophy* it has been used with great advantage in cases in which the electro-muscular contractility was not lost.

In paralysis of cerebral or spinal origin, without wasting of the muscles, the injection may be made under the skin. The dose of strychnia will vary, with the age of the subject, from $\frac{1}{60}$ to $\frac{1}{10}$ of

---

* Eulenberg, p. 243.　　　　　　　　† Ibid.

a grain.   In local paralyses, in infantile paralysis, in progressive muscular atrophy, the injection must be made into the affected muscles.   If the electro-contractility be not lost, the following effects may be expected:

Rise in temperature of the limb, and increase of capillary circulation.

Increase in muscular power with growth of muscles.

Cure of the paralysis.

If, however, the electro-muscular contractility to the galvanic current is lost, fatty degeneration has so far proceeded that the injection of strychnia will be useless.

The method of practising the injection into the muscles is as follows:

The affected muscle or group of muscles is grasped with the left hand and made prominent, and with the right the needle is plunged quickly and boldly into the muscular tissue.   When inserted as far as necessary, the needle is withdrawn a short distance to clear any vessel it may have penetrated, at the same time moving the point about, and then the fluid is slowly injected. It is important, of course, to avoid the blood-vessels, and to insert the needle into the para-lyzed muscles.   The pain of this operation is not greater than the subcutaneous injection, and little danger of deep-seated abscess is to be feared. Muscular tissue, as is well known, does not readily take on the morbid action called inflammatory.

The systemic effects do not follow so quickly nor are they as powerful after injection into the muscular tissue as after the subcutaneous injection. Both local and systemic effects are produced; but it is chiefly the local effects which are desired in cases of local paralysis. Some cases of local paralysis of the bladder cannot be reached in this way. In paralysis of the sphincter ani the needle may readily be thrust into this muscle.

The subcutaneous injection of strychnia has been used in *progressive locomotor ataxia*, but with a negative result. In my own experience I have observed no decided influence for good or evil.

Neuralgia. — The hypodermatic injection of strychnia has been used by Dr. Anstie in *gastralgia* and *cardiac neuralgia*, with advantage. "My decided opinion is, at present," says Dr. Anstie, "that there is no such remedy for gastralgia as strychnia subcutaneously injected in doses of $\frac{1}{120}$ to $\frac{1}{60}$ of a grain." Although I cannot speak so positively as Dr. Anstie on this subject, I can say that I have observed good effects from the strychnia injection in the class of cases to which he refers.

Amaurosis and Amblyopia.—According to Eulenberg, Fremineau was the first to employ the hypodermatic injection of strychnia for the cure of a case of amaurosis following typhus. Sacmann soon after reported a cure of amaurosis by the same means, and Spaeth one of amblyopia,—

"functional paralysis of the retina." Dr. Lacerda,* of Lisbon, employed the hypodermatic injection of strychnia with success in a case of "amaurotic amblyopia." Talko, of Tiflis,† also succeeded in curing amblyopia by repeated injections, ranging in strength from $\frac{1}{40}$ to $\frac{1}{4}$ of a grain. The most important contributions to our knowledge of this subject have been made by Prof. Nagel, of Tübingen, who reports cures, of amblyopia and amaurosis, and even cases of the latter in which there was white atrophy of the optic disks.‡

Weinow § employs the nitrate, $\frac{1}{50}$ grain, injected into the temple every two or four days. If no improvement occur after three injections, he discontinues the practice. In an excellent paper on the subject, Bull‖ gives a *résumé* of Nagel's observations, and follows with an account of twenty-four cases. He concludes that in functional amblyopia we may expect good and permanent results from strychnia; and even in some cases of organic origin, provided there be no extensive atrophy of the nerve structures, some

---

* Gazette de Lisboa, xi., 1867, and Schmidt's Jahrbücher der gesammten Medicin, vol. cxliii. p. 67.

† Ibid., vol. cxlv. p. 74.

‡ Berliner klinische Wochenschrift, viii. p. 6, 1871. Also, Dr. Nagel's special treatise, which, however, I have not had the opportunity to consult.

§ Quoted in the London Medical Record, vol. i. p. 156.

‖ The American Journal of the Medical Sciences, 1872.

improvement is obtained from the use of the remedy. If actual atrophy of the nerve exists, he thinks strychnia useless. All authorities are agreed that it is in alcohol and tobacco amaurosis, especially the latter, that the injection of strychnia renders such important service. It is conceded that the remedy will do no good if no improvement has occurred after three or four injections.

To these must be added the amblyopia of disuse, of hysteria, and allied states.*

The Antagonisms of Strychnia.—The discovery of chloral hydrate and the subsequent announcement of strychnia as its physiological antagonist, made by Liebreich, have been followed by numerous researches, monographs, and clinical reports. Liebreich demonstrated that animals in a deep stupor from chloral intoxication, the dose administered being lethal, were aroused, and death was averted by strychnia. If, for example, two rabbits of equal weight—say three pounds—receive $\frac{1}{96}$ grain of strychnia sulphate, a fatal dose, and to one of them fifteen grains of chloral be also given, the former will die in tetanic convulsions in ten minutes, while the latter will sleep two hours or more quietly, and will wake up in a normal state. Such a striking exhibition would seem to be conclusive, but other observations are necessary. The most important

---

* L. De Wecker, Thérapeutique Oculaire, p. 640.

and elaborate research, undertaken to determine
the supposed antagonism of chloral and strychnia, is that of the Committee of the British Medical Association, Dr. J. Hughes Bennett, Chairman.* The Committee first, rightly, settled the
lethal dose of each agent; they next ascertained
the result of the simultaneous administration of
chloral and strychnia; and then the result of the
administration, at varying intervals, of one subsequently to the lethal dose of the other agent.
Their general conclusions are as follows: " 1.
That, after a fatal dose of strychnia, life may be
saved by bringing the animal under the influence
of chloral hydrate; 2. That chloral hydrate is
more likely to save life after a fatal dose of
strychnia than strychnia is to save life after a
fatal dose of chloral hydrate; 3. That, after a
dose of strychnia producing severe tetanic convulsions, these convulsions may be much reduced, both in force and frequency, by the use
of chloral hydrate, and consequently much suffering saved; 4. That the extent of physiological
antagonism between the two substances is so
far limited that (1) a very large fatal dose of
strychnia may kill before the chloral has had
time to act; or (2) so large must be the dose of
chloral hydrate to antagonize an excessive dose
of strychnia that there is danger of death from
the effects of the chloral hydrate; 5. Chloral

---

* Brit. Med. Jour., Oct. 3, 1874, p. 437, et seq.

hydrate mitigates the effects of a fatal dose of strychnia by depressing the excess of reflex activity excited by that substance, while strychnia may mitigate the effects of a fatal dose of chloral hydrate by rousing the activity of the spinal cord; but it does not appear capable of removing the coma produced by the action of chloral hydrate on the brain."

A careful investigation of the supposed antagonism of chloral and strychnia has been undertaken by Husemann.* He holds that chloral is an antidote to strychnia, prevents the spasms, and averts death, and that it has a corresponding effect in the case of the strychnia bases sold under the name of brucin. One of the earliest attempts to ascertain whether the antagonism existed was that of Rajewski,† who found that chloral prevented or relieved the cramps caused by strychnia, and also to a certain extent the cardiac depression, but that strychnia was not in the same degree an antagonist to chloral. In a memoir on the treatment of poisoning by chloral, Erlenmeyer‡ holds that, while chloral is useful to oppose some of the effects of strychnia, the converse does not hold good, and strychnia is not useful in chloral-poisoning. The influence which Erlenmeyer's opinion might otherwise

---

* " Antagonistische und antidotarische Studien." Arch. f. exp. Pathol. und Pharmacol., vi. p. 345.

† Centralbl. f. d. med. Wissensch., 17, 1870, p. 261.

‡ Prakt. Arzt, xiv. p. 11. Quoted in The Practitioner.

have is decidedly weakened by a statement made in this connection, intended to illustrate and enforce his views, that, while morphia is an antagonist to atropia in poisoning by the latter, atropia is not an antagonist in poisoning by morphia. Arnould,* who has also investigated this question experimentally, regards the antagonism as more limited in scope than Liebreich has maintained. This question has also been studied by Prof. Oré, of Bordeaux,† who concludes that strychnia rather promotes than prevents the poisonous action of chloral.

What is the teaching of clinical experience? I have found recorded seven cases of strychnia-poisoning, in which chloral was the chief or only means of treatment employed. An equal number of cases I find in which chloroform inhalations were practised successfully. Although the latter do not come within the range of the present subject, yet, as the effects of chloral are attributed by Liebreich to the disengagement of chloroform in the blood, they may serve to illustrate and confirm the former. Of the seven cases of strychnia-poisoning, in which chloral was the chief or only agent used, all proved successful. No facts could be stronger. I am unable to find any cases of chloral-poisoning in

---

* Presse Méd. Belge, 1870, No. 9, p. 69. Quoted by Husemann.

† Bull. Gén. de Thérap., lxxxiii. p. 403, et seq.

which strychnia was properly and adequately used, as it is in animals.

If we now sum up the evidence, we cannot fail to be convinced of the antagonistic action of chloral and strychnia; but chloral is an antagonist to strychnia-poisoning, rather than strychnia is an antagonist to chloral-poisoning. The experience on rabbits shows that $\frac{1}{90}$ grain of strychnia is equivalent to fifteen grains of chloral. In the cases of poisoning in man, thirty grains of chloral subcutaneously was sufficient to allay the spasms and avert death from four grains of strychnia. But no absolute rule can be laid down, since the susceptibility to the action of these poisons varies greatly in different individuals. As in the published cases emetics were used, and in many instances the quantity of strychnia was merely estimated, no positive conclusions can be drawn from them. Artificial respiration materially retards the action of strychnia, and warmth, as Brunton * has shown, exercises a remarkable influence in lessening the effect of chloral. Thus, " Dr. Brunton found that an animal wrapped in cotton-wool may recover perfectly from a dose of chloral which is sufficient to kill it when exposed to the cooling action of the air, and that recovery from the narcotic action is much quicker when the temperature is maintained in this way, and still more rapid when the animal is placed in a

---

* Jour. of Anat. and Physiol., May, 1874, No. 14.

warm bath, provided this is not excessive." Heat would therefore seem to be an antagonist to chloral, and for an obvious reason, for heat increases the action of the heart, and thus opposes the depression of the heart, which is a main factor in the toxic effects of chloral. In the treatment of the toxic effects of strychnia by chloral, the amount of the latter administered should be determined by the symptoms. Sufficient chloral should be given to suspend the strychnia spasms, for the danger consists in the stoppage of respiration by tetanic fixation of the respiratory muscles. The amount required for this will, doubtless, vary within considerable limits, as I have already intimated. In the case of the Sioux Indian, treated by Dr. Turner,* the quantity of strychnia was not known, but the return of the spasms from time to time required repeated doses of chloral, one hundred and five grains in all being given within five hours. When strychnia is used against chloral-poisoning, the objects to be accomplished are different. By stimulating the cardiac and respiratory centres with strychnia, the tendency to cardiac and respiratory failure is prevented. The quantity required will be determined by the effects; but it is probably much less than theory indicates. The initial dose may be $\frac{1}{60}$ grain, and each succeeding dose $\frac{1}{120}$ grain, which may be repeated every half-hour,

---

* Med. and Surg. Reporter, June 15, 1872.

or more frequently, until an approximation to the maximum is reached.

Chloral and strychnia can hardly be regarded as antagonistic in their actions on the functions of the brain, since chloral suspends them, and strychnia does not affect them in any way. In one respect they have opposed effects,—chloral producing cerebral anæmia and strychnia rather increasing the intra-cranial circulation. On the spinal cord the antagonism is very complete,— chloral suspending the reflex and motor functions of the cord and strychnia exalting both. Strychnia stimulates the respiratory and vaso-motor centres in the cord, and thus opposes and counteracts the most dangerous tendency of chloral narcosis. The chief danger from strychnia— the tetanic fixation of the muscles of respiration due to the exalted reflex function—is removed by the action of chloral. This antagonism is more certain and effective than the opposite one, or the stimulation of the chloralized spinal cord by strychnia; whence it follows that chloral is a more useful antagonist in strychnia-poisoning than is strychnia in chloral-poisoning.

An antagonism has been demonstrated between strychnia and *bromide of potassium*. Notwithstanding the difference in the rate with which they act, bromide of potassium has been used successfully in several instances to counteract the toxic effects of strychnia. The doses administered must be large and must be frequently repeated. One drachm may be given every half-hour, sufficiently diluted in water. The limitation of the doses will be determined by the effect on the spasms. Bromide may also be used in conjunction with other remedies,—with those more prompt, but evanescent in effect, as ether or chloroform inhalations.

Strychnia as a Stimulant of the Respiratory Function.—The importance of atropia as a special stimulant of the respiratory function has been frequently alluded to. The resemblance in the spinal actions of atropia and of strychnia has been manifest in the study of these agents. Atropia, in therapeutical works, is sometimes suggested as an opponent and antagonist of strychnia; it is so placed in Gubler's " Commentary on the French Codex." Hardly any statement could be more fallacious. In some experimental investigations made some years ago, I found that atropia intensified the effects of strychnia, and hastened death by contributing to the tetanic fixation of the muscles of respiration. We find that strychnia stands next to atropia as a stimulant to the respiratory function. Through the heightened reflex activity of the spinal cord and of the respiratory centres in the medulla, strychnia causes death by spasm of the respiratory muscles and asphyxia. It must therefore antagonize those agents which, like aconite, cause death by paralysis of the respiratory muscles. This supposition is confirmed by experi-

ment. In an interesting series of experiments
to test this antagonism, Dr. Fothergill found that
a lethal dose of aconitine was entirely overcome
by a quantity of strychnia twice as great as the
lethal. The animals given the aconitine alone
died; the same animals receiving the aconitine
with the strychnia, in previous experiments, recovered. The existence of the antagonism is,
therefore, undoubted.

An opposition of actions has been determined
to exist between *strychnia and nitrite of amyl.*
These substances act in an opposite manner on
the nervous system of animal life and on the
sympathetic system. Amyl nitrite suspends the
reflex function of the spinal cord and causes
paralysis of the muscular system, and death ensues from paralysis of the respiratory muscles.
The most characteristic effects are those on the
heart and the arterial system. It depresses the
arterial tension to the lowest point, and increases
greatly the action of the heart, a necessary result
of the enormous dilatation of the peripheral vessels. The reflex and spinal effects, the cardiac
and arterial disturbance, are the opposite of those
produced by strychnia. From the physiological
stand-point, then, an antagonism must be presumed to exist between them. An experimental
research by Dr. Gray,* of Glasgow, strongly
supports this view. Thus, he found that one-

* Glasgow Med. Jour., 1871, p. 188.

fourth of a grain of strychnia proved fatal usually to the rabbits which he used for experiment. He was able to administer half a grain of strychnia and ten drops of the nitrite of amyl simultaneously, by subcutaneous injection, without any marked disturbance following. Of course, further investigations are necessary, but sufficient is now known to justify the inhalation of nitrite of amyl in cases of strychnia-poisoning.

CONIA.

THE SOLUTION.—When this alkaloid was first used subcutaneously, the only preparation available was the alcoholic solution. The following formula, proposed by Burman, is an advance on previous attempts:

> ℞ Coniæ, ʒiii, ℳxii;
>   Acidi acetici fort., ʒiii, ℳxii;
>   Spts. vini rect., ʒi;
>   Aquæ destillatæ, ad ℥ii. M.

Sig.—One minim of this solution is a sufficient dose to begin with. Five minims contain one minim of conia.

As the alkaloid conia readily undergoes decomposition and varies greatly in strength, preparations made from commercial samples must be very unequal in power. It follows, therefore, in beginning a new solution care is necessary to determine its strength. The salts of conia, consisting of the hydrobromate, hydriodate, and tartrate, are, on the other hand, more permanent. These salts crystallize in large, transparent, vitreous crystals, those of the tartrate being especially fine. Solutions prepared from the tartrate of conia will, no doubt, prove more advantageous in all respects.

Physiological Effects.—The local effects of the injection are the same as those of other alkaloids. In the largest dose which can be safely administered, it induces sleepiness, vertigo, coldness of the surface, diminished sensibility, and weakness of the inferior extremities. The respiration becomes slower and less full. The pulse diminishes in number and force, falling so much as thirty to forty beats per minute.

In a case of poisoning carefully observed by Dr. Bennett,* weakness of the legs and staggering were first noticed. Loss of all power of voluntary movement next followed. He became unable to swallow, and completely lost his power of vision. "His pulse and breathing were perfectly natural," but at the expiration of a half-hour after this, paralysis of the muscles of respiration had taken place, the action of the heart continuing, but was "very feeble." Meantime his intelligence was preserved, but he was without power of articulation.

The mode in which conia produces these effects has been elaborately examined by Kölliker and Guttman. The last-named observer has shown that conia does not act on the spinal cord, nor does it destroy the irritability of muscle, but paralyzes the peripheral terminations of the motor

---

* Clinical Medicine, p. 413, Am. ed.

nerves. Death is produced by asphyxia—paralysis of the muscles of respiration—and not by cessation of the heart's movements, for these continue after respiration has ceased.

THERAPY.—The therapeutical applications of conia by the hypodermatic method are neither numerous nor important.

It has been used in the treatment of *asthma* by Pletzer. Although it appears to be a rational remedy, paralyzes the muscles of respiration, and in this way may be supposed to antagonize that condition of things which exists in asthma, experience is not in its favor, and a careful examination of its physiological effects discloses the fact that the influence which it exerts on respiration is a toxic action only. In the treatment of asthma it is not at all equal to morphia and atropia; nevertheless, in cases in which these agents disagree, or in which it is undesirable to use them, it may be tried.

Erlenmeyer procured relief, by the hypodermatic injection of conia, to the difficult breathing of *emphysema*. The same authority reports having cured a case of *angina pectoris* by two injections of conia. He therefore recommends it in these affections.

Lorent, influenced by theoretical considerations,—the action of conia on the pulse and respiration,—has employed this agent hypodermatically in pneumonia and pleuritis, with the effect to reduce decidedly the pulse-rate. It does not appear that this treatment is worthy of serious consideration. In the spasmodic affections of the thoracic viscera, Lorent has had experiences with conia similar to those of Erlenmeyer.

Conia is also one of the numerous remedies proposed for the cure of *tetanus.* Successful cases have been reported, cured by conium administered internally; but we may be permitted to distrust these, since Harley has shown that the extract is entirely devoid of conia, and therefore innocuous. For the treatment of tetanus, the hypodermatic injection of conia may be used with a reasonable expectation of benefiting the patient.

As conia produces motor paralysis, it has been held to be *antagonistic to strychnia;* but since it has been shown by Guttman that conia paralyzes the peripheral terminations of the motor nerves, and does not act upon the cord, this view must be abandoned. Besides clinical experience is wanting.

In a careful course of investigation, Burman * has studied the combined effects of conia and morphia on the condition of mania. He finds the combined remedies very useful to allay the excitement of *acute mania.* The indications are intense motor activity and wakefulness as concomitants of mania.

---

* The West Riding Lunatic Asylum Reports, vol. ii. p. 1, et seq.

WOORARA OR CURARA.

The Solution.—The strength of the solution usually employed for hypodermatic use is one per centum,—one grain to one hundred minims of water. The dose is $\frac{1}{10}$ of a grain, or ten minims of the solution. The repetition of the dose will depend on the effects produced, and on the character of the malady for which it is prescribed.

The active principle—woorarin or curarin—may be employed in place of woorara. In the form of sulphate it is readily soluble in water. The dose is $\frac{1}{200}$ to $\frac{1}{100}$ grain. The solutions should be carefully filtered, especially those of the crude drug, as it contains a great many impurities.

Physiological Actions.—The actions of woorara have been investigated in the most thorough manner by Bernard, Kölliker, Kühne, and others. It is a necessary part of the equipment of a physiological laboratory since Bernard* made his historical observations on its action.

Woorara is locally an irritant. If the solutions are carefully prepared, no little pain and

---

* Leçons sur la Physiologie et Pathologie du Système Nerveux. Tome i. p. 196.

smarting are felt at the point where the injection is made,—inflammation follows, an abscess forms, and an ulcer remains. This is not an invariable, but a very frequent result, and should be mentioned before the injections are practised.

Applied to the unbroken skin or mucous membrane no effect follows. Introduced into the stomach it rarely produces any toxic symptoms, although it is probable slow absorption may take place, and ultimately characteristic effects appear. Applied to a denuded surface, or subcutaneously, diffusion into the blood is rapid. It is a paralyzer of the nervous system of animal life. An early symptom is disturbance of vision, strabismus, double vision, ptosis,—the upper eyelids falling well over the eyes. Next, weakness of the lower extremities (paresis) comes on, extending ultimately to all the voluntary muscles. Death ensues from paralysis of the respiratory function. The paralyzing action of woorara is not in the muscles, for they retain their Hallerian irritability, but in the terminations of the nerves in the muscles,—the end-organs of the motor nerves. It is this complete paralyzing action, involving the nerves only, and leaving the muscles intact, that renders woorara such an important agent in physiological research.

The careful experiments of Hammond and Mitchell * on two varieties of woorara—*carroval*

---

* The American Journal of the Medical Sciences, July, 1859.

and *vao*—throw some important light on the subject of the action of woorara. The two varieties were similar in mode and character of action, but differed in power,—vao being much feebler. In their experiments, death was caused by paralysis of the heart, its muscular tissue having lost contractility.

According to the observations of MM. Voisin and Lionville,* when woorara is injected subcutaneously, a state of shivering and feverishness, trembling, a rapid and weak pulse, sweating, quickly follow. In a few minutes the paralysis begins, and extends to all the voluntary system. If pressure by a ligature is made above the point where the poison is inserted, its entrance into the general mass of the blood is impeded. If artificial respiration is maintained in animals, death may be averted, even when a lethal dose has been given, so rapidly is it eliminated by the urine, which, indeed, may be actively poisonous. Distinct traces of sugar are also found in the urine, whence the condition is entitled " curara diabetes."†

Therapy.—When the first publications were made, setting forth its peculiar action, very confident hopes were entertained that a specific for *tetanus* had been discovered. It failed in the hands of Follin, Gintrac, Cornoz, and Richard,

---

* Archives Général de Médecine, Oct. 1866.

† L. Hermann, Lehrbuch der experimentallen Toxicologie. Berlin, 1874, p. 305.

and was successful in the hands of Gherini, Demme, Lochner, and Spencer Wells.* In most of the successful cases it was used endermically as well as hypodermatically. Of twelve cases treated by the hypodermatic injection, four terminated favorably. According to the statistics of Demme, of twenty-two cases treated by woorara, administered in either mode, eight recovered. Prof. Busch treated eleven cases of tetanus by woorara, and six recovered; but, as the professor thinks this agent is adapted only to the more chronic cases, our estimate of its value must not be too high, for chronic cases often terminate in recovery under the most diverse methods of treatment.

In the successful cases, large doses of woorara were administered. Spencer Wells injected one-twelfth of a grain at a dose. The dose ranges from one-sixtieth to one-thirtieth of a grain. The frequency of administration will be governed by the effects upon the spasms.

Woorara has also been used in *strychnia-poisoning*, but without sufficient success to justify its employment in this class of cases. It does not bear the relation of a physiological antagonist to strychnia, and hence should not be used against the toxic symptoms caused by this agent.

Although the reports are contradictory in respect to the utility of woorara in *epilepsy*, it yet

---

* Eulenberg, op. cit.

deserves a more careful trial than has been accorded it hitherto. Kunze* advocates its use, and reports that in many cases marked improvement followed its administration. He practised the injections once a week, using two and a half grains each time, and this quantity he says produces no distinct physiological effects. Of 13 old epileptics, 3 were cured by this treatment.

Dr. Watson† reports a case, which he diagnosticated hydrophobia, an opinion in which Prof. Flint concurred, in which recovery ensued after the hypodermatic injection of woorara. The first dose was $\frac{1}{16}$ grain, and subsequently $\frac{1}{8}$ grain and $\frac{1}{6}$ grain were injected. The details of the case are well and accurately told, and the conclusion seems entirely justified.

Very recently an Italian case of hydrophobia has been reported cured by curara. Injections of morphia and inhalations of chloroform had been used without success. Then curara was used until paralytic symptoms occurred, when it was suspended. Then the symptoms of hydrophobia occurring, curara was used again with like success.‡

---

* Deutsche Zeitschrift. fur prakt. Med., 1877, No. 1.

† Am. Jour. of Med. Sciences, July, 1876.

‡ La France Médicale, Aug. 1879, p. 541. From *Indipendente.*

NICOTIA.

The Solution and Dose.—Erlenmeyer recommends the following formula:*

> R Nicotiæ, gr. ss ;
> Aquæ destil., ℥ij.   M.

Four drops (minims) of this contain one-sixtieth of a grain,—a suitable dose. The official Vinum Tabaci may be used as a substitute for the alkaloid. The dose will range from one to five minims.

Physiological Effects.—Nicotia is one of the most deadly poisons, ranking in this respect with prussic acid. In its local action it is somewhat irritant. In its remote or systemic action it strongly depresses the nervous and vascular systems. At first respiration is slightly accelerated, and is accompanied by a bruit, produced, according to Bernard, by a very abrupt contraction of the diaphragm. Slowness and feebleness of respiration soon succeed to this acceleration. The

---

* Die subcutanen Injectionen, op. cit., p. 85.

270

pupils dilate, and convulsive phenomena make their appearance in the eyes and extremities, partly of a clonic, and partly of a tonic or tetanic character. Complete adynamia supervenes, accompanied by muscular trembling; the action of the heart becomes exceedingly feeble, and death takes place by failure of the circulation (paralysis of the heart).*

THERAPY.—Nicotia has been employed with success in the treatment of *tetanus.* About one-half of the traumatic cases treated with it get well,—a proportion of recoveries greater than with any other remedy except physostigma.

Prof. Houghton, of Dublin, who was probably the first to employ this agent in tetanus, ascertained experimentally that it is a physiologica. antagonist to strychnia.

Nicotia is indicated in *spasmodic asthma,* certain cases of *angina pectoris, colic, strangulated hernia,* etc., but I know of no instance in which it has been used for the relief of these conditions.

Cases of obstinate *convulsive tic,* " *histrionic spasm,*" and local *muscular spasm* are of a nature, theoretically speaking, to be benefited by the subcutaneous injection of nicotia.

---

* Gubler, Commentaires du Codex Méd., op. cit., p. 847.

HYDROCYANIC ACID.

THE SOLUTION AND DOSE.—The *Acidum Hydro-cyanicum Dilutum* of the U. S. Pharmacopœia is the preparation which I have employed for hypodermatic use. The maximum quantity which I have used is four minims, but this amount is hardly safe in many cases. It should not be forgotten that the action of hydrocyanic acid is so rapid that a toxic dose introduced under the skin would infallibly destroy life before any measures could be employed for relief. For ordinary purposes, two minims of the official solution will be sufficient for hypodermatic use. As its effects are quickly expended, it may be repeated frequently,—as often as every two hours.

PHYSIOLOGICAL EFFECTS.—Locally, the effects are somewhat irritant, but are not more so than a solution of morphia. A metallic taste, slight salivation, faint nausea, giddiness, and sighing respiration are the only systemic effects which I have observed from the doses I ventured to administer.

THERAPY.—The good effects sometimes produced in *mental disorders* by prussic acid, when administered by the stomach, are more conspicuously exhibited when the remedy is injected under the skin.* It is adapted to acute cases, in which power is in excess. Cases of mania or melancholia, in which the subcutaneous injection of morphia proves hurtful, are benefited by prussic acid, and *vice versa.*

I have used hydrocyanic acid hypodermatically in spasmodic asthma, but without moderating the paroxysms. It is indicated in *angina pectoris*, and other cardiac neuroses, but I am not aware of any instances in which it has been tried.

As a remedy for *gastralgia* when a simple neurosis of the stomach, it is undoubtedly useful. In *nausea* and *vomiting* due to functional disturbance, and especially those cases in which morphia and atropia disagree, it may be used with a confident expectation of affording relief. But, as a general practice, the subcutaneous injection of prussic acid in those stomach disorders is, in respect to promptness and efficiency, greatly inferior to morphia and atropia.

The injection may be practised over the epigastrium in cases of vomiting.

W. Preyer,† who has carefully investigated the physiological action of prussic acid, affirms that atropia is a physiological antidote. His researches have conducted him to the conclusions that prussic acid acts by depriving the blood of

---

* McLeod, Medical Times and Gazette, March, 1863.

† The Practitioner, vol. i. p. 106.

its oxygen, and that in very large doses it paralyzes the heart. He considers atropia the antagonist to this action by maintaining the action of the heart. I have carefully repeated the experiments of Preyer, and am unable to confirm them.* I find that animals (cats) fully under the influence of atropia are speedily destroyed by poisonous doses of prussic acid,—just as speedily, indeed, as if atropia had not been administered. If administered simultaneously, or atropia soon after prussic acid, the result is the same.

---

* Prize Essay of American Medical Association, for 1869, on Atropia.

THE SOLUTION.—The extract of physostigma was formerly the only preparation available for hypodermatic use. Recently the active principle —the alkaloid *eserine*—has been substituted. The existence of two alkaloids possessed of different properties seems to be established, but that which is known as eserine is now universally employed in place of the crude drug and its preparations. The muriate or hydrochlorate is the salt generally used.

℞　Eserine muriat., gr. iv ;
Aquæ destil., ʒi.　M.
Sig.—Two minims contain $\frac{1}{60}$ of a grain.

Eserine is now also added to disks of gelatine in proper proportion. One may be dissolved in water when required for use.

The dose of the alkaloid ranges from $\frac{1}{60}$ grain to $\frac{1}{10}$ grain.

The extract may also be used hypodermatically: it is simply rubbed up with distilled water and then filtered. From one-fourth to one-half a grain is the ordinary dose of the extract, but in tetanus a much larger quantity can be injected. It is highly important to obtain a genuine preparation, otherwise disappointment must ensue.

Physiological Effects.—The effects of physostigma and eserine are the same in what mode soever they may be administered, but are more rapid and pronounced by the subcutaneous areolar tissue. When a full dose is administered, giddiness, a sense of weakness and fatigue, and difficulty in maintaining the vertical position and in walking are experienced. The action of the heart and the arterial tension are lowered for a brief period at first, but in a short time the tension rises, and the heart-beats become more vigorous. Toxic doses in man cause death by paralysis of respiration and of the heart, the whole muscular system, including the sphincters, being in a state of complete muscular relaxation, but the consciousness is preserved until carbonic acid poisoning clouds the mind. It is a paralyzer, but before complete resolution occurs, the voluntary muscular system is agitated by tremors, which consist in alternate muscular contraction and relaxation. The contractility of the muscles is not destroyed, nor even impaired.* The peripheral nerves (end organs) and the trunks of the nerves are not concerned in the paralysis, but it is spinal entirely. Physostigma heightens rather than impairs the sensibility of the sensory

---

* Fraser; from Transactions of the Royal Society of Edinburgh. W. Laschkewich, Virchow's Archiv, Band 85, p. 201.

nerves. After merely lethal doses have been administered, the action of the heart continues after respiration; but, as already stated, large, toxic doses paralyze the heart in the diastole, and this organ is found after death flaccid, not at all or very feebly responding to galvanic excitation.*

Contraction of the pupil is a constant result of the action of physostigma, whether instilled into the eye or introduced into the general system. This result is doubtless due to paralysis of the sympathetic fibres and to stimulation of the third nerve.

As respects the intestinal canal, the effects of physostigma are not very distinctive. It increases secretion somewhat, and therefore the number and density of the alvine discharges.

THERAPY.—The applications of physostigma in the treatment of disease are directly deducible from its physiological action. Its principal effect being on the cord, destroying its reflex function, obviously it is adapted to the treatment of conditions in which the reflex function is abnormally excited, as in *tetanus, hydrophobia, strychnia-poisoning*, etc. A great many cases of tetanus have been treated, chiefly by the extract, and the average proportion of recoveries to death is one-half. The result in many more cases would

* Arnstein u. Sustschinsky, Abstract in Schmidt's Jahrbücher, vol. cxlii. p. 286.

have been favorable if a better mode of administration had been followed and a purer drug obtained. In tetanus, the ability of the patient to swallow and the absorption powers of the stomach are alike impaired. Hence the hypodermatic method should always be adopted instead of the stomachal. Furthermore, the quality of the extract used in many of the cases was poor, and the quantity prescribed was too seldom governed by the effects produced. Eserine hypodermatically and in quantity sufficient to keep the spasms in check, so that the nourishment of the patient can be efficiently carried on, is the proper mode of treatment. I know of no cases of hydrophobia treated by physostigma.

Although theoretically a very perfect antagonism exists between strychnia and physostigma, in actual trial, according to the report of the British Association committee, "although the symptoms produced by either substance were modified considerably by the action of the other, there was no instance of recovery from a fatal dose."

A very perfect antagonism, through almost the whole range of their effects, has been demonstrated by Fraser * to exist between atropia and physostigma,—only, however, in respect to lethal doses, and not to large toxic doses. The com-

---

* An Experimental Research on the Antagonism between the Actions of Physostigma and Atropia. Edinburgh, 1872.

mittee above referred to admits that this antagonism exists to a "slight extent," but is "more limited than even Dr. Fraser has indicated." This committee has also shown that "chloral hydrate modifies to a great extent the action of a fatal dose of Calabar bean (physostigma), and in some instances saves life from a fatal dose."

The use of physostigma in *epilepsy* and *chorea*, based on theoretical grounds, has not been satisfactory. In *progressive paralysis of the insane* the results obtained by Browne, although discredited by Williams, justify further trials by the subcutaneous injection of eserine. Agents acting decidedly as paralyzers of the respiratory function, as conium, gelsemium, lobelia, etc., have long been known to act favorably in *bronchitis*, *pulmonary congestion*, and *pneumonia*, and to them must now be added physostigma, which is reported to have good effects in these diseases.

Next to the use of eserine in tetanus, its most important applications in the treatment of disease are in the field of ophthalmic practice. It is now largely used to counterbalance the effects of atropia on the pupil; in iritis to break away or prevent the formation of adhesions; in ulceration and suppuration of the cornea; after extraction of cataract to prevent suppuration, and in the operation of iridectomy. The curative influence of eserine in these cases is due to its action in lowering the intraocular tension, in diminishing the conjunctival secretions by contracting the blood-vessels, and in checking the migration of the white blood-corpuscles.* To effect these important purposes, eserine is used chiefly by the subcutaneous areolar tissue.

---

* Weeker on Eserine, Pilocarpine, and Atropine in Ophthalmic Diseases, Bull. Gén. Thérap.

PILOCARPINE.

Pilocarpine is the active principle of Pilocarpus pinnatus,—a member of the Rutaceæ,—commonly known as *Jaborandi*.

The Solution.—The alkaloid is freely soluble in water. The nitrate is the salt usually found in the market, but the sulphate, acetate, phosphate, chlorhydrate, and bromhydrate have been prepared.

> ℞ Pilocarpin. nitratis, gr. xvi;
> Aquæ destillat., ℥i.   M.
> Sig.—Five minims contain ¼ of a grain.

As pilocarpine is expensive, and the solutions spoil in a short time, a small quantity may be readily prepared, when required, in the proportions of the above formula.

The Dose.—Children are proportionally less susceptible to the action of pilocarpine than adults. Hypodermatically, the dose ranges from ⅙ of a grain to ½ grain. Rarely is it necessary to exceed ¼ of a grain.

Physiological Effects.—Within a few minutes (2 or 3) after the injection a subjective sense of heat, accompanied by a feeling of fulness of the head, is experienced, followed speedily by a flush extending over the face, forehead, ears, and neck. Simultaneously the action of the heart increases, but there occurs at the same time a general fall of the blood-pressure. The most characteristic effect is the increase of the perspiration and the secretion of the salivary glands. As the flushing of the face takes place the saliva begins to flow plentifully, a profuse perspiration breaks out over the whole surface of the body, the nasal and bronchial mucus and the tears are also increased, and sometimes a profuse watery diarrhœa occurs. The amount of perspiration discharged from the skin is enormous, and the salivary flow is measured by pints. It sometimes happens that the amount of saliva is immense and the perspiration small, and *vice versa*, but usually both secretions are very greatly increased. A distinct fall of temperature—from 0.5°–2° Fahr.—takes place when the sweating occurs, and is maintained for about four hours. Pallor of the face succeeds to the flushing, the pulse becomes weak, drowsiness, an extreme degree of languor, and chilliness of the surface * are experienced. These effects of pilocarpine are due to the action of this agent on the vaso-motor nervous system.† Paresis of this system causes dilatation of the arterioles, increased

---

* Albert Robin, Étude Physiologique et Thérap. sur la Jaborandi. Journ. de Thérap. for 7 nos., 1875.

† Kahler u. Soyka, Kymographische Untersuchungen über Jaborandi, Cent. f. med. Wissenschaft., 31, 541.

afflux of blood to them, whence the flushing and the increased action of the heart. The sphygmographic and kymographic tracings show a considerable lowering of the vascular tension, and to this diminution of the vaso-motor tonus is the increased secretion of saliva and sweat due,—for Prevost has demonstrated that ablation of the spheno-palatine ganglion is followed by an enormous effusion from the Schneiderian mucous membrane. The reduction of temperature is referable to the discharge of fluid from the salivary glands and skin, the evaporation from the surface cooling the adjacent tissues, and a portion of the heat of the body converted into another mode of motion.

Pilocarpine contracts the pupil, and the accommodation is impaired. In the language of Mr. Tweedy,* when pilocarpine is instilled into the eye it causes "contraction of the pupil, tension of the accommodative apparatus of the eye, with approximation to the nearest and farthest points of vision, and amblyopic impairment of vision from diminished sensibility of the retina."

In consequence of the great loss of fluid by the skin the urinary secretion is diminished in amount, and, as more or less urea and salts are contained in the sweat, the urine is pale and watery. The bladder is irritable, and pain is felt

---

* Lancet, 11, 1875.

along the urethra during the action of the pilocarpine.

THERAPY.—In *mumps* and acute affections of the parotid, submaxillary, and sublingual glands, and in *acute tonsillitis*, jaborandi has been used with success.*   When the *metastasis of mumps* takes place it is said to afford great relief.   Obstinate *hiccough*, which had resisted ordinary means, yielded to pilocarpine hypodermatically. *Hoarseness* (acute catarrh of larynx), *bronchitis*, *bronchorrhœa*, are cured or relieved by this agent. The *asthmatic paroxysm* has been promptly arrested by the hypodermatic injection of pilocarpine.   The paroxysms of difficult breathing accompanying emphysema are often quickly relieved by the same agent.   In cardiac dropsy it is often beneficial by removing the surplus fluid. It is more especially adapted to the dropsy of acute albuminuria, and in the treatment of eclampsia, but the warning given us by Barker ought to be heeded.   In all cases of disease in which there is a weak heart, pilocarpine must be used with caution, if at all.   A further caution is necessary in respect to pregnancy, but it is doubtful if it possesses any real abortifacient property.

---

* Besides the references already mentioned, the following should be consulted: Ringer and Gould, Lancet, 1875; Ringer and Murrell, Brit. Med. Jour., 1875; Hardy et Rochefontaine, Gaz. Méd. de Paris, 25, 1875; De l'Action des Alkaloïdos du Jaborandi sur les Sécrétions des Glandes; Carville, Ibid., i. p. 9; Rosenbach, Berl. klin. Woch., 23, p. 315.

It is especially serviceable in the case of effusion into cavities and to effect the removal of
recent products of inflammation. The good effects are conspicuous in the case of inflammatory
effusions into the eyes.

The very important observation has recently
been made,* that the hypodermatic use of pilocarpine has the power to abort an impending
ague chill. If given at chill time, just at or near
the paroxysm, the sweat is induced and no febrile
stage occurs. It appears further that in a considerable proportion of cases, the paroxysms are
suspended permanently. Further experience is
necessary to determine the actual value of this
new expedient, but if it accomplish no more than
abort single paroxysms of ague, it is a valuable
addition to our resources. If a paroxysm has
been prevented, but recurrences take place in the
multiples of the regular periods (so-called sep-
tenary periods), it seems important to administer
the pilocarpine in anticipation of, and without
waiting for, such periods.

---

* Medical Record, August 16, 1879.   Dr. Caspar Griswold,
House Physician to Bellevue Hospital.

ACTIONS AND USES.—Being an extremely volatile and diffusible substance, it is difficult to preserve and use amyl nitrite. When administered in vapor by inhalation, the usual mode of giving it, the form of perl, or of solution in alcohol, is sufficiently convenient. For subcutaneous injection the agent itself is used,—from two to five drops being given at a time.

The effects of amyl nitrite, when given by the hypodermatic method, are similar to but less rapid than by inhalation. The effects are uniformly the same. Increased action of the heart; lowering of the arterial tension; flushing of the face; fulness and distention of the head, and headache sometimes very violent; singing in the ears; vertigo, confusion of mind, and even unconsciousness, result from the inhalation of the vapor. Whilst these effects occur as the inhalation is proceeding, when thrown under the skin an interval of appreciable duration is observed before the action begins. The dilatation of the vessels, a result of the paralyzing action exerted by amyl nitrite on the vaso-motor system, is the central fact of its physiological powers, for on this depend all the other phenomena. The applications of the remedy are based on this property. Although inhalation is a convenient mode of administration, it is not practical when the respiration is ceasing. Consequently, the subcutaneous injection of amyl nitrite may be of immense utility in failure of the heart and of the respiration, in cases of *angina pectoris, chloroform narcosis, surgical shock, cholera asphyxia,* and allied states. The indication is to take off the vascular tension, and the result is the heart is freed from restraint. Dr. F. A. Burrall, of New York,* states that he has "a record of nine cases, in all of which impending death from chloroform seems to have been averted by nitrite of amyl" administered hypodermatically.

---

* The New York Medical Record, March 25, 1882, p. 335.

CHLOROFORM.

THE injection of chloroform is not practised by the ordinary subcutaneous method, for the action is local and not systemic. It is not, therefore, adapted to the treatment of internal maladies, and is only useful in external neuralgiæ so situated that the injected chloroform may act on the nerve-trunk or on the peripheral distribution of the nerve. I have therefore entitled the method the " Deep Injection of Chloroform," in the articles I have written calling attention to the efficiency of this plan in the class of cases to which it is adapted.*

The needle is inserted deeply, in the case of the infra-orbital division of the fifth, underneath the lip, passing up so that its point is in the neighborhood of the nerve at its point of emergence; in the case of the sciatic, passed down near the trunk of the nerve at its exit from the pelvis. In the case of any superficial neuralgia the same plan is pursued,—the needle inserted deeply, so that its point rests in the neighborhood of the affected nerve. I am the more dis-

---

* The Clinic, 1873, vol. v. p. 145; The Practitioner (London), 1874, vol. xiii. p. 9.

288

posed to reiterate this instruction because it is too often supposed that the treatment consists in the subcutaneous injection of chloroform. This practice was long ago condemned or regarded as improper, owing to the violent local inflammation which follows its introduction into the subcutaneous areolar tissue. Thus, Dr. Anstie,* in an article on the "Hypodermic Injection of Remedies," says of chloroform, that it is " an agent entirely unfit to be used in that way." Hunter,* after some trials with it, had made a similar declaration : " The injection of chloroform is not to be recommended for the human subject." This remark is all the more noteworthy because Hunter was one of the earliest and most enthusiastic advocates of the hypodermatic method. Eulenberg† simply repeats the remark of Hunter, and mentions an experience of Sandras, in which ten drops of chloroform were injected.

PHYSIOLOGICAL EFFECTS.—The effects produced by the injection of chloroform into the areolar tissue are these : vaporization of the chloroform, and consequent gaseous distention of the surrounding parts, painful swelling, inflammation, and, occasionally, the formation of an abscess. The pain experienced by the patient at the moment of injection is also considerable, and as the needle is withdrawn the chloroform acts energetically on the wounded skin. These are very

---

* Op. cit.　　　† Hypoder. Injectionen, *supra.*

serious and almost insuperable objections to the *hypodermatic injection* of chloroform. They are, to a large extent, obviated in the method of *deep injection.* It is true, in the latter method, considerable pain is felt and swelling arises, but the pain soon subsides and the inflammation rarely proceeds to suppuration. The pain is felt at the moment of injection and for some minutes subsequently, but this disappears and is succeeded by a feeling of numbness and anæsthesia of the parts into which the chloroform diffuses. A puffy swelling quickly forms at the site of the injection, and an induration of variable size forms, which is afterwards slowly absorbed. The numbness persists for a week or more. Systemic, or rather cerebral, sensations are felt usually only when the injection is inserted into the deeper parts of the face, and then are very transient, consisting only of a little giddiness followed by drowsiness. Indeed, the results, so far as systemic effects are concerned, may be regarded as absolutely free from danger. So much swelling and induration occurring at the site of an injection must occasion apprehension of the formation of an abscess. Thus far this untoward result has not happened in any of my cases or in any of the reported cases, with one exception. This was a man suffering from *tic douloureux,* in whom repeated injections were made about the supra- and infra-orbital foramina, a locality unsuited for *repeated injections.*

To ascertain more satisfactorily than is possible from patients the degree of suffering which attends the deep injection of chloroform, and the extent and duration of the resulting numbness, I practised an experiment on myself by injecting ten minims of Squibb's chloroform deeply in the calf of the leg. The pain was by no means so severe as I had anticipated, and could easily, indeed, be borne. Considerable swelling resulted, and an induration as large as a filbert continued for two weeks, when it was absorbed entirely. Immediately after the injection numbness was experienced about the site of the injection; it then extended downwards, and on the following day had reached the bottom of the foot. A space in which the sense of touch and the appreciation of pain and temperature were decidedly diminished existed from the point at which the chloroform was inserted to the hollow of the foot, although somewhat irregular in shape, at least two inches in transverse diameter at any point. This condition of altered sensibility persisted for several weeks.

It is obvious, from the foregoing considerations, that chloroform injected into a part modifies the conductivity of the nerves. As *pain* means an irritation of a nerve or nerves, the perception by the centres of consciousness of this impression, and its reference outwardly to the peripheral distribution, we may assume, with some confidence, that chloroform causes an interruption in the route or circuit of transmission. It has long been known that swelling of a part, the seat of a neuralgia, is a signal of the cessation of the pain.

When the chloroform is injected into the deeper parts of the face, it comes into relation to vessels having an intimate connection with the intra-cranial circulation. It is, of course, perfectly well known that the facial vein communicates with the pterygoid plexus and the cavernous sinus. This anatomical fact explains the greater cerebral effect of an injection of chloroform in the deeper parts of the face as compared with the same injection elsewhere.

THERAPY.—Since the publication of my original cases of *tic douloureux*, various cases of *neuralgia*—of the *fifth, cervico-brachial, sciatic*—have been treated by me successfully by the chloroform injection. This method is especially adapted to the treatment of sciatica. I have had under treatment since 1874 twelve cases of sciatica, all of great severity and all chronic, in which I used the chloroform injections, and of these eight were cured, two improved, and two received no benefit. I do not include in this summary those cases of sciatica which were symptomatic of spinal or cerebral disease. Other cases have been reported in this country and abroad in which this method succeeded after other approved methods had failed.*

* Dr. de Cérenville, La Tribune Médicale, August 20, 1876; Dr. Collins, The Clinic, 1875.

One of the most remarkable cases demonstrating its utility is that reported by Dr. J. B. Mattison,* in which not only was the neuralgia cured, but also the opium habit with which it was complicated.

Strictly localized *spinal pain* and *coccydinia* have been cured by me by injecting the chloroform deeply near to the point of emergence of the sensory branches, or, in case of the pain in the coccyx, as deeply as possible about the point of greatest pain.

The official spiritus chloroformi, U. S. P., has been substituted for pure chloroform with good results in cases of chronic sciatica coming to the Jefferson Medical College clinic.

---

* Medical Record, New York, May, 1874.

ETHER AND ALCOHOL.

ETHER has been more or less used, in the past few years, subcutaneously, to procure its stimulant and anodyne effects. In cases of emergency various alcoholic liquors have, also, been injected. A practice has thus grown up which must receive some attention.

ACTIONS AND USES.—When ether is thrown under the skin, it causes an emphysematous swelling and an intense burning pain, fortunately of brief duration. Almost immediately the effects are perceived, the pulse becomes stronger and fuller, the face flushed, and the skin warm and perspiring. In two or three minutes the odor of ether is observable in the breath. Exhilaration, inco-ordination of muscular movements, and sopor follow in the order named when full doses are repeated. The quantity given at one time varies from five minims to twenty, and as frequently as may be required.

In cases of sudden depression of the powers of life, whiskey and brandy are sometimes injected subcutaneously. An ordinary syringeful —from 20 to 30 minims—may be administered. These remedies act similarly to ether, but less promptly, whilst, at the same time, their effects are more sustained. They cause the same local distress, and alike increase the organic movements, especially of the heart. Whiskey and brandy are more apt to be followed by local inflammation, abscess, and sloughing than ether. An anæsthetic area is usually left about the site of the injection.

In France bromide of ethyl has been proposed as a substitute for ether in subcutaneous medication, but it seems to me with doubtful propriety. Ether has also been used as a substitute for chloroform in the cases for which the latter has been employed successfully. After the author had brought forward and demonstrated the utility of chloroform in certain painful states, a certain physician, without any reference to the remarkable results which had been achieved by chloroform, published some observations on the use of ether in the same group of cases, as if his idea and practice were novel! In the treatment of *sciatica* and other painful affections ether is less efficient and more painful than chloroform.

Dr. Barth has employed subcutaneous injections of ether in *pneumonia* with striking results. Of 14 cases of severe and adynamic pneumonia and broncho-pneumonia treated by the ether injections, there were 11 cures and 3 deaths.*

---

* Gaz. Hebdom. de Méd. et de Chirurg., Nos. 50, 51, and 52, 1881.

Very soon after the injection is practised, a grateful sense of stimulation is experienced, the respirations grow more easy, the pulse becomes fuller and stronger, the face gains in color, and the tongue moistens. The amount required at each injection is about 15 minims, and the number of injections from two to four a day, according to the amount of depression present in each case. The same method has been pursued in the treatment of *variola*, by M. du Castel. It is probable that in various maladies characterized by sudden and profound depression of the powers of life the hypodermatic injection of ether will prove a valuable resource. *Chloroform narcosis* is, however, a condition which will be intensified by ether injections, and also by injections of alcoholic liquids. The depression caused by the *bites of venomous snakes, surgical shock, cholera Asiatica* and *cholera morbus*, the passage of *biliary* or *renal calculi*, the action of arterial sedatives, as *aconite, veratrum viride*, etc., and cardiac failure from hemorrhage are alike conditions in which the prompt action of ether may be a most precious resource.

If it is necessary to give repeated injections, the administration should not be practised at the same site even twice, but should be at distant points.

Whiskey and brandy are given subcutaneously when the patient is unable to swallow the stimulant, or the urgency will not admit of the delay necessary for absorption by the stomach. The depression caused by hemorrhage is the particular state justifying this practice. I must reiterate the injunction against the use of alcoholic stimulants in chloroform narcosis. When the stimulant action of alcohol is desired, it must be given in small doses.

25*

CHLORAL HYDRATE, AND CHLORAL AND MORPHIA.

The Solution.—Crystallized chloral only is suitable for the preparation of solutions for hypodermatic use. A saturated solution in water contains 50 *per centum* of chloral. Although this is rather irritating to the tissues, a weak solution may be more objectionable, as two punctures will be necessary to introduce the required amount.

> R Chloral. hydratis, ℥ss;
> Aquæ destil., ℥i. M.
> Sig.—Thirty minims contain 15 grains of chloral.

The Dose.—Chloral diffuses into the blood more rapidly from the subcutaneous areolar tissue than from the stomach. Under ordinary circumstances, ten grains will be a sufficient quantity for an adult; but special conditions may require more.

Physiological Effects.—Very great pain and smarting are felt at the point of puncture, and it persists, unfortunately, for a half-hour or longer. Considerable swelling, an erythematous blush, and urticaria-like eruption take place about the puncture. A hard nodule, very prone to suppurate, usually forms. Especial pains are necessary to avoid penetrating a vein, for, although Oré has proposed the operation of intra-venous injection for the purpose of inducing anæsthesia, the direct admission of chloral to a vein is considered so hazardous that the proposed expedient is almost universally condemned. The production of sleep is the result of the chloral injection, and this follows promptly, usually without any disturbance of function. In some subjects, however, just as when taken into the stomach, a period of excitement, with headache, precedes sleep, or, it may be, prevents it altogether. If the dose be sufficient, sleep is very sure to follow, and the drowsiness comes on within five minutes after the injection is practised. The sleep of chloral is very like that of natural sleep, and there are no after-disturbances,—no headache, nausea, nor constipation.

Administered subcutaneously, chloral possesses distinct pain-relieving power, differing in this respect from the effects of its stomach absorption.

A weak heart, especially a fatty heart, is an important contraindication to the hypodermatic injection of chloral, still more than to its administration by the stomach. Numerous deaths have resulted from its incautious use in cases of weak heart when taken by the stomach; the danger is greater, of course, when it is thrown under the skin.

Therapy.—So unpleasant is the local action of chloral that its use by the hypodermatic injection is restricted, usually, to cases in which the stomachal administration is prevented by the condition of that organ, or by the inability or the unwillingness of the patient to swallow.

Vomiting, not controlled by the ordinary means, may sometimes, frequently indeed, be arrested by the injection of five to ten grains of chloral in the epigastric region. Obstinate *hiccough*, not amenable to the usual treatment, may also be stopped in the same way. In violent *cholera morbus* and in true *cholera* excellent results are obtained from the chloral treatment, better, in the author's experience, than from any other treatment. In the cholera epidemic at Riga in 1871, the injections were remarkably successful.* Similar successes attended the practice of Mr. Hall, an English army surgeon, at Kheri, Oudh, India,† of Nepven,‡ and others. During a short epidemic of cholera in Cincinnati in 1873, I had the most convincing proofs of its efficiency. When the cramps are severe and the algid state well advanced, very considerable doses must be used. In one very formidable case, in which there seemed but little hope, sixty grains were administered hypodermatically in two hours, with the

---

* O. Liebreich, Berliner klinische Wochenschrift, 1871, p. 408.   Letter from Dr. v. Reichard.

† The Practitioner, July, 1875.

‡ Gaz. Méd. de Paris, September 13, 1873.

effect to stop the cramps, restore warmth, and to remove, indeed, all unfavorable symptoms.

In *asthma* decided relief is produced by the injection of chloral. Other *neuroses* of the chest organs are equally benefited; but the utmost circumspection is needed lest a fatal result follow, by paralysis of a weak heart.

The hypodermatic injection of chloral is indicated and may be employed in all *cerebral disorders* in which chloral is so much prescribed by the stomach: to procure sleep, to allay the excitement of mania, and to prevent convulsive attacks. The remedy is employed in this group of cases hypodermatically, when the patient cannot or will not swallow it in the usual way. In superficial *neuralgiæ* the local use of chloral may be substituted for the deep injection of chloroform.

Chloral and Morphia.—In most of the cases for which chloral is directed in the preceding paragraphs the combination with morphia is to be preferred, generally speaking, to the chloral alone. As is perfectly well known, the pain-relieving power of chloral is greatly inferior to that possessed by morphia. A combination of the two makes an anodyne and hypnotic of the highest order of excellence; that which is wanting in one is supplied by the other, and in respect to their special properties each adds to the power of the other. In a paper read before the New York Neurological Society, I showed that whilst morphia increased the physiological effects of chloral in all other respects, it prevented the depression of the heart's action caused by the latter, and thus obviated the chief danger from its administration. The combination is rendered still more efficient by the addition of atropia. The following formulæ are intended to illustrate and embody the above principles, and may be employed for the hypodermatic injection of these remedies:

      ℞ Chloral hydrat., ʒiij;
         Morphia sulph., gr. iv;
         Aquæ destil., ʒi. M.

Sig.—Twenty minims contain $7\frac{1}{2}$ grains of chloral and $\frac{1}{8}$ grain of morphia.

      ℞ Chloral hydrat., ʒiij;
         Morphiæ sulph., gr. iv;
         Atropiæ sulph., gr. $\frac{1}{8}$;
         Aquæ destil., ʒi. M.

Sig.—Twenty minims contain $7\frac{1}{2}$ grains of chloral, $\frac{1}{8}$ grain of morphia, and $\frac{1}{120}$ grain of atropia.

CAFFEIN.

The Solution.—The preparation now used is the citrate, and as it is soluble in water, can be dissolved in that menstruum for hypodermatic use.

R. Caffeinæ citratis, gr. xxiv;
Aquæ, ℥i. M.
Sig.—Twenty minims contain 1 grain.

The Dose will range from ten to twenty minims of the above solution, or from one-half to one grain.

Physiological Effects.—The local effects are similar to those produced by other alkaloids. Slight drowsiness is an immediate effect, but this is quickly followed by stimulation of the brain and the other animal functions. In very large doses it produces decided excitement of the nervous and vascular systems, violent palpitation of the heart, with frequency, irregularity, and sometimes intermittence of the pulse, oppression and pain in the head, disorders of the senses, ringing in the ears, flashes of light before the eyes, priapism, and delirium.

Therapy.—Caffein has been used hypodermatically for the relief of *neuralgia.* Eulenberg found it useful in a case of occipital neuralgia. Dr. Anstie says with regard to it : " In one case of severe neuralgia of the superficial branches of the circumflex in the shoulder, two successive injections of caffein (over the biceps) appeared to cut short the malady altogether. In a case of dorso-costal neuralgia, attending shingles, the patient was injected daily, for five or six days, with the effect of notably mitigating the pain on each occasion." Lorent used the hypodermatic injection of caffein in *hysterical headache* and *migraine.* Dr. Anstie relieved by it the *insomnia* attendant upon chronic alcoholism without delirium. In these affections, as Anstie suggests, caffein will probably be found a valuable remedy.

Caffein is indicated in simple *melancholy*, in *hysterical paroxysms*, in certain cases of *delirium tremens ;* but our knowledge is not yet sufficient to pronounce positively on these points. It has also been used with success against *opium narcosis ;* in this state it is certainly inferior to atropia, yet, as there is no therapeutical incompatibility, these agents may be used simultaneously in the same case.

As a solution of apomorphia rapidly changes, —becoming greenish and unfit for use,—it should be kept in powder and the solution made when required. The dose for an adult by the subcutaneous areolar tissue is $\frac{1}{16}$ grain, and for children a proportional amount. As very serious symptoms have been produced by full doses, it is necessary to be circumspect, especially in the case of children.

PHYSIOLOGICAL EFFECTS.—In a few minutes after the injection is made some nausea, giddiness, and headache are experienced, and vomiting occurs abruptly and thoroughly in from five to twenty minutes. At the first effort the stomach is well emptied; but the vomiting recurs a few times at intervals of a quarter to a half hour. Such is the ordinary course of action of a sufficient but still small dose. If a full dose is given by the subcutaneous areolar tissue, there occur headache, vertigo, nausea, a cold sweat, a quick, small, feeble pulse, depression and drowsiness, and profuse vomiting, followed by prolonged sleep.

A very alarming condition of depression—a state of collapse, indeed—has been caused in children and inebriates by the hypodermatic injection of a full dose. Toxic doses in animals cause at first great excitement, vomiting, followed by muscular trembling, paralysis, and convulsions.* It does not seem to affect the blood-pressure,† nor the motor and sensory nerves; the respirations at first greatly increase in number, but ultimately become more shallow and infrequent, death occurring from paralysis of the respiratory function.‡

THERAPY.—The use of apomorphia hypodermatically is confined to the production of vomiting.§ It is the most useful of all the emetics for *narcotic poisoning.* The evidence is convincing that profound insensibility hinders the emetic action, but an increase of the dose suffices to overcome this. If then in the treatment of poisoning by narcotic substances the usual dose does not have the desired effect, it must be repeated until vomiting does occur. It is highly probable that very much larger doses can be administered in the condition of insensibility from poisons than in ordinary cases of disease. It is extremely questionable to employ apomor-

* E. Harnack, Archiv f. exp. Path. u. Pharmacologie, vol. ii. p. 201.

† Dr. Vincent Siebert, Untersuchungen über Apomorphia. Abstract in Schmidt's Jahrbücher, vol. clv. p. 14, et seq.

‡ Harnack, *supra.*

§ Gee, Note on Apomorphia, etc., St. Bartholomew's Hospital Reports, vol. v., 1869.

phia in opium-poisoning, since this agent has an effect on the cerebrum, and causes death by paralysis of respiration. If the patient is too profoundly narcotized for the action of emetics, the stomach-pump is an available and effective resource, and should unquestionably be preferred to the subcutaneous use of apomorphia.

In *capillary bronchitis*, to free the tubes of their contents, and in *croup*, to dislodge the false membrane, apomorphia is used to obtain the mechanical effect of powerful emesis. In common with other emetics it is supposed to possess expectorant properties, but it is never used hypodermatically for this purpose.

ERGOTIN.

Tᴴᴇ Sᴏʟᴜᴛɪᴏɴ.—The *Ergotin*, so called, employed in medical practice is not the supposed active principle, but an aqueous extract. Perfectly good ergotin is now to be obtained from various manufacturers, but the aqueous extract prepared by Squibb, of Brooklyn, for hypodermatic injection is an excellent preparation,—the best, doubtless, to be obtained at present. This " extract of ergot is almost entirely soluble in cold water, and represents good rye ergot in the proportion of one grain of extract for five grains of ergot. Sixty grains of this extract dissolved in two hundred and fifty minims of water—the solution filtered and made up to three hundred minims by passing water through the filter to wash it and the residue upon it—makes a solution which represents ergot in the proportion of minim for grain, and is of the same strength as the fluid extract of ergot, but is free from alcohol or other irritant substance." Such are Squibb's instructions for the preparation of a solution. A much more concentrated solution can be prepared from Squibb's extract, which is soluble in water in the proportion of grain to minim, by simply rubbing up the extract with distilled water until saturated,—then filter. Of this solution, so prepared, from five to fifteen minims may be injected, —the largest quantity in cases of great urgency and danger. The following formula may be used as a guide in the preparation of a solution:

> ℞ Ergotin (aq. ex.), ℈ij ;
>   Aquæ destil., ℥ij.
> M. Filter.
> Sig.—From five to twenty minims at each injection.

Dragendorff and Podwissotzky propose their newly-discovered sclerotinic acid, in aqueous solution, for hypodermatic injection, but at present this substance is too difficult to procure and too expensive to be used. Furthermore, the conclusions of these experimental physiologists are not yet well established in professional opinion, and may prove to be erroneous; nevertheless they assert with confidence that "the special, active substances in ergot are sclerotinic acid and scleromucin."*

As solutions of ergotin undergo important changes in a short time, it is desirable to prevent them, if this result can be accomplished without impairing the quality of the material. The addition of one per cent. of carbolic acid

---

* Archiv für experimen. Pathologie u. Pharmakologie, vol. vi. p. 153. Ueber die wirksamen und einige andere Bestandtheile des Mutterkornes.

will prevent any change for several months, and this rather increases than lessens the therapeutical power of the solution.

PHYSIOLOGICAL EFFECTS.—Considerable pain, lasting for several minutes, attends the injection, and a tumefaction, subsequently sometimes hardening into a firm nodule, forms at the site of the puncture. It is rare, however, for suppuration to occur, if proper care is exercised in the preparation of the solution, and in injecting.

If a moderate dose is injected, there may be no symptoms whatever produced. Frontal headache, transient giddiness, more or less dilated pupils, are produced by full doses in from fifteen minutes to a half-hour. In a somewhat longer time,—an hour or two after the injection,—sometimes quite severe rhythmical pains come on, referrible to the region of the uterus, and undoubtedly uterine in seat. Women experienced in the sensation, spontaneously, liken the pains to those of the first stage of labor. In a case of uterine fibroid expelled from the cavity by the action of ergotin hypodermatically used, severe rhythmical pain always came on in a half-hour after the injection. That these pains are uterine seems highly probable, not only in respect to the examples cited above, but because of the unquestionable action of ergot on the parturient uterus. The cases are parallel, for when subinvolution exists, or when a fibroid is contained in the uterine cavity, the muscular development of the organ is sufficient to permit the action of ergotin to take place. On the other hand, ergot unquestionably affects the muscular fibre of the intestine, but in the examples of pain above referred to there was no increased intestinal action.

When considerable daily doses of ergotin are injected, the patients complain of a sense of pressure, with pain and numbness in the muscles of the thighs and legs. They also complain of fatigue on slight exertion, of a sense of coldness of the limbs at night, especially, and muscular cramps of varying severity and persistence. The bladder, too, or, rather, the sphincter, is kept in a state of spasm when daily doses are administered, so that micturition becomes slow, difficult, or impossible, the catheter becoming necessary in rare instances.

The actions of ergot have been studied by many observers, and their reported observations differ widely, and are often, indeed, diametrically opposed. Faulty methods are frequently responsible for discordant and contradictory views. Thus, attempts have been made to arrive at a knowledge of the influence of ergot on the blood-pressure by injecting a quantity of the infusion or fluid extract into the jugular vein. We are told, with a remarkable *naïveté*, that under these circumstances the blood-pressure at first falls and then rises remarkably. Prof. Wood confirms what Dr. Holmes has asserted

with regard to this experiment. Brown-Séquard
long ago demonstrated that ergot had the power
to contract the vessels, and this fact has since
been confirmed by a number of observers at different periods,* and he also asserts that which in
itself has a high degree of probability, that the
vaso-motor spasm which first comes on is followed by vaso-motor paralysis. The results of
the very numerous experiments made are nearly
uniform in proving that ergotin causes a rise in
the blood-pressure, a necessary sequence of the
contraction of the arterioles. The particular
constituents of ergotin effecting this result have
been ascertained by recent investigations. Köhler devoted himself especially to determine the
physiological effects of the " Ergotin" of Bou-
jean, and of the " Ergotin" of Wiggers,—the
former being an aqueous extract merely, and the
latter a conjectural active principle. His researches proved that the former possessed the
properties belonging to ergot, the latter exhib-

---

* Among those who have demonstrated the narrowing of
the vessels caused by ergotin are the following : Dr. H. Koeh-
ler. Vergleichend-experimentelle Untersuchungen über die
physiologischen Wirkungen des Ergotin Bonjean und des
Ergotin Wiggers. Virchow's Archiv, vol. lx. p. 381. M.
Laborde, Gazette des Hôpitaux, March 10, 1877. Dr. A. Wer-
nich, Beitrag zur Kenntniss der Ergotinwirkungen. Virchow's Archiv, vol. lvi. p. 505. This research was in part
determined by some experiments of Handelin, made under
the direction of Schmiedeberg,—these experiments having
shown that ergotin causes the blood-pressure to fall.

ited powers of a different kind. The most recent and valuable contribution to our knowledge of this subject is the research of Podwissotzky on sclerotinic acid, a new product of ergot, a knowledge of which we owe—as has been shown —to Dragendorff and Podwissotzky.* These experiments have demonstrated (apparently) that this new substance is the true active principle, as the discoverers had previously affirmed. Sclerotinic acid is tasteless, odorless, freely soluble in water, and without any irritating effect on the tissues when injected, so that it is perfectly adapted for hypodermatic use. It is much to be desired that it shall prove to be all that its discoverers claim for it.

It is said that sclerotinic acid has been largely used in Germany by Prof. Von Holst, in solution in water, the dose being one-half to three-quarters of a grain hypodermatically. This substance appears to possess a high degree of activity.

Ergot exerts an influence on the heart in accordance with that on the arterioles,—it diminishes the number and lessens the power of the heart-beats. A toxic dose arrests the heart in the diastole, not by reason of a poisonous action on the cardiac muscle, but through the agency of the pneumogastric nerves, for when these nerves are divided the heart is not arrested by

---

* St. Petersburger med. Wochenschrift, Aug. 27 and Sept. 8, 1876.

the same or a larger toxic dose.* Paralysis not due to an action on the motor nerves or on the muscles, and therefore centric in origin, is a result of the poisonous action of ergot on the lower animals. Convulsions are also produced by it. An explanation of these symptoms is afforded in the extreme cerebral anæmia induced in animals by the large quantity of the drug administered.

The following is a summary of the symptoms of *acute ergotism* in man: nausea, vomiting, abdominal pain, dryness of the throat, thirst, anorexia, itching of the extremities, numbness, lassitude, vertigo, dilatation of the pupils, drowsiness, delirium, and stupor, diminution of the force and frequency of the pulse (rarely the opposite state), with tendency to syncope, pallor and lividity of the face, etc.

Chronic ergotism, witnessed occasionally on a large scale by reason of the consumption of diseased rye as food, exists in two forms,—*convulsive* and *gangrenous*. Generally the convulsive form begins by vertigo, disorders of vision, *tinnitus aurium*, numbness of the fingers and toes, and afterwards of the whole integument. Tetanoid cramps follow,—of the fingers, of the forearms, on the arms, and of the arms against the chest; of the toes, on the palmar surface of the foot; of the leg, on the thigh. The muscles of the

---

* Eberty, Abstract in Schmidt's Jahrbücher, vol. clviii. p. 126.

thorax, abdomen, and diaphragm are also attacked, making respiration difficult and painful, and inducing attacks like asthma. Cramps of the same character attack the intestine,—the muscular layer,—and pains like colic and diarrhœa ensue, but the appetite continues ravenous. Usually, or at least frequently, the uterus becomes affected, expulsive pains come on, and abortion takes place. The action of the heart is weak and slow, the pulse feeble, the surface cold. At first the spasms are occasional, but they become more frequent, ultimately continuous, resulting in opisthotonos or emprosthotonos. Complete anæsthesia of the whole surface succeeds to the tetanoid attacks, and gangrene in spots of small extent may occur. The organs of sense lose their power to react to their physiological stimuli, and taste, hearing, and smell are abolished. The pupils are dilated, sometimes unequal, and various disturbances of vision ensue. Epileptiform attacks may occur as well as the spasms; delirium sets in, and the poor victim passes into a state of complete insensibility.

The convulsive and gangrenous forms, although clinically separable, are not pathologically very different. The gangrenous form sets in by tingling, numbness, formication, an insupportable sense of fatigue in the members, an earthy hue of the skin, coldness of the surface; nausea, vomiting, and diarrhœa then occur; muscular contractions take place; an eruption of

vesicles filled with a dark ichorous fluid appears
on one or more extremities; and gangrene, dry
or moist, quickly destroys the toes, the legs, the
nose, or other parts. Doubtless, not unfrequently,
owing to the contraction of the arterioles in front,
a weak heart behind, and blood containing a
great excess of fibrin, sudden coagulation of the
blood in a large vessel takes place, and gangrene
of a member is the result. These are the factors
probably concerned in the formation of gangrenous spots of greater or less size.

To enter so largely in the consideration of
these topics may seem an unnecessary elabora-
tion, but at the present time so freely is ergotin
used, and in such large doses, that any details in
regard to the results of its administration should
not be omitted.

THERAPY.—The therapeutical uses of ergot are
based on the modern conception of its physiological actions.

One of the most effective remedies against
hemorrhage in any situation not remediable by
surgical means is the hypodermatic injection of
ergotin. Originally used against *uterine hemorrhages*, it has become generalized in its application to the treatment of hemorrhage in general.
Not to enter into tedious details, it will suffice to
state that the hypodermatic injection is the most
effective way of treating all cases of uterine
hemorrhage to which ergot is adapted.

Subinvolution of the uterus, a state of things fruitful of mischief, is most effectively treated by a daily hypodermatic injection of ergotin.* The same treatment used persistently, about twice a week, will cure the so-called *chronic metritis.* Local thickening and *hypertrophy* of the uterine wall just developing into, or well-formed, intra-mural *fibroids* can be cured in a large proportion, and are being cured since the beneficent discovery of Hildebrandt † was announced. The relative proportion of cures to cases cannot be stated in numbers, notwithstanding the enormous experience now accumulated. Selecting out of a mass of reports, probably no better or more accurate can be found than that of Prof. Byford, of Chicago. Of his group of 101 cases, 22 were cured, and all the rest, except 21, were more or less ameliorated. Various modes of introducing the agent were employed, and probably not all were treated by the best method, or by ergotin of the best quality. Besides the arrest or diminution in the growth, it is, as Prof. Hildebrandt remarks, " of great significance that those distressing symptoms, the profuse hemorrhages, the debilitating serous discharges, and the harassing pains, totally disappear."

Hypodermatic injections of ergotin are also used to effect the expulsion of *polypi* from the

---

* Keating, Amer. Journal of Med. Science, July, 1873.
† Berliner klinische Wochenschrift, June 17, 1872.

uterine cavity. The *hydatid mole* may be most effectively expelled by the same agent.

Hypertrophied prostate, as Prof. Langenbeck has shown, may be reduced in size by the subcutaneous injection of ergotin. I have succeeded better, I think, by injecting the lobes of the prostate through the rectum, an expedient which is easily practised. A bivalve rectal speculum must be first introduced; then vessels felt for, and the point for puncture selected, when the needle may be introduced and some five minims inserted. The utmost care must be exercised in regard to each detail, for inflammation and suppuration of the prostate would be a serious addition to the sufferings and hazards of the case. Hemorrhoids that are recent, not previously inflamed, and bleeding in consequence of increase of pressure in the portal system, can be relieved greatly by ergotin injections.

Varicocele, if not too far advanced in respect to the size of the vessels and atrophy of the testis, may be cured by the injection of ergotin. The needle must be inserted between the vessels, and entrance into a vein avoided,—a fact which must be ascertained with absolute certainty,—and the fluid must be sufficient in amount to diffuse among the vessels. Great pain attends the operation, so great that the patient may faint or suffer considerable shock, and there will be subsequently a good deal of inflammation and swelling, with the usual concomitants of feverishness and pain. An injection of ergotin on the dorsum of the penis in the neighborhood of the dorsal vein is an efficient expedient to promote the vigor of the *erections* when they are not well maintained. Injections in the perineum once a week is an excellent remedy in cases of *spermatorrhœa* with feeble erections and a discharge of mucus from the urethra.

Probably the most efficient means we now possess for the arrest of *hæmoptysis* is the hypodermatic injection of ergotin. It acts promptly, and does not interfere with the simultaneous use of other means of treatment, but the injection is usually sufficient of itself. Numerous cases of hæmoptysis have been reported in the treatment of which ergot was the principal. or only agent employed, but the most careful recorded and instructive series of cases which have come under my observation are those of Dr. Anstie.* His conclusions are as follows:

"We have now established the facts (*a*) of the direct action of ergot in the cases which I have recorded; (*b*) of its superiority in several of these cases to other styptics that had been tried; (*c*) the probability, from physiological analogies, that ergot would act more universally as a checker of hæmoptysis than the routine remedies with which we are familiar; (*d*) also, that it is perfectly safe for the purpose in view, and in this respect is

---

* The Practitioner (London), vol. x. p. 279

superior to digitalis, which otherwise resembles it a good deal." These good effects were obtained by the stomachal administration, but Dr. Anstie makes a remark which has been abundantly confirmed since,—"For getting the best results, I can scarcely doubt that the hypodermic injection of ergotin is a decidedly superior method."

Scarcely less important than Hildebrandt's discovery of the value of ergotin in uterine fibroids is the observation of Langenbeck with cases showing the curative power of the ergotin injections in *aneurism*.* Soon after the cases of Langenbeck were reported, Plagge,† of Darmstadt, published a case of traumatic popliteal aneurism, in which the ergotin injections were signally beneficial. In a case of femoral aneurism, Schneider has succeeded by the ergotin injections, and Dutoit in one of the subclavian.‡ I have myself seen remarkable diminution in size and great improvement in condition in a case of aneurism at the transverse arch of the aorta, death being due to other causes entirely. After death the walls of the aneurism were very thick and firm by deposition of successive layers of fibrin, and rupture was not possible. In Langenbeck's and

---

* Berliner klinische Wochenschrift, No. 2, 1869.

† Betz's Memorabilien. Quoted in London Medical Record, vol. ii. p. 87.

‡ Berliner klinische Wochenschrift, 1872, p. 115. Quoted from Langenbeck's Archiv, Band xii.

other successful cases the aneurisms treated were on superficial arteries, except that of Dutoit. It has been asserted that these injections are idle in the case of aneurism of the aorta, since this vessel possesses but rudimentary elements of the organic muscular fibre to be acted on by such an agent as ergot. Such critics overlook the fact that ergot, by slowing the heart and raising the tension at the periphery by contracting the arterioles, offers the most suitable conditions for securing the coagulation of blood in the aneurismal sac.

In *varicose veins*, Voit* has proposed and has used successfully injections of ergotin in the immediate neighborhood of the diseased vessels.

Enlarged spleen has been cured by the injection practised at any indifferent point,† but preferably under the integument of the abdomen.

The disease *leukæmia*, which is closely connected pathologically with a condition of the spleen, has been cured by Dr. Da Costa, and *exophthalmic goitre* benefited by the same treatment.

Brown-Séquard was undoubtedly the first to use ergot systematically, and from the standpoint of a correct appreciation of the nature of its action, in disease of the brain and nervous system. It has been used with advantage, hypo-

---

* Berliner klinische Wochenschrift, *supra*.

† Dr. Miller, N. Y. Med. Rec., April 15, 1876, and Dr. Da Costa, who was the first, in Amer. Jour. Med. Sci., Jan. 1875.

dermatically, in the treatment of the *acute affections* of the *meninges* of *the brain and spinal cord,* and in *cerebro-spinal meningitis.* It is highly serviceable in these affections if used at the proper time—during the stage of excitation—and before depression comes on, when it is harmful. It ought to be serviceable in those cases of *cerebral hemorrhage* in which the escape of blood occurs slowly and there is a gradually deepening coma.

In the congestive form of *migraine*—flushed face, injected conjunctivæ, quick pulse, severe pain, coincident with each arterial pulse—the hypodermatic injection of ergotin is highly useful, and often affords immediate relief. In ordinary *headaches* of the congestive variety, but not in the headaches of anæmia, it is equally efficient and curative. The most ardent and comprehensive advocate for the use of the subcutaneous injection of ergot is Dr. Marino,* who finds it superior to all remedies in *sunstroke, tic douloureux,* and *hemicrania.* In *sciatica,* the results of its use are sometimes "brilliant," but it often fails without apparent cause.

---

* Quoted in London Medical Record, vol. v. p. 456.

QUINIA.

The Solution.—Opinions are divided in respect to the proper solution of the sulphate, and as to the salt of quinia which should be used for the hypodermatic injection. Since the last edition of this monograph was published, and very recently, important recommendations have been made in respect to the particular salt which should be employed. As the sulphate has been chiefly used, I first submit to the reader the best formula with which I am acquainted for the administration of this salt hypodermatically:

> R Quiniæ di-sulph., gr. 50;
> Acid. sulphuric. dil., m 100 ;
> Aquæ font., ℥i ;
> Acid. carbolic. liq., m 5.
> Solve.

"Place the quinine and water in a porcelain dish over a spirit-lamp; heat to the boiling-point, and add the sulphuric acid, stirring with a wooden spatula. Filter at once into a bottle, and add the carbolic acid. This gives six grains to the drachm. Even this solution will deposit some crystals at a temperature of 50°, and, of course, at or below that temperature requires to be warmed before using."—Lente.*

Kinate of quinia is soluble in the proportion of one to four of water. It can readily be obtained by a reaction between solutions of kinate of barium and sulphate of quinine. At Guy's hospital, the strength of the solution used is one to four, prepared according to the following process: "Put into a beaker ℥vi of distilled water and ℨij of kinate of quinia, and heat until the salt dissolves, which it does almost immediately, and then add enough distilled water to make up to ℥i."

The use of so concentrated a solution of kinate of quinia is attended with some difficulty, as the neck and stopper of the bottle become encrusted with a deposit of the kinate, and the syringe used to make the injection must be frequently cleaned.

Lactate and sulpho-vinate of quinia have also been recommended for hypodermatic use. By Prof. Gubler the hydrobromate of quinia was preferred to all other salts.

> ℞ Quiniæ hydrobromat., gr. 48;
> Aquæ destillat., ℥iv.
> M. Dissolve, if necessary, by heat.
> Sig.—Twenty minims contain 4 grains.

Very recently a new compound salt of quinia

---

* The New York Medical Journal, March, 1874.

has been introduced for hypodermatic injection, and it seems to possess very distinct advantages over all other preparations hitherto proposed. It has been "termed *quinia bimuriatica carbamidata*, and is formed by Drygin from a combination of twenty parts of muriate of quinia, twelve parts of muriatic acid, and three parts of urea. The resulting salt is soluble in equal parts of water.* The trials that have been made of it at Hamburg have proved so successful that it is highly desirable it should be known more widely. A 50 per cent. solution has always been employed, and the quantity injected has varied from a half to three syringefuls. The local irritation was in most cases very slight, and at the worst consisted in a circumscribed burning pain, without redness or swelling."

ACTIONS AND USES.—Beside the local irritation, little is to be said respecting the physiological effects of quinia. The solutions of quinine, when injected beneath the skin, excite considerable burning and a zone of more or less intense redness for some distance around the puncture. If care be not used in the preparation of the solution, inflammation will follow at the site of the puncture, matter will form, and possibly a diffuse inflammation of the areolar tissue will ensue. Before I had learned the necessity for

---

* Centralblatt f. d. med. Wiss., June 14, 1879. Quoted in the Medical Times and Gazette, July 12, 1879.

caution, accidents of this kind occurred in my own hands, and lately some very bad cases have been reported as occurring in New Orleans, where, it is said, a *mixture* of quinia sulphate and water was injected under the skin. Some cases of tetanus have been reported caused by subcutaneous injection of quinine, but there must have existed a peculiar state of the nervous system, in which, as is well known, very slight injuries may be followed by this malady. But little systemic effect follows the subcutaneous injection of quinia. The actions are similar in character to those produced by the stomach administration, and, as they are so well known, require no description here.

Dr. Chasseaud published, in 1862, an account of the great success which he had obtained in the treatment of *malarial fevers*, in the hospital at Smyrna, by the subcutaneous injection of quinine. He ascertained that this agent, administered in this way, had a more decidedly curative power, without occasioning its usual physiological effects, than when given by the stomach. This practice has since been continued with undiminished success at the same hospital by Dr. J. McCraith. Dr. Moore, of the Bombay Medical Service, repeating these experiences, concludes "that four or five grains of quinine injected beneath the integument are equal to five or six times that amount taken into the stomach."

Not only is the immediate therapeutic effect of

the quinine given in this way greater, but more permanent cures thereby result. In one hundred and fifty cases treated in this way, Dr. Chasseaud had but a single relapse. Such has been my own observation.

From five to ten grains, injected under the skin, will suffice to cure an ordinary intermittent. Fevers of the remittent type, and pernicious fevers, will require a larger amount. In those deadly malarial attacks, known as *pernicious*, is the efficacy of this treatment most conspicuous. Much depends, as everybody knows, upon bringing the patient promptly under the quinine influence; the subcutaneous injection is the quickest and most powerful means of accomplishing this object.

Recent malarial fevers may be aborted at the beginning of the cold stage by a full injection, but it is better to anticipate the attack by an hour or two, in order to procure the physiological effects before the onset of the expected paroxysm. It is true that the injection may be administered at any time during the febrile movement, but it is better to anticipate and prevent it. The ultimate cure will depend upon the amount of quinia received by the patient, and not upon the period at which it was administered.

The subcutaneous injection is much more effective also against *chronic malarial poisoning* than the stomach administration, but here we meet with new conditions, requiring other management than the use of quinine. We may confidently expect to prevent the febrile movements by frequent repetition of the injection; but we do not thereby cure the disease, for the changes induced by the long-continued action of malaria, in the liver, spleen, gastro-intestinal mucous membrane, cerebro-spinal axis, must be corrected if we would arrest the objective phenomena of fever and cure the patient.

Dr. Eulenberg sums up his conclusions in regard to the cases in which the subcutaneous injection of quinia in malarial fevers may be desirable as follows:

In intermittents complicated with gastric disorder.

In children in whom the disagreeable taste and the large doses necessary produce strong aversion and stomach derangement.

In poor and hospital practice, where economy in the use of the drug is desirable.

These conclusions seem to the writer well founded. But he has omitted chronic malarial poisoning, in which the subcutaneous injection of quinia has undoubted utility.

The antipyretic effects of quinia are constantly made use of in the treatment of continued fevers, as all the world knows, the administration being by the stomach; but Dr. Ravicini* urges the

---

* Revista Clinica di Bologna. Quoted in the London Medical Record, vol. ii. p. 324.

hypodermatic use of quinia in typhoid. He combines a minute quantity of morphia with it. He gives three injections daily, making in the aggregate about 70 grains, and this practice he continues for several days. The results are most favorable: the sordes disappear from the mouth and teeth, the headache, meteorism, and gurgling in the right iliac fossa are greatly diminished, the spleen is reduced in size, and the countenance becomes more composed. The disease, although not cut short, is much abbreviated, as nearly all convalesce at the end of the second week, or, at most, of the third. The morphia, he thinks, affects the nervous phenomena favorably. If these statements can be relied on, nothing can be more satisfactory than this mode of treating typhoid. By using the new compound—muriate of quinia and urea—there need be no apprehension, which otherwise might be felt as to the effect of an irritant on the tissues of a typhoid fever patient.

Mr. Hall,* of the British army, serving in India, reports remarkable success in the treatment of *heat-apoplexy* (sunstroke) by the hypodermatic injection of quinine. He reports in all seven cases of a severe type in which this treatment proved uniformly and invariably successful. He refers also to the experience of Mr. Waller, of Calcutta, which was equally favorable.

---

* The Practitioner, March, 1876.

In some cases of *neuralgia* good results have been obtained by quinia, subcutaneously. One notable example of ovarian neuralgia, accompanied by, or caused by, menorrhagia, has been reported, and I can confirm from personal observation the special utility of quinia under these circumstances.

CARBOLIC ACID.

The Solution.—The following formula is a suitable one for the preparation of a solution of carbolic acid for hypodermatic use:

R Acid. carbolic. purif., gr. x ;
Aquæ destil., ℥i. M.
Sig.—Two *per centum* solution of carbolic acid.

The Dose.—From fifteen to thirty minims—even as much as ℥i—of the above solution may be injected, but not more than the largest amount once in six hours. The minimum dose may be administered very frequently, until the maximum amount prescribed is reached. The quantity at each injection and the frequency of repetition will, however, depend on the character of the case.

Physiological Effects.—Some smarting attends immediately, but declines rapidly, and is replaced by a local anæsthesia and analgesia extending for some distance around the puncture. Usually very little irritation is produced, and it is rare for an inflammatory induration and suppuration to follow. No change occurs in the feelings and condition of the patient, due to the carbolic acid. Elimination takes place by the bronchial mucous membrane to a slight extent, also by the skin, but chiefly by the kidneys. If the injections have been practised frequently and in considerable quantity, the characteristic changes in the appearance and reaction of the urine are observed. A slight smoky appearance may be disregarded, but if the urine becomes persistently blackish, the administration should be lessened or suspended.

THERAPY.—Important results have been obtained from the subcutaneous and parenchymatous injection of carbolic acid. The original conception suggesting its employment was the supposed relation of certain morbific ferments to diseased processes. Influenced by these notions, Kunze,* of Halle, employed it in these maladies (Infectionskrankheiten), notably in *erysipelas*, and, as it proved, with excellent results. Some experience of my own is quite confirmatory. By injecting five minims of a two per cent. solution just at the margin of the inflammation, and at several points, two or three times a day, a very favorable influence on the case is at once apparent. Kunze found the same practice very beneficial in *pleuro-pneumonia*. The injections had the effect to lower the temperature and the pulse-rate. Aufrecht† has repeated the same practice and confirmed the results of Kunze.

The practice has been greatly extended by

---

* Schmidt's Jahrbücher, vol. clxiv. p. 147.   † Ibid.

Hüter,* under the title of "parenchymatous injections,"—*Form parenchymatöser Einspritzungen*,—and applied to the treatment of *synovitis, white swelling, adenoma, bubo, fibroma*, etc. A two per cent. solution is thrown into the cavity of the joint every day or two, and into the substance of the abnormal growths. In some cases remarkable results of a curative kind follow, as I have ascertained by actual trial. In several instances I have seen ulcers of the face, which had all the external signs and appearances of *epithelioma*, heal and cicatrize permanently under the influence of carbolic acid injections so practised that the medicament came into contact with the tissues immediately adjacent to the diseased tissue. The needle was entered in the sound tissue just at the margin of the disease, and passed well under the ulcer, so that the carbolic acid solution could diffuse thoroughly through the parts. If necessary, two or more punctures can be made at one sitting.

In *acute rheumatism* decided relief has been produced by these injections about the affected joints; they are still more efficient in *chronic rheumatism*, and also do good in *myalgia*. Superficial *neuralgiæ* may not unfrequently be promptly cured by deep injections of the two per cent. carbolic acid solution instead of chloroform.

---

* Schmidt's Jahrbücher, vol. clxiv. Also Dr. Rothe, Die Carbolsäure in der Medicin, Berlin, 1875, p. 40, et seq.

The Solution and Dose.—Applying the rules already given, I reject all insoluble preparations of mercury. Scarenzio* used in 1864 a mixture of calomel, glycerine, and water. Hebra† injected a solution of sublimate,—gr. i to ʒss water. Hill, of England, made use of a solution of sublimate containing $\frac{1}{8}$ of a grain to the dose. Lewin,‡ who first submitted this practice to systematic examination, employed a weak solution of corrosive sublimate. The following is a suitable formula for hypodermatic injection of mercury:

> ℞ Hydrarg. chlor. corrosiv., gr. i ;
> Aquæ destil., ʒi. M.

Ten minims of this contain $\frac{1}{48}$ of a grain. As Lewin, and especially Liégeois, have shown that concentrated solutions are not desirable and that large doses are not necessary, this formula will

---

* Eulenberg, op. cit., p. 307.

† Ibid. Also, Bulletin de Thérapeutique, vol. i., 1869, p. 297. De l'Application de la Méthode hypodermique au Traitement de la Syphilis par les Preparations mercurielles. Par le Dr. F. Bricheteau. Ibid., vol. ii., 1869, p. 158, by M. Liégeois.

‡ Ibid.

be strong enough for ordinary purposes. Recognizing the fact that induration of the tissue, and frequently unhealthy and sloughing ulcers, were produced by these injections of sublimate, Bricheteau requested M. Bouilhon, a Paris pharmaceutist, to prepare a salt of mercury soluble and free from irritant properties. M. Bouilhon suggested the double iodide of mercury and sodium as supplying the conditions required.

> ℞ Hydrarg. et sodii iodid., gr. xxiv;
> Aquæ destil., ℥iij. M.

Fifteen minims of this contain $\frac{1}{4}$ of a grain. Ten minims, or $\frac{1}{6}$ of a grain, will generally be sufficient for an injection. "This salt," says M. Bouilhon, "fulfils perfectly the object; it introduces into the economy only the active substance combined with a small quantity of a salt of soda." But as this salt is difficult to prepare, and as the corrosive chloride is more readily procured, the latter will generally be employed. With suitable precautions, abscess will not frequently result from its use. Thus, Lewin, who used his solution—which is stronger than that I have recommended—many hundred times, found small abscesses to occur in the proportion only of two to three for one hundred injections.

The formula of M. Liégeois * is as follows:

---

* Bulletin Général de Thérapeutique, 30 Août, 1869, p. 158.

R̶ Hydrarg. chlor. corrosiv., gr. iij;
   Morphiæ sulph., gr. iss ;
   Aquæ destil., ℥iij.   M.

Fifteen minims of this solution contain $\frac{1}{32}$ of a grain, the quantity recommended by Liégeois for a single injection. It will be perceived that this solution contains the same quantity of sublimate as the formula I have proposed, but only about one-third of that used by Lewin. In two cases only has Liégeois observed abscess and eschar follow his injection. This comparative immunity from ill effects is to be attributed, unquestionably, to the small proportion of sublimate. The injection is preferably inserted under the skin of the back.

Physiological Effects.—The injection of the corrosive chloride is accompanied by severe burning pain and considerable local heat and redness. If the solution be concentrated it will produce induration of the areolar tissue, inflammation and abscess, and sometimes a dry eschar, leaving an ulcer slow to heal. The intensity and persistence of the pain will depend upon the quantity of sublimate injected; weak solutions do not occasion much distress; the pain of any solution may be much mitigated by the conjoined use of morphia, as in the solution of Liégeois.

Salivation is frequently produced, according to Lewin, who had fifty-one cases of mercurial stomatitis in one hundred and forty-four men treated in this way. On the other hand, Liêgeois found salivation an "exceptional" occurrence, there being only four in one hundred and ninety-six subjects, and these were mild cases. The difference in result here is plainly due to the difference in the strength of the respective solutions. It is a curious and important circumstance that this physiological effect has no relation to the therapeutical results in syphilis, for Liégeois's cures are even more numerous, proportionally, than Lewin's.

The subcutaneous injection of sublimate does not impair any of the functions, but increases the activity of the digestion. and assimilation, so that decided increase in weight takes place in most of the cases in which it is employed.

THERAPY.—The therapeutical applications of mercury by the hypodermatic method are confined to the treatment of syphilis, in which results of the greatest value have been obtained.

It is applied to the treatment of primary (infecting chancre), secondary (constitutional), and tertiary forms of this disease. I have used it with great advantage in the tertiary, but have not had the opportunity to give it sufficiently numerous and prolonged trials to enable me to pronounce as to its utility in primary and secondary syphilis. I therefore avail myself of the very full reports and statistical evidence published by George Lewin, of Berlin, and M. Liégeois, of Paris. The following are the statistics of Lewin:

Cases * treated exclusively by injections of sublimate, 107; relapses 24, or 22 in 100.

" Cases treated by injections of sublimate, after sarsaparilla decoction and sweating, 58; relapses 19, or 30 in 100.

" Cases treated simultaneously by injections of sublimate, sarsaparilla decoction, and sweating, 24; relapses 7, or 33 in 100.

" Cases treated by injections of sublimate and iodide of potassium, 60; relapses, 14, or 23 in 100.

" Cases treated by injections of sublimate and chloride of potassium, 60; relapses 14, or 23 in 100."

To sum up—356 patients have been treated by injections of sublimate, either singly or joined to other means; the relapses have been 89, or 25 in 100.

With the ordinary means of treatment, the relapses are 81 in 100 cases.†

The conclusions arrived at by Lewin,‡ as a result of his large observations, are the following:

1. The syphilitic phenomena disappear quickly, and with a rapidity proportional to the quantity of sublimate daily injected.

---

* These statistics are based upon cases of constitutional syphilis.

† Bulletin de Thérapeutique, vol. i., 1869, p. 300. Abstract of Lewin's researches by Bricheteau.

‡ Ibid.

2. Certainty and precision of the method, as ascertained by nine hundred observations made during two years and a half.

3. Lessened number of relapses, and those that occur are light.

4. Facility of execution.

The statistics of Liégeois are even more favorable. Thus, of 196 cases of constitutional syphilis, treated by injections of sublimate, 127 were cured, and 69 were ameliorated. For the cured, the number of injections were 68; for those ameliorated, 50. The number of relapses in those noted as cured were 12 (9.45 in 100); for those noted as ameliorated, 14 (20.30 in 100). The greater number of injections, and the increased length of time required by Liégeois's method as compared with Lewin's, are due to the small quantity injected, but these disadvantages are more than counterbalanced by the greater proportional number of cures. The production of salivation, then, is unnecessary in order to secure the best results from the hypodermatic injection of mercury. The longer the constitutional symptoms have existed, the greater the number of injections required to effect a cure.

In practising the injection, the back should be selected for the site of the puncture. Two injections, of eight minims each, may be practised at one sitting, one on each side. This quantity should be inserted daily. If the symptoms be not urgent, if time is of little consequence, and if it be desirable to avoid salivation, the daily quantity may be much less.

With the view to avoid the irritation produced by subcutaneous injections of corrosive sublimate in the ordinary way, and also to administer it in larger doses, Dr. Staub conceived the idea of using it in the form of an albuminous solution in alkaline chlorides. He prepared his solution as follows:

> Corrosive sublimat., 1 gr. 25.
> Chloride of ammonium, 1 gr. 25.
> Chloride of sodium, 4 grs. 15.
> Water, 1 gr. 25.

After filtration this solution is added to an albuminous solution (white of one egg to 125 parts of water). Twenty drops of this contain 5 milligrammes of sublimate. It produces no irritation when injected under the skin. The results of treatment with this solution have been very favorable in the hands of M. Staub. He reports 44 observations, the treatment varying from 17 to 34 days, and the amount injected being 1 centigramme daily. He observed no relapses.*

The subcutaneous use of the albuminous solution of mercury is greatly extending. Within the past two years especially, numerous reports have been published, showing the rapidity and

---

* Archives Générales de Médecine, Juillet, 1872.

permanence with which cures have been effected. It has also been established by the recent experience in the hypodermatic treatment of syphilis, that relapses are much less apt to occur by this method than by the stomachal or epidermal administration.

29

ARSENIC.

THE first actual trial of arsenic subcutaneously was made by Dr. C. B. Radcliffe, in a case of chorea, and the announcement of this fact is to be found in the article on chorea in Reynolds's "System of Medicine."* As an interesting subject historically, I quote those paragraphs concerned with this topic:

"This patient had suffered for nine years with a distressing choreal affection of certain muscles of the neck, by which the head was kept continually turning and bobbing. At different times various modes of treatment had been tried, including the hypodermic injection of morphia and atropia, without the least benefit. . . . The idea of injecting arsenic hypodermically occurred to me on the 12th of January, 1866, and was carried out the same day. Fowler's solution was chosen, and the part selected was the most tender point over the contracting muscle." Commencing with three minims, the quantity injected was finally raised to fourteen minims. "Before the fourth injection was practised, a marked

---

* Vol. ii. p. 133, et seq.

change for the better had taken place; before the eighth, the choreal movements were almost at an end, and a change for the better had gone on steadily from the beginning." Dr. Radcliffe reports another case in which amelioration, equally as great, was produced by the hypodermatic injection of arsenic, the patient being a lady sixty years of age. He has also employed " with results more or less satisfactory the hypodermic injection of arsenic in certain cases of neuralgia, epilepsy, and other affections of the nervous system."

In the choreal cases above referred to, Dr. Radcliffe's " object in introducing the arsenic hypodermically was not to escape gastric irritation, but to produce some local change in the nerves of the parts which were the seat of the disorder, as well as to bring about some more general change in the system."

Dr. Radcliffe employed for these injections at first the undiluted Fowler's solution, but as considerable local irritation followed, he afterward diluted it by one-half water. This proved much less irritant. It is probable, I think, that the *Liquor Sodæ Arseniatis* will be found much better for hypodermatic use than Fowler's solution. This being a higher oxide than the arsenite of potassa, is less irritant in its local action and less apt to produce arsenical poisoning. Moreover, it is a clear solution, possessed of a considerable degree of osmotic power. The solution of the arseniate of soda may be injected in quantities of five to ten or even fifteen minims. Every alternate day is sufficiently often in ordinary cases to make the injection. It will be found advisable not to insert the solution frequently in the same neighborhood.

Dr. Radcliffe's example has been followed with success. Not only local but severe general chorea has been treated with good results. Successful cases have been reported by Perroud, Garin, Hammond, and others.

Remarkable results have been obtained from the hypodermatic injection of arsenic in *lymphadenoma* by Billroth and Czerny. Fowler's solution is used, and the injection made into the substance of the enlarged glands. The quantity depends somewhat on the susceptibility of the patient, and therefore varies,—from 5 to 10 minims of the official solution being injected daily. The same practice has been followed with good results in *enlarged spleen* and in *splenic leucocythemia.*

M. Lipp * has proposed to use arsenic subcutaneously in cases of *psoriasis* and chronic *eczema.* He reports three cases thus treated successfully. He injected from one to two centigrammes of arsenious acid. The general symptoms produced by these injections were elevation of temperature, acceleration of pulse,

---

* Archiv für Dermatologie und Syphil., No. 3, 1869.

diminution of appetite, increased thirst and diuresis, nervous excitement, headache, vertigo, cough, redness of conjunctiva, etc. The advantages which M. Lipp claims are the smallness of the dose, the shorter duration of the treatment, and the absence of injury to the digestive organs. Excellent results have since been obtained in numerous instances of cutaneous diseases of an obstinate character by this practice, in the hands of dermatologists, in all parts of the world. The class of cases benefited by arsenic subcutaneously is the same as those heretofore treated by the stomachal administration of the same agent.

AQUAPUNCTURE.

THE method now designated *aquapuncture* consists merely in the subcutaneous injection of water at ordinary temperature. A special instrument has been invented by M. Guérard for the simultaneous introduction of a number of fine streams of water (*douches filiformes*), but an ordinary hypodermatic syringe will answer the purpose very well by making a number of punctures within a certain area.

The immediate effect of the sudden introduction of a fine jet of water is a sense of burning, which lasts a few minutes, a feeling of distention and warmth lasting longer, for about the point of puncture considerable swelling takes place, presenting the appearance of a wheal of urticaria. The immediate effect of the introduction of cold water is to cool the nerve-filaments; of hot water to raise their temperature, and the distention of the parts stretches the nerve-filaments. Undoubtedly, therapeutical effects are produced by such impression. What difference of physiological or therapeutical effects will follow the introduction of very warm or very cold water, or greater or less stretching of nerve-fibres, remains to be determined by further investigations.

The method of aquapuncture has been used in fourteen cases of various forms of *neuralgia* by Servajan,* with the result of a cure in all but one. Among these were examples of facial, sciatic (5), lumbar (3), and other forms.

The injection of water has been gravely proposed † as a substitute for morphia in the treatment of painful affections, and a medical eccentric has propounded the extraordinary theory that the systemic effects of a solution of morphia are due not to the morphia, but to the water! If this was not intended as a practical joke, if the author is really sincere in his proposition, it is a curious example of that morbid desire for notoriety which is indifferent to the means employed to secure it.

Water injections have been used with success to deceive the patient in cases of morphia habit of a few days' or few weeks' duration; but ancient and experienced morphia-takers cannot be so deceived, for they quickly realize the difference in the amount of effect produced. In making an effort to cure them, it is never useful to practise any deceit; their co-operation must be sought and their confidence gained. If water merely is to be injected, let them be informed,

---

* De l'Aquapuncture, par J. Servajan, Paris, 1872, p. 41.

† Lafitte, Union Médicale, No. 113, 1875.

but do not commit the professional error (not to speak of moral wrong) of being concerned and caught in an attempt to deceive.

I have had excellent results from the injection of water into paralyzed and wasting muscles: it promotes their nutrition, and contributes indirectly to the regeneration of voluntary power.

In the various cases to which the aquapuncture is applicable, the quantity injected will range from thirty minims to a drachm. When the first injection does not relieve in two minutes, another should be inserted. As far as practicable the "painful points," or the tissue in which the pain is felt, should be the site of the injection.

IRRITANT INJECTIONS.

Dr. Luton,* of Rheims, under the singular designation "parenchymatous substitution," described a method of treating neuralgias, new formations, hypertrophies, etc. This method consists in the injection into the substance of the affected part of such irritants as tincture of iodine, nitrate of silver, chloride of sodium, etc. The term applied to this process was intended to express the theoretical views of its author in regard to the nature of the therapeutical action which takes place. The pain and irritation set up in the part were assumed to be *substituted* for the morbid process.

Dr. Ruppaner imitated this method of Luton in the treatment of sciatica and other neuralgias. Dr. Bertin (de Gray) also, attracted by the results obtained by Luton, practised the method for several years and then published the results.† I have had myself a limited experience with this method.

The substances employed in this way are chiefly the following:

---

* Archives Générales de Médecine, Oct. et Nov. 1863.

† Ibid., Avril, 1868, p. 444.

A solution of iodine.

A saturated solution of common salt.

A solution of the nitrate of silver.

The tincture of cantharides.

The following is the solution of iodine employed by Bertin:

> R Potassii iodidi, gr. xv;
> Tinct. iodinii, ʒijss;
> Aquæ destil., ʒx. M.

The quantity of tincture of iodine may be increased to v.

The tincture of iodine is sometimes employed alone and undiluted.

The following is a suitable formula for the nitrate of silver solution:

> R Argenti nitrat., ʒij;
> Aquæ destil., ʒi. M.

To illustrate at the same time the class of cases to which this method is applicable, and its therapeutical power, I subjoin the statistics of Bertin:

1. Tumors formed by development of the thyroid gland 8
       Cured... 5
       Ameliorated 1
       Failed... 2
2. Lymphatic ganglions..................................... 3
       Cured... 3
3. Bursæ... 1
       Cured... 1

Ruppaner employed the nitrate of silver injection in one case of cervico-brachial neuralgia, and in four cases of sciatica; two cases were ameliorated, and three cases of sciatica were cured.

As respects *neuralgia*, this method of treatment seems specially adapted to cases of sciatica,—obstinate cases in which structural alterations have probably taken place in the neurilemma. In order to be effectual, the injection—five drops of the nitrate of silver solution—should be thrown into the vicinity of the nerve. It produces great pain and burning, and is followed by considerable inflammation, not diffused, but localized to the site of the injection. Abscesses, of course, frequently happen from this practice, and, indeed, sufficient irritation to result in this way seems necessary to produce the best effects. It is probably true that the irritation, and not the agent, is the principal factor in the curative process.

Injections of the iodine solution have been

practised with success in *goitre.* The tincture of iodine may be thrown into the substance of an enlarged thyroid without producing violent irritation. Five minims of the tincture will be sufficient for this purpose, and it may be repeated every other day. Recent cases are quickly cured by this treatment. I have seen excellent results from the same application in those *cystic and glandular tumors* so frequently found in the cervical region. After evacuating the cyst with a trocar, the tincture of iodine may be freely thrown into the sac, and the solid parts of the tumor injected by the hypodermatic syringe, the needle point being well introduced into the substance of the growth.

Enlarged bursæ are best treated by the same means; evacuate the contents and inject the solution of iodine. Slight inflammatory action follows, the tumor becomes indurated, and finally disappears.

Solid tumors may be destroyed by injecting such irritants into them as will give rise to violent inflammatory action and sloughing. Into the substance of cancerous new formations various corrosives may be injected; but this practice, although rational, has not hitherto proved satisfactory,—a remark equally true of Dr. Broadbent's method of injecting dilute acetic acid,— of the success of which such confident expectations were at first entertained. Solutions of chloride of zinc of varying strength have lately been proposed for " interstitial injection" as a means of curing certain cystic tumors. It is asserted that when the air is excluded eschars are not produced. The strength of the weaker solution is about five grains of the chloride of zinc to the drachm of water, and of the stronger solution about a half-drachm to a drachm. The method consists in introducing an aspirator and withdrawing some part of the contents of the cyst, and then injecting from five to twenty drops of the zinc solution.

Recently* considerable success has been claimed for the treatment of tumors by the injection into their intimate structure of *gastric juice.* As this practice is devoid of danger in suitable cases, and as the gastric juice is not difficult to obtain from the stomach of the pig, it is desirable to have further experience in order to form decided opinions as to its utility.

The natural digestive fluid, the juice of *Carica papaya,* has been used successfully to effect the solution of morbid growths, in the same way as pepsin. It deserves further investigation.

It would be foreign to my purpose to speak of such uses of the iodine solution as the injection in hydrocele, in hydrothorax and empyema, in cystic disease of the ovary, etc., and of the use of perchloride and persulphate of iron in nævus.

INJECTION OF AMMONIA INTO THE VEINS.—As

___

* Bulletin Général de Thérapeutique, Août 15, 1869.

the hypodermatic syringe is the instrument employed in this operation, it may be proper to include in my account of hypodermatic medication some references to the injection of ammonia into the veins. We owe to Prof. Halfourd, of Melbourne, Australia, the introduction of this important means of relief. He used it to overcome and remove the lethal effects of the poison of venomous snakes. A number of successful cases have now been reported occurring in the practice of Prof. Halfourd and others. The solution used consists of one part of *aqua ammoniæ fortior* and two parts of distilled water. By means of an ordinary hypodermatic syringe this solution is injected into a vein. The quantity is determined by the effect; one or more syringefuls may be injected. Care must be used to prevent the introduction of air. The operation appears to be devoid of danger, and to be free from ulterior bad effects.

The injection of ammonia is indicated not only in the case of poisoning by venomous snakes, but in various conditions in which the danger to life consists in depression of the heart's action. In *poisoning by hydrocyanic acid* it may be used with a good prospect of success. The report of a case of poisoning by chlorodyne has lately come to us from Australia, in which life was saved by the injection of ammonia. In cases of danger from thrombus of an important vessel, as, for example, thrombus of the pulmonary artery, a cause of sudden death after delivery, this mode of treatment is strongly indicated. In failure of the heart's action during the chloroform narcosis, the injection of ammonia should be promptly practised.

Recent experiences by Brunton and Fayrer have demonstrated that the intravenous injection of ammonia is not effective against the poisoning by the venomous snakes of India, and grave doubts are now entertained in respect to the same practice in the poisoning by Australian snakes, the apparent cures heretofore reported being instances of the *post* rather than the *propter hoc.*

INDEX.

THE END.